# RAW
# EDGES

Introduction and notes copyright © D. Edward Wright, 2024

Originally published in 1908 by William Heinemann Ltd.

This edition published in 2024 by Glowbug Publishing

Illustrations by Alberto Martini

Contact us at glowbugpublishing@gmail.com

Browse other Glowbug publications at
www.glowbugpublishing.com

ISBN: 978-1-3999-8084-5

Typeset by Glowbug Publishing

Printed and bound in Great Britain by Imprint Digital

# TABLE OF CONTENTS

# INTRODUCTION

*Raw Edges: Studies and Stories of These Days* is a collection of thirteen short stories by the English writer and journalist Perceval Landon (29 March 1869 – 23 January 1927).[1] Following its original 1908 publication by William Heinemann Ltd., *Raw Edges* was not reprinted for 116 years; as such, copies were (until now) incredibly rare: in late 2023, a copy in good condition was able to command a price of just under £2000. Today, *Raw Edges* is best remembered for the ghost story *Thurnley Abbey*, which has been reprinted in many anthologies over the last century. A handful of other stories from *Raw Edges* have occasionally found their way back into print, but at the time of writing, only *Thurnley Abbey* and its fellow ghost story *Railhead* are readily available to read online, while the greater part of Landon's short stories remain hidden in private collections and university archives. It is thus with great pleasure that Glowbug Publishing brings these stories back to life with the publication of this 2024 edition of *Raw Edges*, which will eventually be followed by an electronic version.

The long hiatus in the reprinting of *Raw Edges* necessitates that some words be said about the author, his times, and his work. Perceval Landon was born in Hastings on the south coast of England on 29 March 1869 to Rev. Edward Henry Landon and his wife, Caroline Perceval.[2] He was named for his mother's family: his grandfather Rev. Arthur Philip Perceval (a prolific writer himself) was a nephew of Spencer Perceval (1762–1812),[3,4] the only British prime minister to have been assassinated. Landon followed in his learned forebears' footsteps by enrolling at Hertford College in 1888, where he obtained a Third Class Honours in Classical Moderations in 1890, and served as Secretary of the Oxford Union in 1891. In

# INTRODUCTION

1892, he graduated with a Third Class Honours in Law, and was called to the bar at the Inner Temple in 1895.[5,6]

Landon would not pursue a career as a barrister for long, and instead embarked upon the nomadic life of a journalist, as well as briefly serving as private secretary to William Lygon, 7th Earl Beauchamp. Landon accompanied the Earl to Paris in late 1898 and then to Greece in early 1899. Lord Beauchamp invited Landon to accompany him to Australia, where he had been appointed governor of New South Wales; however, the Earl's diary notes that 'P.L. was found impossible.'[7] Fate would instead pull Landon to a different corner of the British Empire: South Africa.

In 1899, the Second Anglo-Boer War (or South African War) broke out between the British Empire and the two Boer republics: the South African Republic, also known as the Transvaal Republic, and the Orange Free State. The origins of the war lay in the long and uneasy history between the Boer republics and Britain; the expansionist ambitions of British mining magnate Cecil Rhodes, Cape Colony Governor Sir Alfred Milner, and others; and crucially, the discovery of gold-bearing ore south of Pretoria, then the capital of the South African Republic. The resulting gold rush flooded the area with predominantly British *uitlanders* ('outlanders' in Afrikaans), which threatened to destabilise Boer power. A British ultimatum that uitlanders with at least five years residency be granted the vote, combined with the threat posed by a British military build-up at the borders, forced the Boers to declare war against their old foe on 11 October 1899.[8]

The declaration saw Landon despatched to South Africa to serve as war correspondent for *The Times*. Following the capture of Bloemfontein (at that time the capital of the Orange Free State) on 13 March 1900 by British forces, Landon and three other journalists (F.W. Buxton of the *Johannesburg Star*, H.A. Gwynne of Reuter's Agency, and Julian Ralph of the *Daily Mail*) were asked by the Army's chief censor, Lord Stanley, under orders from Field Marshal Lord Roberts, to manage a 'daily newspaper published for the entertainment and information of the army.' To this end, a newspaper called *The Friend of the Free State*, owned by an Englishman named Barlow and managed by his son, was commandeered and renamed *The Friend*.[9] Landon was later described by one of his fellow editors, the American journalist Julian Ralph, as follows:

> Perceval Landon, representing the *Times*, is a university man, who has been admitted to the bar, and who took up the work of a war correspondent from an Englishman's love of adventure, danger, and excitement. It can be nothing but his English blood that prompted him to this course, for in mind and temperament, tastes and qualifications, he is at once a scholar and a poet rather than a man of violent action. Had the *Times* so desired he would have charmed the public with letters from the front as human and picturesque in subject and treatment as any that were sent to London. His charms of manner and of mind caused his companionship to be sought by the most distinguished and the most polished men in the army, and all were deeply sorry when, at the close of the army's stay in Bloemfontein, illness forced him to return to London, though not until he had served in the war as long as any man at that time on the west side of the continent.[9]

It was through his tenure as editor of *The Friend* that Landon became acquainted with Rudyard Kipling (1865–1936), with whom he formed a close friendship that lasted until Landon's premature death.[10] Landon had secured Kipling's involvement in the project by sending a telegram to the famous poet's winter holiday home in Cape Town. Kipling was sufficiently enthused by the prospect of a return to his newspaper days that he travelled the 600 miles to Bloemfontein, where he contributed to the editorial office by writing poems and fables, conscientiously reading poems submitted to the newspaper by 'Tommy Atkins,'* correcting proofs, and even personally distributing copies of the newspaper to wounded soldiers in the hospitals. Kipling departed Bloemfontein on 1 April 1900 to prepare to sail back to England with his family, but before leaving, he wrote a poem to celebrate Landon's 31st birthday on 29 March:

A BIRTHDAY GREETING

BY RUDYARD KIPLING

Tell the smiling Afric morn,
Let the stony kopje know,
Landon of the *Times* was born
One and thirty years ago.

Whisper greetings soft and low,
Pour the whisky, deal the bun,
Only Bell and Buckle know
All the evil he has done.[9]

Landon and the other editors were also able to secure an article, entitled *A First Impression*, from a second famous writer, Sir Arthur Conan Doyle, who was then in Bloemfontein serving as a volunteer physician in the Langman Field Hospital. Landon himself was kept busy with both his obligations to *The Times* and to *The Friend*, with his

---

\*        British soldiers.

contributions to the latter including battle reports, a comedic column called *The Military Letter Writer* in collaboration with Rudyard Kipling, and news articles on despatch riders, horse theft, and other items of interest to the occupying army. He also wrote an article on the battle at Karree Siding (a railway siding about 20 miles north of Bloemfontein), where William Lygon's younger brother, Lieutenant The Honourable Edward Hugh Lygon, was shot and killed. Julian Ralph wrote that Lygon 'was an intimate and beloved friend of Mr. Landon, who mourned him deeply and most lovingly looked after his burial and the proper marking of his grave.' By mid-April, Landon became ill and returned to England; *The Friend* was handed over to the proprietor of the *Johannesburg Star* shortly after on 16 April 1900, barely a month after the newspaper was commandeered by the army.[9]

After a short period serving as private secretary to Lord Beauchamp in New South Wales, Landon returned to his journalistic duties, first as special correspondent for the *Daily Mail* at the second Delhi Durbar to mark the coronation of Edward VII as Emperor of India.[11] It was at about this time that Landon, perhaps inspired by his new friend Kipling, started to work on his first book: *Helio-Tropes or New Posies for Sundials*.[12] This work, published in 1904 by Methuen & Co., consists of thirty-two posies and one incomplete fragment, all of which are related in some way to sundials or the passage of time, and most of which are accompanied by an explanatory note written in a 17th century style. The title page claims that these posies were 'written in an old book partly in English and partly in Latin and expounded in English by John Parmenter, clerk, of Wingham in the county of Kent, 1625,' with Landon as editor; however, it seems more likely that Parmenter is fictional and Landon is the true author: the British Library catalogue entry for *Helio-Tropes* notes that it is 'edited [or rather written] by Perceval Landon.' In support of this hypothesis, Landon writes in the introduction that 'My sincere thanks are due to Mr. Rudyard Kipling, who has given me a singularly appropriate "posy" (XXVII) for this collection.' The pretence is that Kipling assisted Landon by (very loosely) translating the Latin posy *Me neque Sol radiis placat nec paenitet Umbra*,' but it is more likely that the posy, reproduced below, is purely Kipling's invention.

> I have known Shadow:
> I have known Sun.
> And now I know
> These two are one.

In further support of the hypothesis that Landon is the author, an anonymous commenter on a post about *Helio-Tropes* on the *Wormwoodiana* blog observed that the Landon family is descended from the Palmer baronets of Wingham, the supposed hometown of 'John Parmenter.'[13] This connection is documented in the *Encyclopædia of Heraldry* by John Burke.[14] Furthermore, the Palmer Baronetcy, of Wingham in the County of Kent, was created in the Baronetage of England on 29 June 1621 for Thomas Palmer,[15] four years before the purported original publication date of Parmenter's book. Perceval Landon had a documented interest in heraldry, and authored an article in 1895 on the heraldry of the Oxford colleges.[16] As such, it is likely that he would be familiar with his own family's right to quarter the arms of the Palmer line. And finally, Landon may have intended to more directly hint at the Palmer-Parmenter secret in the eighth posy in his work, which reads:

> I am nothing but a name.
> (*Nemo nisi Nomen*)

# INTRODUCTION

(I should note that the 'original' Latin helio-trope, *Nemo nisi Nomen*, is a palindrome, Landon no doubt enjoying the opportunities for wordplay that this project afforded.)

In early 1904, Landon joined the British expedition to Tibet, once again as correspondent for *The Times*. The expedition was despatched on the orders of Lord Curzon, then Viceroy of India, ostensibly to formalise diplomatic relations, establish trading rights, and resolve border and treaty disputes—but in reality to pre-empt the Viceroy's (misplaced) fears of Russian influence in Tibet. Curzon received permission from London to send the Tibet Frontier Commission, led by Colonel Francis Younghusband, to the Tibetan fortress of Kamba Dzong just beyond the border with India, but no further; however, the refusal of Tibetan and Chinese officials to open discussions until the British forces left Tibetan territory, combined with the personal ambitions of Younghusband and others to reach the forbidden city of Lhasa, ultimately resulted in a series of largely one-sided military engagements that collectively caused the deaths of between two and three thousand Tibetan soldiers. On reaching the capital, Younghusband unilaterally forced a treaty on the Tibetan National Assembly, the monasteries, and the representatives of the Dalai Lama (the 13th Dalai Lama himself having fled to Mongolia before the arrival of British forces in Lhasa).[17]

Landon was not witness to the signing of the treaty, for by then he had already left Lhasa to return to India, ostensibly to carry important despatches to the acting Viceroy Arthur Oliver Villiers Russell, 2nd Baron Ampthill, who happened to be an old Oxford chum of Landon's. Colonel Younghusband claimed that Landon's willingness to depart so soon was simply because 'he wanted to get home and get his book out first'; Landon had been open about his plans to write a book on Tibet, causing some consternation among his fellow journalists, all of whom harboured similar ambitions. On returning to England in September 1904, Landon visited Kipling at his house Bateman's in East Sussex,[18] where he started writing the work that would be published in 1905 as *Lhasa: An Account of the Country and People of Central Tibet and of the Progress of the Mission Sent There by the English Government in the Year 1903-4*.[19,*] This was not merely an account of the mission itself: Landon's insatiable curiosity, eye for detail, and journalistic instincts compelled him to provide exhaustive details on the history, geography, ecology, customs, and folktales of Tibet. In his introduction to *Lhasa*, Colonel Younghusband wrote that '[Landon] appreciated to the full the wonderful scenery which to my mind was infinitely the most fascinating of all our experiences' and that 'no more competent chronicler of what the Tibet Mission saw and did could be found, and we were indeed fortunate in having with us one of his enthusiasm and powers of description.'[19]

With the completion of his Tibetan assignment, Landon defected from *The Times* to join *The Daily Telegraph*, to which he would contribute articles for the rest of his life, starting with reports of the Indian tour taken by the then Prince of Wales (later George V) in 1905–1906; Landon's evocative descriptions of India were subsequently published as *Under the Sun: Impressions of Indian Cities* in 1907.[20] The same year, a collection of articles Landon had written for *The Telegraph* 'in commemoration of the 50th anniversary of the Indian Mutiny' were collected and published as *"1857."*[21] *Raw Edges* followed in 1908, and was generally well received by critics (see below).[1] In 1909, Landon turned his attention to the stage, writing a play called *The House Opposite* that was performed at the Queen's Theatre, London in the 1909–1910

---

\*     Doubleday published the same book as *The Opening of Tibet: An Account of Lhasa and the Country and People of Central Tibet and of the Progress of the Mission Sent There by the English Government in the Year 1903-4.*

season.[22] A description of the play in a 1910 issue of New Zealand Graphic (reproduced here in Appendix C) reveals that it is an adaptation of one of Landon's own short stories from *Raw Edges: Mrs. Rivers's Journal*.[23] The play dispenses with the supernatural ending, and the falsely accused maid is vindicated by outside forces, releasing the protagonists from their moral quandary with no need for substantial action on their part. The central role of Richard Cardyne was played by the actor Harry Brodribb (H.B.) Irving (1870–1919); Irving's biographer, Austin Brereton, noted that:

> He [H.B Irving] was 'frightfully busy' with the rehearsals of a new play, written by a friend of the Oxford days, Mr Perceval Landon (the Earl of Pembroke of *King John*), entitled *The House Opposite*. Unfortunately, the piece did not hit the public taste, being possibly too morbid or too psychological. Nor was there any capital to be made out of the character of Richard Cardyne.[24]

Despite this muted reception, the play was later adapted by the British Broadwest Film Company into a 1917 silent film, directed by Walter West and Frank Wilson, and starring Ivy Close as Mrs. Rivers and Gregory Scott as Richard Cardyne.[25] Landon also wrote a second play, *For the Soul of the King*, which was performed at the Queen's Theatre on 28 December 1909.[26] This work was a translation of the short story *Un épisode sous la Terreur* (*An Episode during the Terror*) by Honoré de Balzac, in which two nuns and a priest encounter the king's executioner while in hiding during the French Revolution. In Landon's adaptation, H.B. Irving played the role of 'the stranger' who follows one of the disguised nuns home. Austin Brereton's account of this play is no more favourable than that of *The House Opposite*:

# INTRODUCTION

> In order to strengthen the bill a one-act play, *For the Soul of the King*, translated from the French by Mr Landon, was brought out in December and played as a first piece. It was a sad little play, and although there were one or two fine moments in it, it did not call for much more than the mournful appearance made by the impersonator of the Stranger.[24]

Both of Landon's plays were ignobly replaced by Joseph William Comyns Carr's adaptation of *The Strange Case of Dr. Jekyll and Mr. Hyde* in 1910,[24] and Landon returned to his true calling as journalist for *The Daily Telegraph*, travelling to India again for the third Dehli Durbar in 1911 at which George V was proclaimed Emperor of India, as well as to Persia, Nepal, Russian Turkestan, Egypt, Sudan, Syria, and Mesopotamia.[11] In 1910, Landon started to rent a cottage, 'Keylands,' on his friend Kipling's estate, which served as his base between his many overseas jaunts.[18] After the First World War, Landon was present at the Paris Peace Conference of 1919–1920 and the Lausanne Conference in 1923.[11]

Landon's health took a turn for the worse in 1924: in a letter dated 17 December 1924, Kipling informed his daughter Elsie Bambridge that Landon 'isn't half as well as I'd wish to see him, and most anxious to get away to his beloved East (*via* Egypt) again'; a postscript in the same letter added that Landon had been diagnosed with 'blood poisoning, enlarged liver, and ulcerated stomach,' but that 'he has the grit of a dozen men and only talks of lying up for "a little while." ' In a letter to Lord Burham sent the same month, Kipling again described Landon's maladies, adding, 'I want to get him down here if he'll only come.'[10]

Despite his illness, Landon joined the Kiplings on a trip to France in March 1925.[10] Landon had also been invited to attend the Third Empire Press Conference in Melbourne in September of that year; it seemed that his sojourn to Australia as private secretary to Earl Beauchamp twenty years earlier had not been forgotten, for his impending arrival was announced by 'The Salamander' in the Melbourne newspaper *The Sun News-Pictorial* on 29 June 1925:

> Flickers of grimly smiling reminiscence will, no doubt, flit across the mind of Perceval Landon, one of the most interesting figures of the coming Empire Press Conference, in Melbourne, when he falls in with some of Sydney's folk. He had to encounter everyone who was in the social swim there about a quarter of a century ago, also all the others who hadn't exactly got into the swim, but were trying their toes in pretty cool water. I had some sympathy with poor Landon, for his job as Governor's private secretary was more delicate than usual.[27]

The reason for this delicacy lay in the ill-considered decision of the governor, Earl Beauchamp, to greet the population of New South Wales by cabling a poem adapted from Kipling's 'Song of the Cities' for publication in *The West Australian* newspaper on 12 May 1899; the offending verse read as follows:

> Greeting! Your birth-stain have you turned to good;
>   Forcing strong wills perverse to steadfastness:
> The first flush of the tropics in your blood,
>   And at your feet success![28]

This was most likely intended as a compliment, but mention of the former penal colony's past did little to endear the new governor to its residents. Landon did not arrive in Australia until after this blunder, as noted by 'The Salamander':

# INTRODUCTION

> His [Landon's] particular Governor was Earl
> Beauchamp, who quoted Kipling's 'birthstain' verse
> to the descendants of Sydney's involuntary pioneers
> and was never forgiven. I don't think he was actually
> helping the young Governor at the time of the blunder,
> but he came along soon after. His experiences in
> dealing with the social rough and tumbles at Sydney
> Governmen [sic] House probably afforded him an
> excellent training as a war correspondent. That has
> since been his preference, varied by a lot of peaceable
> travel and the writing of plays.[27]

Landon ultimately decided not to attend the Empire
Press Conference, and instead departed for China on 17 July
1925—to the 'huge disgust' of Kipling, as the latter wrote in a
letter to his daughter dated 4 July 1925.[10] However, it was not
long before Landon was compelled by his illness to return to
England.[11] On 12 January 1927, Kipling persuaded the very
ill Landon to enter a nursing-home.[10] Kipling himself had
been suffering from poor health, and his physician, Sir John
Bland-Sutton, had persuaded him to leave Europe for the
winter.[18] Before leaving for Brazil on the 28th, Kipling wrote
to Lord Beauchamp on 22 January 1927 to inform him that
Landon had 'crocked' badly, adding that 'he'll have to be in
the home for weeks and will have to have a nurse for some
time after he comes out.' He asked Beauchamp to 'keep a
kindly eye on him' while Kipling was travelling.[10] However,
Landon died one day after the letter was written, at the age
of 57. Kipling's poem, *A Song in the Desert*, is dedicated 'P. L.
Ob. Jan. 1927'[29]; this tribute to Landon has been included as
Appendix B.

Landon's final completed work, *Nepul*, was published
posthumously in two volumes in 1928.[30] His writings and
letters were inherited by Kipling, but these were likely

destroyed by Kipling's widow and daughter following the poet's death in 1936.[18] While much has been written about Kipling, Landon and his works have been neglected by scholars, and he remains a somewhat enigmatic figure; although it is clear from his own history and the writings of others that he was a charismatic, inquisitive, and adventurous man, we know little about Landon's innermost hopes and fears. In the absence of his letters, perhaps we can still learn something about Landon's inner life from his short stories.

## THE RAW EDGES OF LIFE AND DEATH

Much like Landon himself, *Raw Edges* has been largely forgotten in the 21st century. The breakout story was, of course, *Thurnley Abbey*, which has been republished in at least 47 short story collections and magazines (excluding reprints), according to the Internet Speculative Fiction Database.[31,*] Evidence that *Thurnley Abbey* eclipsed its creator early on is provided by its introduction in the first issue of *The Magazine of Fantasy*,** in which the editors Anthony Boucher and J. Francis McComas remarked that:

> Unfortunately, we have learned but little about Perceval Landon, whose *Thurnley Abbey* was published in England in 1908. But the story itself is sufficient evidence of its author's stature, though it has occasioned long and serious arguments between us. One editor claims that it is unequaled among the

---

\*      Of the twelve other stories in *Raw Edges*, only *Mrs. Rivers's Journal*, *Railhead*, and *The Crusader's Mass* were subsequently reprinted prior to the publication of this volume.

\*\*      Renamed *The Magazine of Fantasy & Science Fiction* from the second issue onwards.

innumerable chronicles of haunting and the horror thereof, while the other holds that it is merely one of the three most terrifying stories in the English language. We leave the final decision to you, with the warning that in the supernatural field, things are not always what they seem … or even what they seem not to be.[32]

The strong, contemporary association between *Raw Edges* and its famous ghost story *Thurnley Abbey* may lead the reader to suppose that all of the stories are of the supernatural. This is hardly the case: two of the other stories (*Mrs. Rivers's Journal* and *Railhead*) conclude with apparently paranormal events, but the others are substantially more corporeal in nature. However, all of the tales are strongly infused with the macabre, being variously described as 'grim and terrifying,'[33] 'having a 'taste for the bizarre,'[34] and as 'chiefly ghostly or gruesome.'[11] Some of the contemporary reviews of *Raw Edges* (which, baring a rather scathing review in *The Nation*,[35] were generally positive) have been reproduced in appendices D to G of this volume.

*Raw Edges* is named for a line in the story 'And Our Ignorance in Asking': 'There was no understanding there, and no one to whom she could bring the raw edges of her sorrow.' The book's title is apt, as all its stories are concerned with the raw edges of life and death. Landon had already seen much of death by the time he wrote *Raw Edges*, and had lost at least one good friend in the Second Anglo-Boer War.[9] Death is indiscriminate, and in *Raw Edges*, so is Landon: he slays men, women, and children, sparing neither the innocent nor the wicked, and even those who survive to live another day are left shells of their former selves. To quote the unnamed young woman in *Thurnley Abbey*, 'all true art…[is] shot through and through with melancholy' and 'it has always been tragedy that embodied the highest attainment of every age'—sentiments that, if the contents of *Raw Edges* are any indication, reflect Landon's own.

Several of the stories explore the possibility of life after death. Some, like *Thurnley Abbey*, *Railhead*, and *Mrs. Rivers's Journal*, hint strongly at the supernatural without unequivocally proclaiming the reality of ghosts: even *Thurnley Abbey's* immured nun may be a parlour trick, the skeletal pieces perhaps picked up in the dark by one of Broughton's hunting pals, or a servant in on the act. Other presented cases of life after death are more prosaic: Kane's return from the dead in *'And Our Ignorance in Asking'* is merely a case of mistaken identity, and the man moving in the coffin in *Railhead* was very much alive when he entered, the magical made mundane (until the reversal of the ending). In *A Deathbed Comedy*, a more blessed afterlife is bestowed upon the neglected child Miriam Gilchrist, as her faith sees her ascend to a happy ending in Heaven. This is Landon at his most saccharine, but few would begrudge the child the happiness she barely knew in life. Befitting its historical primacy in the explanation and acceptance of death, religion features prominently in several of the other stories, and Landon frequently presents a Catholic faith more in sympathy with sin and death than its Protestant cousins: in *'And Our Ignorance in Asking'*, a widow's prayers are answered by the Virgin Mary while parsons can offer nothing but platitudes, and in *Overtried*, a death-haunted priest sees into the soul of a sin-weary vicar.

Death and vengeance go hand in hand in an endless bloody cycle, and Landon does not let the deaths of women or children go unavenged in *Raw Edges*. In *Between Thee and Him Alone*, the protagonist Andersen manipulates both the Boer and British armies to take revenge on a former comrade complicit in the death of his family. In Andersen's mind, this is no vendetta, but the will of God, and he, God's Angel of

Death. Andersen takes his eye for an eye in accordance with what he sees as God's justice, knowing full well that he will have to face man's justice in turn. We the reader can have little sympathy for Van Cloete and his deception, but we would perhaps struggle to argue that two war crimes make a right—although, with the knowledge of the terrible conditions of the British concentration camps, in which many Boer civilians died from disease and malnutrition, perhaps Andersen was right not to leave his grievance to be settled by British justice. In *An Outpost of the Empire* (the sole excursion into poetry in this volume), vengeance is enacted against an entire people for the horrifying torture and death of Margaret Daubeny and two others. The poem is written in loose anapestic tetrameter, which, much like its use in Lord Byron's *The Destruction of Sennacherib*, suggests the pounding of horses' hooves as the rescuers gallop in vain to save the captives. Elsewhere, the dead return to wreak their own vengeance: the wrongfully convicted Martha Craik returns to face the woman who might have saved her life, and the nun of *Thurnley Abbey* is perhaps waiting for someone to ask her where her body is immured—we shall never know, for Colvin never asked, and Landon never told us.

Landon also pits the death of the body against a different type of death: that of one's reputation and social standing. In *The Recording Angel's Peerage*, Noreen Leighton feels no guilt upon killing her own biological father to prevent her mother from suffering the shame of being known to have borne an illegitimate child. Likewise, in *Mrs. Rivers's Journal*, the titular chronicler fears being shamed were it known that Cardyne had been in her chambers more than the guilt of condemning an innocent woman to death. Mrs. Rivers prays that God will deliver her from her dilemma by saving Craik's life—failing to consider that perhaps she was the intended instrument of God's will. We might observe that faith in God allows both

Mary Rivers and Lucas Andersen to justify the death of others: Rivers by passively ceding responsibility to God, and Andersen by actively appointing himself the murderous hand of the Almighty. Cardyne, who might also have saved Craik from the gallows, is bound by a strong sense of honour that prevents him from betraying his social better, Mrs. Rivers. This Edwardian sense of honour is perhaps very rare indeed a hundred years later, and most would consider it deeply immoral to put the reputation of a lover or social superior above a stranger's life. Actions that would have once led to dishonour are now openly accepted in most circles: few today would bat an eyelid at someone bearing an illegitimate child (like Mrs. Burleigh), marrying a married man (like Lady Beatrice), or having an extramarital affair (like the Reverend Carteret), but a hundred years ago, the fear of shame could have conceivably justified the murder, manipulation, and self-imposed penance presented in *Raw Edges*. Landon's stories of the social imbroglios of the upper classes may well have been inspired by gossip he heard while moving in these circles, and one of his good friends did eventually find himself at the centre of a scandal: William Lygon, 7th Earl Beauchamp, who Landon served as private secretary, was exposed as a homosexual by his brother-in-law, the Duke of Westminster, in 1931.[36] It will likely remain unknown whether or not Landon knew that his friend and employer was hiding this secret from his own recording angel.

In *Raw Edges*, even those characters who personally confront physical death must still consider social propriety. In *Skin for Skin*, the president of a young republic narrowly escapes assassination, only to be confronted with a complex moral dilemma while recuperating: spare the life of the failed assassin, or uphold the integrity of the law. The moral imperative to save a man's life is muddied with the selfish desire to preserve his own presidency and the earnest belief that only in doing so can he secure the best interests of the republic. Like Mrs. Rivers, President Carmichael ultimately leaves the decision to the law, losing the would-be assassin his life and himself the presidency. In *The Crusader's Mass*, the dying Milbank, although unable to warn the British army of the Boers' plans, is at least able to protect the reputation of the woman he loved. It is only in *Thurnley Abbey* that the fear of social shame is eclipsed by the fear of death: after their ghoulish visitation, Alastair Colvin and John and Vivien Broughton are unconcerned about any scandal resulting from the butler seeing them in bed together.

Landon was arguably a man more of the British Empire than of Britain, and at the time *Raw Edges* was written, the empire was approaching its zenith, with colonies on all continents except Antarctica. The imperialistic ambitions of men such as Cecil Rhodes in South Africa and Francis Younghusband in India had seen the empire grow in territory and influence at the cost of many lives, lost not only in battle, but also to the attendant horsemen of famine and pestilence. Landon's stories do not shy away from these horrors, and his tales of South Africa in particular highlight the reality of conflict: the lonely death of a war correspondent on the veldt in *The Crusader's Mass*, the lists of those sent to their death in *'And Our Ignorance in Asking'*, and the stark brutality of the concentration camps in *Between Thee and Him Alone*. Cessation of war does not mean the end of conflict, and in *An Outpost of the Empire*, Landon shows the cycles of violence that can erupt between two peoples following colonisation.

The adoption of technological marvels during the Victorian and Edwardian eras also had the potential to bring about death and misery: in *Railhead*, it is casually noted that 'all engineers know that their lives must be sacrificed to carry out any important work.' But it is in the thirteenth and final tale, *The Gyroscope*, that this theme of the dangers of technology comes to the fore. *The Gyroscope* is an early science fiction horror story that is both truly inventive and horrific, a nightmare that surpasses even *Thurnley Abbey* in its ability to unsettle. The machine run amuck in a crowded auditorium recalls such tragic accidents as the Victoria Hall disaster of 1883 and the Iroquois Theatre fire of 1903. In *The Gyroscope*, Landon does not appear to be criticising technology itself, but rather those who, in their ignorance, unleash its destructive, diabolical power. The unlikely survivor, Alston, retreats to the countryside to live a simple rural existence, far away from the latest technological advances. By the final page, Alston balks at the task of killing rats, the parallels with the gyroscope's emotionless extermination perhaps too much to bear.

And finally, what of the missing fourteenth story mentioned in the preface? All we know is that the publisher refused to include it, and yet Landon claims its publication 'might have saved some children from ill treatment by reason of its very ugliness.' Considering the nature of the tales that were published, this story must have been very ugly indeed. Sadly, it is most likely that the story no longer exists, destroyed along with Landon's other papers after Kipling's death.

## ALBERTO MARTINI

It would be remiss of me to fail to mention the illustra-tions commissioned to accompany *Railhead*, *Thurnley Abbey*, *Between Thee and Him Alone*, and *The Gyroscope*, which were printed on plate sections and protected by tissue guards in the original 1908 publication, and are reproduced here. These four illustrations were drawn in ink by the Italian painter, illustrator, and engraver Alberto Giacomo Spiridione Martini (24 November 1876 – 8 November 1954), whose beautiful, grotesque, and intricate linework remains just as shocking and compelling as it was over a century ago.

# INTRODUCTION

In a review of the original edition of *Raw Edges* that appeared in the *Athenæum*, Martini's illustrations were described as 'rather clever and very fanciful, after a grotesque fashion.'[34] A second review, published in *The Spectator*, declared:

> It is not too much to say that there is not one of these stories which does not leave the reader either unhappier for having read it, or with a tendency to look over his shoulder at the dark corners of the room. The four illustrations by Mr. Alberto Martini do nothing to lessen this effect, anything more horrible than the picture which faces p. 64 having surely never been offered to the public by way of an illustration to a volume of light fiction.[33]

The picture facing page 64 is that which accompanies *Thurnley Abbey*, in which the shadowy, emaciated, and eyeless figure of an undead nun pierces the remorseless darkness that lies between the ornately carved columns of a four-poster bed. In the picture accompanying *Railhead*, a wild-eyed man struggles out from a coffin buried prematurely beneath packing-cases and steel tools. *The Gyroscope*, released from its bonds, cruelly reflects the ghoulish faces of the audience as it spins towards its entranced victim. And finally, the illustration for *Between Thee and Him Alone* takes the greatest liberties with its source material, depicting a monstrous angel of death and bullets, blindfolded as it bravely faces the firing squad. All four illustrations are couched deep in death and madness, the meticulous hatching engendering an almost nauseating and intoxicating effect, the areas of light drawing the eye to gruesome apparitions, and the darkness hiding worse sights still. Whereas Landon hoped his tales 'have been written from a point of view from which other men also have looked,' few perhaps have seen the world in quite the same dazzling horror as Alberto Martini. Of his technique, Martini wrote in his autobiography, *Vita d'artista*, that:

> The pen is the art's scalpel, a tool that is as sharp and tricky as the violin [...]. I worked with the world's thinnest pens, 'Made in England,' on *piccolo cavallo* paper that I had sent from Germany and that you can no longer get hold of today, with India ink that came from Japan. I sharpened the extremely fragile pen on Indian stone, never enough, and to obtain certain greys I had to turn it over, and if it still wasn't enough, dilute the ink. Depending on the case, my pen was as strong as a burin and as light as a feather...
> For the transition from white to black, modelling flesh, veils, velvets, hair, water, clouds, light and fire I used a very fine weaving of traits, that I elaborated with the back of the pen, later stippling and finally retouching with the steel tip. [...] With this passionate technique, I composed the drawings for Poe, Shakespeare, Mallarmé, the erotics and others.[37]

The cover of the original *Raw Edges* included the small upper section of Martini's illustration for *Between Thee and Him Alone*, showing the Maxim gun used by the story's powerfully principled protagonist at the climax. The Angel of Death below is hidden beneath a black background, upon which is emblazoned the book's title in red. One may wonder whether this was a purely stylistic decision (and certainly the unadorned design makes a bold statement), or whether the publisher's original intention to display the illustration in its bizarre glory ran afoul of the censors. Regardless of the reasoning, we have decided to unveil the full illustration for this 21st century release, in part to distinguish the cover from the 1908 original, but also to celebrate Martini's mastery of the surreal beauty and madness of the human condition.

To explain how *Raw Edges* came to be depicted with such striking imagery, I must say a few words about the life of the artist. Alberto Martini was born in 1876 in the comune of Oderzo in Veneto in Northern Italy to Giorgio Martini (1845–1910), a portrait painter and professor of drawing, and Maria dei Conti Spineda de' Cattaneis, an aristocrat of the old nobility.[38] The family later moved to Treviso in 1879, where Giorgio Martini taught drawing at the Istituto Tecnico Riccati. The elder Martini was also his son's first teacher of painting and draughtsmanship. In 1897, Alberto Martini exhibited a series of fourteen paintings, entitled *La Corte dei Miracoli* (*The Court of Miracles*), at the second Venice Biennale; these paintings were later exhibited in Monaco and at the International Exhibition of Turin. While staying in Monaco in 1898, Martini worked as an illustrator for the German art magazines *Dekorative Kunst* and *Jugend*.[39]

Alberto Martini spent much of his career illustrating historic works of literature, including Dante's *The Divine Comedy* (1321), Luigi Pulci's romantic epic *Morgante Maggiore* (1483) (translated as *Morgante: The Epic Adventures of Orlando and His Giant Friend*), and Alessandro Tassoni's mock-heroic epic poem *La Secchia Rapita* (*The Kidnapped Bucket*; 1622).[39] From 1905 to 1909, Martini produced 132 ink illustrations based on the works of Edgar Allan Poe[40]; these illustrations, which are stylistically similar to those created for *Raw Edges* in the same period, were eventually published posthumously by Franco Maria Ricci as *Alberto Martini Illustratore di Edgar Allan Poe* in 1985.[41] In 1907, Martini was invited by the publisher William Heinemann to visit London, where he was commissioned to create the artwork for *Raw Edges*. In his autobiography, Martini said the following about his time in London:

# INTRODUCTION

> I was invited to London by William Heinemann, then
> the most important editor in the world. [...] I did
> not stay long in London, as my unquenchable Latin
> sacred fire would not be adjusted like a paraffin lamp
> by the cold, staid English control. I said no to fortune
> and returned happily to gay and spiritual Paris, where
> I spent my earnings well, and then returned almost
> penniless to Milan (it is very easy to return penniless
> from Paris!).[37]

Martini's evident talent for depicting the macabre was put
to powerful use during the Great War: from 1914 to 1915,
he created five sets of propaganda cartoons (54 lithographs
in total) in a series called *Danza Macabra Europea* (*The
European Dance of Death*), some of which were turned into
postcards and distributed to troops in the trenches on the
front line. These disturbing cartoons were created when Italy
was still neutral, and so depicted not only the Central Powers,
but also the Allied Powers as monstrous figures: in one, a
grinning Japanese revenant gloats over the bloated corpse of
a German soldier after the battle of Tsing-Tao; in another, a
British ghoul demands that the *Manneken Pis* fight the Kaiser,
while elsewhere, a French skeleton wearing the bonnet rouge
of the Revolution sharpens a scythe on a whetstone made of
bones. Italy, naturally enough, is depicted as a comely victim
of the insensate violence, caught between the Great Powers.[42]

Martini later moved away from monochromatic ink to
polychromatic paint, working on the theme of woman as
butterfly and other dream-like pastel scenes. Martini's work
at this time is considered to have been an influence on the
Surrealism movement that emerged in the 1920s.[43] Martini
also had a passion for the theatre, creating 84 pen and
watercolour drawings and six tempera panels for the costumes
of the ballet *Il Cuore di Cera* (*The Heart of Wax*).[39] In 1923,

# INTRODUCTION

he proposed a form of theatre on a platform surrounded by water, that he called 'Tetiteatro,' dedicated to the goddess of the sea Teti. In his book *Il Tetiteatro*, published in 1924, Martini illustrated various scenes that might be performed 'on the water,' including the crucifixion of Christ, a city under assault, and *The Eumenides* by the Greek tragedian Aeschylus.[44]

Largely ignored by the critics in his native Italy, Martini decided to move to Paris in 1928, where he continued the work he described as 'painting the colour of the sky' and 'black painting.'[39,45] He also continued to create satirical pieces, now focused against the artistic movement of novecentism, which were published in the journal *Perseo* (*Perseus*) in 1935–1936.[39] In one of his final projects, he created 20 lithographs for *La Vita della Vergine e altre poesie* (*The Life of the Virgin and other poems*) by the Austrian poet Rainer Maria Rilke.[46] Alberto Martini died in Milan on 8 November 1954, leaving behind an enormous body of work that continues to shock, inspire, and unsettle.[39]

## IN CLOSING

In addition to the original text and illustrations, this new edition of *Raw Edges* includes seven appendices related to Landon's life and works. I have also included notes with definitions of selected words, expressions, quotes, references, locations, historical figures, events, and organisations, some of which may not be familiar to modern readers. I take full responsibility for any mistakes in this volume, and I hope that the information provided in this introduction will perhaps serve as a starting point for future scholarship into Landon and his works.

I have taken great care to reproduce the main text of *Raw Edges* with the utmost fidelity, and have resisted the urge to modernise spellings ('to-day' for example, remains in its

# INTRODUCTION

original hyphenated form). Certain terms and expressions contained within these stories may be considered objectionable by some readers in the 21st century, reflecting changes in societal values in the time since *Raw Edges* was originally published. The reader is trusted to draw their own conclusions and to consider the work within the context of the time in which it was written.

Glowbug Publishing is proud to bring *Raw Edges* back to life after the century it spent out of the public eye. We are a strong proponent of preserving the past by reprinting forgotten works; while the Internet has proven to be exceptionally useful in this regard, none of us know what the future holds, and it seems prudent to ensure that we also have some eggs outside of the online basket. I hope you enjoy this volume, and encourage you to visit the Glowbug Publishing website to browse our other publications. I also welcome readers to send any enquiries or comments to glowbugpublishing@gmail.com.

*D. Edward Wright*
*Editor-in-Chief, Glowbug Publishing*
*May 2024*

*D. Edward Wright obtained his doctorate in molecular neurobiology from the University of Warwick, and later studied languages in Japan and Taiwan. He now works in academic publishing, but dabbles in translation, writing, and research. His interests include literature, linguistics, education, history, art, conservation, religion, and philosophy. He would like to thank Craig Hargreaves and David Harry for valuable discussions and insight, and his parents for their kind support and assistance.*

# REFERENCES

1    Landon P. *Raw Edges: Studies and Stories of These Days*. London: William Heinemann; 1908.

2    Landon, Perceval, (29 March 1869–23 Jan. 1927), barrister-at-law; special correspondent, dramatist and author. *Who Was Who*. 2007 Dec 1; doi:10.1093/ww/9780199540884.013.u199031

3    Cokayne GE. *The Complete Peerage of England, Scotland, Ireland, Great Britain and the United Kingdom, Extant, Extinct or Dormant. Volume One*. 2nd ed. London: The St. Catherine Press Ltd; 1910.

4    Mosley C, editor. *Burke's Peerage, Baronetage & Knightage*. 107th ed. Wilmington, Delaware: Burke's Peerage Ltd; 2003.

5    Rao CH. *The Indian Biographical Dictionary*. Madras: Pillar & Co.; 1915.

6    Foster J. *Oxford Men & their Colleges*. Oxford: J. Parker & Co.; 1893.

7    Lygon W (7th Earl of Beauchamp). *Diary written while Governor of New South Wales*. Mitchell Library, State Library of New South Wales; 1899-ca. 1900.

8    Pakenham T. *The Boer War*. New York: Random House; 1979.

9    Ralph J. *War's Brighter Side: The Story of "The Friend" Newspaper Edited by the Correspondents with Lord Roberts's forces, March–April, 1900*. New York: D. Appleton and Company; 1901.

10   Pinney T, editor. *The Letters of Rudyard Kipling. Volume Five: 1920–1930*. Basingstoke: Palgrave Macmillan; 2004.

11   *Obituary: Perceval Landon. The Times*. 23 Jan. 1927.

12   Parmenter J (Perceval Landon). *Helio-Tropes or New*

*Posies for Sundials. Written in an Old Book Partly in English and Partly in Latin and Expounded in English by John Parmenter, Clerk, of Wingham in the County of Kent 1625.* London: Methuen & Co.; 1904.

**13** Valentine M. *PERCEVAL LANDON: A BOOK OF SHADOWS.* 7 June. Wormwoodiana [online]. 2021. [Accessed 19 March 2024]. Available from: http://wormwoodiana.blogsp ot.com/2012/06/perceval-landon-book-of-shadows.html

**14** Burke J. *Encyclopædia of Heraldry, or General Armory of England, Scotland and Ireland: Comprising a registry of all armorial bearings from the earliest to the present time, including the late grants by the College of Arms.* London: H.G. Bohn; 1840.

**15** Cokayne GE. *Complete Baronetage. Volume One (1611–1625).* Exeter: William Pollard & Co.; 1900.

**16** Landon P. *Notes on the Heraldry of the Oxford Colleges.* In: Archaeologia Oxoniensis 1892–1895. London: Henry Frowde, Amen Corner; 1895.

**17** Allen C. *Duel in the Snows. The True Story of the Younghusband Mission to Lhasa.* London: John Murray; 2004.

**18** Lycett A. *Rudyard Kipling.* London: Weidenfeld & Nicolson; 1999.

**19** Landon P. *Lhasa: An Account of the Country and People of Central Tibet and of the Progress of the Mission Sent There by the English Government in the Year 1903-4. Volumes One and Two.* London: Hurst & Blackett, Ltd; 1905.

**20** Landon P. *Under the Sun: Impressions of Indian Cities: with a chapter dealing with the later life of Nana Sahib.* New York: Doubleday, Page & Company; 1907.

**21** Landon P. *"1857": In Commemoration of the 50th Anniversary of the Indian Mutiny: With an Appendix Containing the Names of the Survivors of the Officers, Non-commissioned Officers and Men who fought in India in 1857.* London: W.H. Smith & Son; 1907.

**22**  *The programme of a performance of 'The House Opposite' by Perceval Landon*. London: Queen's Theatre. The British Library. 1910.

**23**  Bayreuth. *Music and Drama*. New Zealand Graphic. 26 January 1910. Volume XLIV, issue 4, page 14.

**24**  Brereton A. *"H.B." and Laurence Irving*. London: Grant Richards Ltd.; 1922.

**25**  *The House Opposite*. [Film] Directed by: Walter West and Frank Wilson. UK: British Broadwest Film Company; 1917.

**26**  *The Era Almanack and Annual*. Chicago: Open Court Publishing Co.; 1911.

**27**  'The Salamander.' *A Place in the Sun*. The Sun News-Pictorial. Melbourne. 29 Jun 1925, page 7.

**28**  Lygon W (7th Earl of Beauchamp). *Lord Beauchamp: Message to New South Wales*. The West Australian. Perth. 12 May 1899, page 5.

**29**  Kipling R. *Rudyard Kipling's Verse: Inclusive Edition 1885–1926. Fourth Impression*. London: Hodder and Stoughton, Ltd.; 1929.

**30**  Landon P. *Nepal. Volumes Ones and Two*. London: Constable and Co. Ltd.; 1928.

**31**  von Ruff A *et al*. *Thurnley Abbey*. The Internet Speculative Fiction Database (ISFDB) [online]. [Accessed 21 March 2024]. Available from: https://www.isfdb.org/cgi-bin/title.cgi?73932

**32**  Boucher A & McComas JF. *Introduction to Thurnley Abbey*. The Magazine of Fantasy. Fall 1949, page 18.

**33**  *Books: Raw Edges. The Spectator*. 4 July 1908, page 26.

**34**  *Short stories: Raw Edges. The Athenæum*. No. 4206. 6 June 1908, page 695.

**35**  *The Short Story of Convention. The Nation*. 6 June 1908, page 354.

# REFERENCES

**36**     Lacey R. *Aristocrats*. Boston: Little, Brown, & Company; 1983.

**37**     Botta A. *Alberto Martini: "The pen is the art's scalpel": Drawings for Edgar Allan Poe and other themes*. Henderson S, translator. Rome: Galleria d'Arte Carlo Virgilio & C.; 2021.

**38**     Monferini A. *Alberto Martini (Oderzo 1876 - Milan 1954)*. Bank of Italy Art Collection [online].[Accessed 22 March 2024]. Available from: https://collezionedarte.bancadit alia.it/en/-/alberto-martini

**39**     *Alberto Martini*. Laocoon Gallery [online]. [Accessed 24 March 2024]. Available from: https://laocoongallery.co.uk/ alberto-martini-2/

**40**     Carlson EW, editor. *A Companion to Poe Studies*. Westport, Connecticut: Greenwood Press; 1996.

**41**     Lorandi M, editor. *Alberto Martini illustratore di Edgar Allan Poe*. Milan: Franco Maria Ricci; 1984.

**42**     Bryant M. *The world's greatest war cartoonists and caricaturists, 1792-1945*. London: Grub Street; 2011.

**43**     Hopkinson M. *Italian Prints 1875-1975*. Burlington, Vermont: Lundon Humphries; 2007.

**44**     Martini A. *Il Tetiteatro: "Il teatro d'arte sull'acqua"*. Milan: Bottega di Poesia; 1924.

**45**     Roberts P. *Alberto Martini, Masks & Shadows*. 23 Feb. London Art Week [online]. 2022. [Accessed 25 March 2024]. Available from: https://londonartweek.co.uk/alberto-martini-masks-shadows/

**46**     Rilke RM. *La Vita della Vergine e altre poesie*. Virgillito R, translator. Milan: Editoriale Italiana; 1945.

RAILHEAD.

# RAW EDGES

## STUDIES AND STORIES
## OF THESE DAYS BY
### PERCEVAL LANDON

#### WITH DESIGNS BY

#### ALBERTO MARTINI

'THERE IS IN THIS TALE,' SAID THE
MAN, 'NO GREAT MATTER THAT I
HAVE LEFT UNSAID, AND THAT
LITTLE I HAVE THOUGHT
THAT I HAD NO
NEED TO
SAY'

LONDON
PUBLISHED BY
WILLIAM HEINEMANN
MCMVIII

# PREFACE

No one reads a preface seriously, so there is not such great importance in it that a man may not speak the truth therein. Short stories have but one recommendation—sometimes they catch a mood that is bound to pass before a novel is read through. The best of them may hold its interest for an hour. If there is any good in these tales at all, it is that they have been written from a point of view from which other men also have looked. For the rest, if they vary the outlook through the window of a railway carriage upon the woods and fields drifting by, they will have done as much as most. One ugly tale I would have added had my publisher permitted. He probably knows best—yet it might have saved some children from ill treatment by reason of its very ugliness.

I wish to thank Signor Alberto Martini for the brilliant designs with which he has illustrated the spirit of these tales.

P. L.

5 PALL MALL PLACE,
LONDON, S.W.

3

TO THE DAWN

# RAILHEAD

THIS story was told me in Rangoon by a man whose name, I think, was Torrens, but I cannot remember very clearly, if indeed I ever knew. Really I hardly know anything about the man except that he was obviously convinced of its truth. He said that John Silbermeister told him the story himself, and I have no doubt that he did. So far as Torrens could recall the man, Silbermeister was an ordinary lanky man, of a singular directness of speech, and totally unable to see a joke. So, for that matter, was Torrens. He said that he had verified the story to this extent, that at the date that Silbermeister mentioned, the N.P. Railway would have reached Enderton; nor is it apparent what motive there could be for Silbermeister lying in the matter. Torrens hadn't the imagination of a 'rickshaw-wallah, so it isn't his lie either. At any rate, I give it for what it is worth.

Torrens was a little man who had taken up Christian Science somewhat earnestly a little beyond middle life. He was really a person of some importance on the railway, and I believe one of the Company's most efficient servants. To listen to him sometimes one would hardly believe that an accident could possibly occur on the railway, except as a mere delusion of the senses. I believe he died about two years after he told me the story, and for his own sake I hope that he was able to maintain his Christian Science doctrines to the end, for he had sore need of them. He died of cholera at Bhamo in 1904.

He had shown me round the curiosity-shops of Rangoon, and with his help I had disentangled one or two interesting pieces of work from the mass of modern substitutes—it is unfair to call them forgeries—which fill up the curio-shelves of Rangoon dealers. One of them was a little bronze serpent, which sat on its rounded tail and blinked at me with ruby eyes as he told the story in the billiard-room of the 'Strand'; and I remember that the Calcutta boat was coming in from the Hastings shoal at the time, and from time to time wailed like a lost spirit up the river. The heat was intense. They have not in Rangoon the mosquito antidotes to which one is used in India. One buzzing electric fan supplied the entire room, but its sphere of influence was entirely monopolised by a pair of German diamond merchants and their jet-clad wives.

'Some years ago,' said Torrens, 'a man called Silbermeister came to me with excellent references, and asked if there was any chance of his being employed on the new construction towards the Yunnan frontier. That was before Curzon had put a stopper on the whole project. I dare say Curzon was right. The railway to the North-East, both on this side and on the other side of the frontier, would have been extremely expensive and possibly impracticable. There are deep ravines, "canyons," Silbermeister called them, across which our line had to be thrown. To zigzag down to the bottom by reversing stations and then up again seemed to be the only possible means of crossing them, and with such enormous initial expenditure it was doubtful whether the traffic would ever pay one per cent. upon the capital. But we in Rangoon wanted to establish a definite connection with China for political reasons, and if the Indian Government had been willing to guarantee half the cost, the Burmah Railways would have gone on with the business.* Silbermeister, who had had a good deal of pioneer railway experience, would have been just the man for the job. While the matter was being decided in Calcutta he remained here, and I saw a good deal of him. One evening Silbermeister told me this story, and, so far as I can judge the man at all, I should say that he was telling me the truth.'

Some years ago, when the big New York Syndicate that employed Silbermeister, among thirty thousand others, was pushing forward the construction of the N.P. Railway in Nebraska, he was for about three months in charge of the railhead station at Enderton. This was merely a solidly built wooden hut by the side of the line. Trains ran up to it and nominally carried passengers, but as a matter of fact very few wanted to go farther than Castleton, a raw pioneer clump of houses, which had already blossomed out into half a dozen stores, seven 'hotels,' an electric generating shed, and thirty or forty pretentiously named wooden houses. Beyond Enderton the railway was at this time actually in course of construction. The navvies were chiefly Italian. It was a difficult piece of work, and about eight miles on matters had temporarily come to a standstill owing to a persistent subsidence along the edge of a small half-dry river. On one Thursday morning a piece of the embankment had given way, and an Italian workman had been killed. This was a matter of no great importance; all engineers know that their lives must be sacrificed to carry out any important work, and on the whole the loss of life on this section of the N.P. line had been less than might have been expected. There were the usual police guards in the navvies' camp, which contained between three to four hundred workmen.

On a Friday evening, between six and seven o'clock, Silbermeister was sitting in his station-house at Enderton running

---

\*        Torrens was scarcely accurate in this matter.

over the week's wages' account, when a light engine ran up from Castleton. Silbermeister was expecting the money with which to pay the navvies' weekly wages on the following day, and a sub-inspector got off the footplate carrying a canvas bag which contained the money that was needed. It was the usual week-end routine. At the same time, a couple of railwaymen took off the tender half a dozen large packing-cases containing materials that had been requisitioned for the work, and put them into the baggage-room, which composed one-half of the station-house. The inspector ran through Silbermeister's accounts, initialled them as correct, and then took a receipt for the money which he brought with him. Silbermeister proceeded to lock the money up in the safe in his own room, and then checked the packing-cases which had just been stored in the baggage-room. Among these cases was a somewhat gruesome object, a coffin sent up by the Company from Castleton in order that the victim of the late accident might be decently buried on Sunday morning.

Another receipt was signed for the cases, and then the inspector told the engine-driver he was ready to return. Before doing so, however, he turned to Silbermeister and said:

'Do you feel quite safe here with all that money? Shall I leave you a man to spend the night here with you?'

Silbermeister shrugged his shoulders, and with a smile declined the offer. He said that the police looked after the navvies' camp, that he and his negro servant had spent many nights together at the station, and that he had no fear of burglars. He had, he said, his revolver beside him, and the money would not remain with him more than that one night. The two men shook hands, and the inspector departed as he had come.

Silbermeister then re-checked the books, re-counted the money, saw that the doors were properly locked, sent away his negro servant for the night—the man had been getting the table ready for his supper while he was escorting the inspector back to the engine—and, after locking the door leading to the platform, occupied himself with some small duties now that his day's work was done. There was no further possibility of being rung up from Castleton, so he took this opportunity of cleaning and re-adjusting the telegraph instrument which stood on a table by the wall, and had not been working quite satisfactorily that morning. For this purpose he disconnected the instrument, and being a fairly skilled electrician—though of an old-fashioned school, Torrens said—he did nearly all that was needed in a few minutes. Leaving the instrument as it was, he lit a pipe and started to get ready his supper. By this time the night had begun to fall in earnest, and he lighted the kerosene lamp on the table. More from habit than from anything else, as he knew that he was not likely to need it, he also lighted the bull's-eye lantern which, on most evenings in the week, he took with him on his final rounds.

Silbermeister then opened the cupboard and took down a loaf of bread, a tin of canned meat, and a pot of marmalade. His preparations for supper were simple. It was a cold night, and he meant to have some hot grog before turning in, so he lighted the spirit lamp and filled his kettle from a pitcher of water. While the water was boiling he opened the tin of meat, cut himself a German slice of bread, and arranged the table. By this time the sun had entirely set, and only the last reflections from the dull western horizon still found their way through the windows. For a moment he looked out through the windows across the platform and the wide level waste beyond. There was not a living thing in sight—not a tree, hardly a bush. Then he shut up the house for the night, and fastened the shutters. He sat down at the table for his meal, propped up a book underneath the lamp, and made himself as comfortable as he could. The bully-beef was not a very appetising dish, and it occurred to him that he had a bottle of sauce put away in a box at the side of the room. He got up, opened the box, and, in order to find the sauce, turned out upon the floor with some noise most of the contents of the trunk. While doing so, he did not notice that the telegraph instrument on the farther table ticked out a short and sharp message: at least, it was only the last few strokes that attracted his attention. He turned from the box, before which he was kneeling, to listen, but the message had already stopped. Leaving the sauce undiscovered, he rose to his feet and muttered:

'I'm sure the thing was talking,' and went across to the table, to ask for a repetition from Castleton, only to discover, as he might have remembered, that he had himself disconnected the instrument while cleaning it. Dismissing the matter as an illusion, he returned to the box where the sauce was, and after a moment or two found what he wanted. He then resumed his seat at the table without thinking again of the telegraph instrument. He began his reading, and was in the middle of an engrossing sentence when the telegraph instrument spoke again. This time there could be no mistake. Silbermeister, who knew that when he had left the machine three minutes before it was entirely disconnected, laid down his knife and fork and listened like a man in a dream. There was no doubt about it.

'E—N—T.'

The signal for Enderton Station had been called up sharply, imperiously, unmistakably. He waited a moment, and then, in spite of the fact that he had not acknowledged the call, came the short message. He muttered the words as they were ticked out:

*'Watch the box.'*

For one full minute Silbermeister sat immovable. There was no question of the fact, yet the man's common sense refused to believe in what his ears had heard. The room was dead silent except for the hissing of the spirit lamp which had just begun to boil. Silbermeister felt that he was the victim of some nightmare. He would not believe his own senses, and decided to test the thing once more. He rose from the table, went across to the instrument, and brought it bodily away from its position. He put it on the table in front of him next the corned beef, and then, blowing out the spirit lamp in order that the silence might be more intense, he resumed his seat and waited, hanging over it with every sense on the alert. The lamp lighted up his angular jaw and deep-set eyes staring at the little contrivance of brass and wood. He had not to wait long. The instrument, with its connecting wires and plugs hanging over the side of his dinner-table, and still swinging to and fro beneath it, once again called out his station:

'E—N—T.'

The sweat leapt to Silbermeister's forehead, but he made no sign. It went on. It was the same message, short, clear, and beyond all doubt:

'*Watch the box.*'

Silbermeister passed a hand over his face and thought. Whatever the origin of this message was, the message itself was unmistakable. He reached for his bull's-eye lantern, saw it was burning well, turned out the lamp on the table, and rose silently. He moved across to the door that separated his living-room from the luggage-room, very quietly opened the door, and waited. One minute dragged its slow length along, then two, then three, and still Silbermeister stood in the darkness as motionless as the jamb of the door. There was no sound inside or outside the station-house. So still was the silence that, as Silbermeister said, a man could hear his blood circulating round the drum of his own ear—rather a good expression, Torrens thought.

At last the tension was relieved. There was a sound, more like the sound of a gnawing mouse than anything else, and Silbermeister sank silently to his knee to listen more intently. A touch which, infinitesimal though it was, could only have been made by iron upon iron, betrayed the whole circumstance to him. There was a man in the coffin, and the man had so contrived the lid that he could get out of the coffin without attracting the notice of Silbermeister till it was too late. There was at the same moment the sound of a cautiously planted footstep on the platform outside. Silbermeister acted at once. Some of the cases of railway material that had been sent up that evening contained steel tools, and were as much as two men could carry into the room. Silbermeister was a strong man, but he hardly knew how he managed unaided to drag down one of the packing-cases and set it on the top of the coffin with a crash that almost crushed it in.

The moment he had done so, all pretence was at an end, and the man within it shouted to his accomplice outside. The answer was a blow on the door like a battering-ram. The packing-case might hold down the man for some time yet, so Silbermeister leapt back into his living-room to meet the new danger, only to find the door on to the platform being battered through just above the bolt. He picked up his revolver, and in order to make sure there should be no attack from behind, aimed at the coffin and pulled the trigger. There was no response. It was clear that treachery had been at work. His black servant had seized the opportunity while Silbermeister escorted the inspector to the engine, of opening and emptying it—an easy task, as it was lying on the table. There was no time to turn back to the baggage-room. Seizing a small crowbar, Silbermeister had only just time to dash to the door, through the hole in which his negro servant's arm was now thrusting itself feeling for the bolt. He gripped the man's hand and pulled it into the room until the negro's arm-pit was forced up against the splintered hole in the door. He struck heavily with the crowbar, and the negro screamed in agony. He struck again, and again, and again. He hardly knows what happened during that awful minute. He went on striking blindly and mechanically at what had suddenly become a man's sleeve. In the baggage-room he had just left the tremendous exertions of the imprisoned man were making the room resound, and the packing-case on the top of the coffin rocked to and fro. Silbermeister paid no attention. He lost his head. Both lamps were now out, and all he could do in the darkness was to go on hitting at what he held.

\*　　　　　\*　　　　　\*　　　　　\*　　　　　\*

Suddenly there was the whistle of an approaching engine. No train was due until the following morning, but Silbermeister admitted that at the moment he hardly regarded anything as unusual. A couple of armed men and the inspector leapt down on to the platform, collared the negro servant, who by that time was hanging half-unconscious from the hole in the door, and burst in just in time to intercept the man in the baggage-room who had at last overturned the packing-case above him and was crashing his way out through the lid of the coffin. It was an extraordinary scene.

The inspector pulled the negro servant, with his arm one pulp of splintered bone and blood, into the room and thrust him roughly aside. He fell without a moan into the corner. The two men then brought the burglar into the living-room between them. Silbermeister went back to the table, sat down, and put his head between his hands. The inspector looked at him for a moment in amazement as he raised his head and said: 'Thank God!' After a pause he added: 'Why did you come?'

The inspector answered:

'Your telegram caught us just before we left Castleton again. It was lucky, wasn't it?' he added grimly.

Silbermeister again raised his head from his hands, and as if he had heard nothing, said:

'But why did you come?'

The inspector, a trifle gravely, said:

'I told you, your telegram just reached us in time.'

There was another pause of ten seconds, and then Silber-meister pointed to the disconnected instrument, and said once more:

'Why did you come?' His eyes turned in his head: 'I sent no message'; and then he fell on the floor in a dead faint.

\*      \*      \*      \*      \*

That is all I know about it. That is the story that Torrens told me, and the story that undoubtedly Torrens believed.

# OVERTRIED

I DO not know if I am guilty of a grave indiscretion in saying so, but it has often seemed to me that the present remembrance of a past and most repentable deed is the surest road to the achievement of that sympathy whereby alone other men may be helped.

There was one hidden chapter in the life of the Rev. Richard Carteret, and there was only one other person in the world who knew it.

I remember seeing him one evening, after service in his great Norfolk church was over, when he could not have known that there was any one left in the darkening building, drop almost like a stone beside the carved oak finial at the eastern end of the choir seats, and lean his forehead against the old browned wood. He said nothing, but he remained there for some minutes, and if it had not been for a certain motionless of the kneeling figure, one might have thought that he was but murmuring the prayer that is said, from habit or in earnest, by most clergymen, when leaving the church.

Certainly Carteret was the finest parson I have ever known. Dissent was as needless as it was futile in Leigh Monacorum, for there was no material in the ranks of Methodism or Congregationalism wherewith to gainsay a priest who sang his song, made his hundred, withstood the unjust, and understood the tired and bewildered with equal simplicity and transparent honesty, without affectation or self-seeking. No man was more welcome in the village, or, when he could be induced to go, up at Middlelees also, where the squire of this and twelve other parishes lived in unmarried solitude, and appreciated to the full the man he had been able to secure for his own home parish. The M.P. for the district had mentioned his name first to him, explaining that he was an old friend of his at Oxford, who had at one time been in India, and had been ordained in a curious state of dissatisfaction with his life. Carteret himself had never known to whom he owed his presentation. From the first day of his arrival he had been a favourite with every one, and the usual silly pursuit of a new clergyman had ensued on the part of some of the women of the neighbourhood. But the report, that had not lost in the telling, of the way in which he had met the advances of a wealthy and otherwise excellent lady, damped the ardour of the pack.

She had written to him delicately suggesting that they should in company pursue the paths of parochial labour, and she had received an answer that he would be glad to do so on one condition,—but he asked her to keep his answer a secret from every one till he had informed her of the condition.

But this was entirely beyond the self-restraint of the lady: she imparted the happy news to three or four of her most intimate friends under the strictest promise of secrecy, and awaited an interview that evening with cooing self-satisfaction. But Carteret's manner from the first discouraged any sentiment, and after sternly reproaching her with the indecency—a word that the poor lady had never heard before, except as applied to quite other and terrible persons—of her behaviour, told her that the condition was that they should postpone the marriage till he proposed to her. She left the parish, and the story was the property of too many for Carteret to be troubled again in that way.

And he went on his way alone, doing his work better than another might have done it, because there was so little that seemed to interest him outside the boundary fences of Leigh parish.

The squire, Mr. Wynnstay, had learned long ago to respect the silence that Carteret rarely broke about his earlier years. He only knew that he had come from a parish in one of the greater manufacturing towns with a letter of recommendation from his late chief—a man who was not given to wasting his praise—that a Lowder or a Damien might have envied. His health was at that time entirely broken down from overwork, and it was long before it was discovered that in the new rector the parish had gained an old blue and a scholar whose final honours would in most years have won him a first.

But he never gave any one the slightest hint that he regretted his decision to come and bury himself in this utterly insignificant parish in the eastern counties; indeed, he had declined the bishop's offer of a more important living in Norwich itself, although his lordship had twice made the offer, the last time with a hint that it would gravely displease him if the refusal were persisted in. However, nothing could move Carteret, and Wynnstay was sincerely thankful that he was willing to remain, though no mention of the matter had been made between them. The squire, who was a man of the world, and would have called himself an agnostic, if he had not known the meaning of the word, realised that he had a most unusual man in Carteret, and would have regarded any attempt on his own part to find out the reason for his rector's unwillingness to avail himself of the really excellent offer of the bishop, as an act in unpardonably bad taste. So the rector stayed on.

Visitors were few and far between at both the rectory and the big house. Now and then, one man at a time would appear at Middlelees, and then Carteret as a matter of course was invited to meet him. Intensely as Wynnstay and, as a rule, his guests also, were out of sympathy with the point of view taken by clergymen, without distinction of cloth, he knew well enough that his friends would never have become his friends if they had been unable to see that the rector of Leigh Monacorum belonged to the small class of 'men who understand.' Often and often, when Wynnstay had seen Carteret out of the front door in the evening and had returned to his guest in the smoking-room, the latter would wheel round from the fire and demand the whole truth about the *rara avis.*

Wynnstay never had a man inside his house who had no qualification besides the power of shooting birds and drinking whisky and soda. They were a curiously assorted crew, but if the chance had offered itself, there was not one who would not have been glad to meet again every one of the rest of them.

If a man had done nothing, Wynnstay had no use for him. Neither rank, money, nor routine service—excellent as they were all admitted to be—was a passport to Middlelees. The only man who resented this state of things was one High Sheriff, who, after a decent period had elapsed, intimated his willingness to stay the night at Middlelees on the occasion of some festivity in the neighbourhood.

The suggestion was received by Wynnstay in blank astonishment. The tale of Carteret's answer had reached the House, and in a fit of mischief he sent back word that it would give him the greatest pleasure to entertain the High Sheriff at any time—after he had had the honour of being introduced to him.

The guests at Middlelees were not numerous, but they came from the ends of the earth: scientists, pioneers, diplomats; one or two refugees were to be found there, and from India there were every year a few tawny, white-haired men whom no one knew in London except the permanent officials of the India Office.

Rarely, indeed, were there more than one at a time, and among the ladies in the vicinity who played croquet, and had long given up any designs upon its owner, Middlelees was indignantly dismissed as the dullest house in the county, and one that was a perfect disgrace to every one concerned.

But one Sunday morning there were no less than three men staying there. One of them was Sir James Manisty, a wizened little old man who had been through the Mutiny, and was the only person, except Colonel Westmacott, who really knew where Nana Sahib was then, and perhaps is now, living. A second was Charteris, the M.P. for the district, who had recommended Carteret to Wynnstay; and the third was a well-known French Monseigneur—well known, that is, to Europe: the village of Leigh was ignorant of his very existence, and righteously concerned that the papistical ecclesiastic should have dared to walk down to the church after luncheon and inspect with the utmost care the font-cover that is considered to be second only to that in Ufford church in the neighbouring county. (It is indeed possible that Leigh would not have thought the better of the Protonotary Apostolic if it had been aware of the story that half Europe connected with De Bernard. It is credibly reported that in reply to the indignant and public expostulations of a certain distinguished princess on a matter of social toleration, he terminated a fruitless and tiresome discussion by remarking with perfect courtesy, 'I am afraid, madam, that you will think me very immoral, but in this matter I have always preferred to err with our Lord.')

De Bernard also noted the 'Tarasque' on the exterior corbel of the rood screen's bracket, and finally filled the cup of his offence in the eyes of Leigh by staying for the afternoon service, and afterwards by blessing with uplifted hand a couple of children who curtsied to a guest at the House.

Carteret was coming to dinner that evening, and Wynnstay, before he went to dress, remarked to Charteris that he never could be sufficiently grateful for the advice that had resulted in the acquisition of the rector.

'As you know, I'm not much at that kind of thing, but I assure you that there is nothing I would not do on the recommendation of that man, church attendance included. In fact, I often do go in the afternoon; I didn't to-day, as I wasn't sure what Monseigneur and you would find to do.'

'I really don't know what his reverence did to-day. I didn't ask him; but he was away nearly the whole of the afternoon, and I haven't seen him since he came in. Well, I was glad your religious fervour failed you, as I wouldn't have missed the gems for anything in the world. Manisty!'

'Hullo.' He was deep in a drawer full of third-century gnostic seals, and did not raise his head.

'Do you know where Monseigneur was this afternoon?'

'Can't think; but here he is to answer for himself. Monseigneur, here's a detective on your track, who wants to know what mischief you've been up to this last three hours.'

'I have been to your church,' said Monseigneur de Bernard, quite simply.

'I thought that you got excommunicated for that, or had to put beans in your shoes for a month, or something mediæval like that.'

'My friend, I do not think anything so distressing will occur to me. For who is there to do these terrible things to me? I am, as you say, out of the jurisdiction. Be reassured.'

'I thought that there was no getting away from the jurisdiction of the Bishop of Rome. You will get Bourne on the top of you if you aren't careful!'

'Ah, yes. Well, I do not think'—(Frenchmen who speak English well always pronounce that word with such betraying perfection)—'I do not think that he will do me very much harm. But'—and he turned to Wynnstay—'you have a most remarkable man here as curate—ah, I mean "vicar"; it is so confusing, you know. Is he to be your guest this evening?' Wynnstay nodded. 'I am glad, for I have not heard so good a sermon for many years, and I wish to ask him of one or two things'—Monseigneur looked across quickly to his host—'unless, of course, there would be any want of tact in my doing so. I did not mean to dispute with him,' he added earnestly.

'Of course, you can do what you like. Did you think, my dear Monseigneur, that I was likely to ask any one to meet you here to-night who was tiresome? Yes, you'll find him worth talking to. Charteris here will undertake that too.'

'And now, may I ask what have you all been doing?' said De Bernard cheerily. 'Upon my word, *you* are pretty people to criticise! Three hours of gnostic gems, and I make no doubt the fullest of full explanations from Manisty. I always believe that you devilled for the *Arabian Nights*—upon my word I do. Talk of Simon Magus! He would be nowhere with our friend over there, and we all know that his reward was worse even than what my friend calls beans in the boots. I shall set the Holy Office at you, my dear and charming people—discipline is needed sorely, and a little match between your toes would save you from these unholy sciences! Besides, I am sure that you have been insisting on your version of the Lesser Limbs, which I have so often—alas, so very often!—proved to you to be wrong, wrong, wrong, my friend. But I see I am only regarded as a *vox clamantis in deserto*, so I will go to dress for dinner.'

Dinner that evening was a meal as it is not understood by many. There were four men who could have held their own with respect against any antagonist in their own lines, and Carteret was no inadequate chorus. The conversation opened with a recognition of the interesting nature of the church and the exterior corbel that had been noticed. Monseigneur found, to his delight, that he had discovered a reliable and fairly extensive authority upon East Anglian architecture, who, as he admitted afterwards, saved him quite a week's travelling, and he was even more pleased with the steady and thorough views of the rector on more serious questions than the orientation or the restoration of churches.

For the talk soon drifted far beyond the eccentricities of architects, who may or may not have been Comacine disciples, to a wider range of incident, experience, and custom. Carteret himself found that his scholarship was but the first step to the breadth and certainty of grasp that distinguished the others. Wynnstay revealed himself in a new light, and the rector realised that he had been quite unable to extend him—as he would have expressed it himself—in all the time the two men had known each other.

Charteris, whose constant pose inside and outside the House was that of a half-educated Philistine, kept pace with the other two with ease, and seemed to have travelled even more than Manisty.

After dinner, in the smoking-room, Monseigneur settled himself into the abysses of an armchair, over the edge of which the single red-shaded lamp glowed on his half-aureole of silver hair and lay richly on the purple sash of his cassock. His white, nervous hand with the deep veins and sharp-cut knuckles lay along the arm, and he gazed long into the fire while Manisty and Wynnstay resumed at the other end of the room their examination of the gems. Two admitted experts were over-hauling one of the finest collections in Europe, and the disputes were prolonged.

Charteris joined them after a moment, and De Bernard and Carteret were left together. The former, without withdrawing his eyes from the red embers, spoke.

# OVERTRIED

'I was in your church this evening, Mr. Carteret, and if I may say these things to you without—what is your word?—not "boring"—I don't like that—*eh bien!* you have no word, but you will understand—I would like to say that I was very much interested in your sermon. I do not remember having heard so good a sermon for a long time. I wish I could preach like that, but my—my—*métier* is different.' Carteret from the recesses of a high-backed chair on the left of the fireplace smiled, but said nothing. The prelate's right hand fingered the chafed piping of his soutane, still staring into the fire. He went on after a moment's pause: 'But will you pardon an old man, a very old man, who has seen so much that all things will, I fear, soon become to him an observation or a memory and nothing more—will you pardon me when I say that you told me this evening more than you meant perhaps to tell me?'

Carteret made no answer, and the white hands clasped themselves on the lap of the cassock.

'We have perhaps been taught to see more in the lives of men than the priests in your church are ever taught to look for. It is not only the inevitable symptoms revealed in the confessional that teach us to see. These latter move in a narrow circle indeed—a narrow circle. Ah, if penitents only knew that there is no new sin under the sun—if they realised that the secret that they believe so unique has perhaps been told in the same place, to the same man, almost in the same words, but the very day before!

'But perhaps the very fact that each one thinks his sin so original is one extra help to abandoning it, and, my faith! they need all the help that they can get.

'But you—you told me much more than the eternal trivialities of a trouble that the moving fingers and the muttered words of the confessor can dispel. For you, as for many others too, there is no help in religion.'

23

Carteret still held his peace, and there was not enough light from the fire for the expression of his face to be seen. Not that Monseigneur looked at him. No small part of the impressiveness of De Bernard's individuality was the unswerving certainty of his demeanour when at last he spoke of any motive or any impulse of his fellow-creatures. He only allowed himself to speak when he felt, beside and perhaps against all reason and all proof, that he was speaking the exact truth, and then neither admissions nor denials affected him.

'If you were an old man, I should be sorry to think that the cloud could never be lifted, for I have rarely heard the note of *accidia*—I love your English "wanhope"—so strongly as I heard it to-night behind the words you used. Do not think that any one else heard the chord; there was no one there who has had the training, perhaps also—*Deo gratias*—the instinct to detect these things. But no man could have preached the words you spoke to us to-night who had not been down into the dark places. And I am not speaking to you to-night in my turn in mere idleness.

'But I will not say more if you contradict me as I now shall speak to you.'

At the farther end of the room the conversation was quick and keen; Charteris was looking for another lamp to get more light, and swooped down upon the table behind the head of Monseigneur.

'You don't want this, do you? Thanks!'

Outside, the wind had risen, and there was a splash of rain against the windows high overhead: an ivy leaf fluttered against a quarrel of loose glass.

De Bernard leaned forward and poked the fire of logs. His face looked like an ivory carving, and he played for a moment with the crucifix that hung from the heavy gold Venetian chain round his neck. His voice was quiet, but as certain as before.

'There are not, perhaps, many of us who can feel the higher degrees of sorrow. And it would be a dangerous doctrine to admit, as priests, that there can be, and that there are griefs that are beyond the healing of religion.

'Not that they are outside the power of God to help, but it is often beyond our earthly strength and perception to lay the health to our souls and live.

'So many have never understood, and have never been called upon to understand this, that it would be indeed unwise to tell those whose strength is unequal to the great truth. Just so, in Rome, the Bambino is exhibited every Christmas, and God only knows what tales are told to the faithful people who come to see for themselves the wax puppet. No one has attended the mummery from the Vatican for many years now, and we are indeed ashamed of it, but the farce has to be played through for those who are not strong enough to receive the disillusionment.

'So, too, we may not cry aloud that in the deepest sorrows the faith we love may at utter need fail us like a broken reed. Do not mistake me. There is indeed a comfort still, but it is not of this world, and in this world the sufferer may not always receive it. There is yet a stay, but it cannot be provided by any power so interwoven with mortality as the Church.

'In the dire extremity of man the religion that has for so long been a garment of honour becomes but a cloak and a hindrance between the agony of man and the abiding mercy of God.'

Monseigneur leaned his head on one hand, and the crucifix lay in the fingers of the other, with the red glow lighting up the worn gold. Almost as though he were speaking to himself, he went on, and the clean-cut features flashed into momentary relief as the logs fell together a little, and a hissing jet leaped into flame for a moment.

' "Deus meus, Deus meus, ut quid dereliquisti me?"—so few have won to the meaning of that cry! So many do not see how nearly in the Garden and again in that cry from the Cross the Man shrank from the last awful test. Yet had the story closed with the word "sabachthani," there would have been our redemption yet to be accomplished. In that He did not shrink, He was divine.

'A man came to me once. He told me that he had reached the stage of despair wherein a man says to himself that God doesn't care, and that he is only making a fool of himself to himself.

'I told him that Christ had gone through the same stage, for who can believe that the bitter agony of the apparent failure of the work of a life, was spared Him?

'And my mouth was moved, and I told him that there was yet another and a bitterer stage still. A few months later he wrote to me that he now saw what I meant, and I asked him to come and see me. I spoke to him, and he told me more of his trouble. I could have knelt before the feet of the man whom, whatever his sins, and they were neither few nor small, God was honouring with all His storms, and I asked him as one asks one's patron saint, if he could tell me how it could be so.

'And he said, so quietly that I could hardly be certain that he had said it: "Oh, I dare say it pleases the Almighty." And I said that it surely did.

'And my lips told him despite myself that there was yet one and only one greater punishment than he had yet endured, and that a Man had survived the trial. And I, not my lips only, told him that night and day, with all the strength I had, I would pray that that might not be his. And he looked on me with wonder and almost in pity, as one who said things that had no meaning, and he went away.

'I kept my word, but it had been but presumption in me. What was ordained was performed, and I had but one more letter from my friend, and that was but a few words. He said that I had been right, and the news of his death two days later was only what I expected. And those who have not known have spoken in hushed words of my friend.'

Monseigneur de Bernard turned at last and for the first time to his companion, who had never moved during the time, and did not seem willing to speak now. The carved amethyst on the prelate's hand caught a line of light as he leaned across the arm of the chair in the direction of the other man, whose face could only fitfully be seen. The other three had gone from the end of the gallery, and there was a silence broken only by the wind in the chimney.

'One of your own Englishmen has used a strange phrase of haunting force. "I speak to you a dying man to dying men"—to dying men, a dying man. Like him, I speak to you a dying man. My name is on the list of those who will at the next Consistory be raised to the Cardinalate. Thereafter there lies a forked path. One way leads me on to all that many'— he paused—'all that most men deem best worth having. The other means that it will not be long before my work is over. Yet I have no choice. Others of us have failed. The "handful of silver" works with us too, and men who are valiant enough in black are often cowards in scarlet. But your case is harder than mine. The church kills me: you it bids live on. My friend, I pray you live on yet, whatever your sorrow.

'Remember always that others have known your agony. Do not believe yourself put away from God because He strips for you His glory of its earthly cloak and offers you Himself and not His sleeve to lean upon.

'And if you should ever say in the darkest hours, "This is not just," then do not lie to your own soul as the friends of Job lied, but whisper very silently the greatest truth of all, the truth that Christ Himself only knew to the depth, that wherein you suffer beyond your deserts, you suffer some part of the punishment that else would fall upon another.'

Carteret caught his breath twice.

'And I pray that though I speak to you a dying man, the other part of Baxter's great line may rest unfulfilled.'

Almost wearily the great ecclesiastic drew himself out of the chair, and raised himself to his full height beside the fireplace.

Then, as one in helpless despair, Carteret dropped from his seat, and knelt with his face in his hands, as Monseigneur's fingers were raised over him, and the hackneyed words of benediction passing slowly from his lips took on a new meaning for both.

The scene held Wynnstay rooted to the spot, as from the door he saw the closing movement. Carteret rose from his knees.

'Well, what have you been discussing? I do hope that neither of you has converted the other, for one doesn't get the chance every day of having a rector who is a friend, and a friend who is going to be a Pope.'

'We have been agreeing that your distinguished poet Browning was untrue to his ideals in using the expression, "He must be wicked to deserve such pain"—an opinion that, if you will do me the honour of remembering your gnosticism, is not unknown in that degrading superstition. But you are all wilful sinners in that matter, none more so than Sir James—a fact that reminds me that if you'— Monseigneur turned to Manisty—'are going to prove to me that Gamaliel was a gnostic, as you once promised, and as you have conspicuously failed hitherto to do, we must set to work at once.'

Carteret, who had recovered his composure during this speech, stayed very little longer, and Monseigneur did not prove very communicative on the subject of their conversation. But later on in the night, Manisty, of whom one could never safely predicate the limitations, said *à propos* of nothing that he felt curiously undecided whether or not the rector was going to die within a short time. 'Generally,' he added, 'I can prophesy to within a week when I have a strong presentiment of death concerning any one I am with, but in *his* case there is a tremendous force acting to save him, while—' His words ceased, and he would have given half his reputation to have recalled them. The keen, amused gaze of De Bernard met his across the table, and both men knew the other man's thoughts. With a shrug of the shoulders, and a face full of affection, Manisty leant over, and the two friends shook hands across the seals over which they continued their argument.

\*　　　　\*　　　　\*　　　　\*　　　　\*

Sir James, however he came to know these things, was right enough in his unspoken prophecy, for within six months Cardinal de Bernard, whom the *Times* described as the most liberal-minded of the College, and one whose elevation but three months before had been universally recognised as reflecting credit on both the Consistory and himself, died while on a visit to one of the small monasteries that shrink among the crannies of the Italian Alps. The Jesuits, with great alacrity, published the certificate of the doctors who had been called in from a neighbouring brotherhood, so the world now knows that His Eminence died of septic tonsilitis amid the inconsolable grief of all the faithful, but especially of the General of that powerful Order.

# OVERTRIED

## II

Some months after the dinner Wynnstay met the rector in the village street, and said that Charteris had given him a message.

'It is a rare thing for him to mention his wife's name,' said Wynnstay, 'but he asks you if you will go and see her in the asylum. He says nothing more, nor gives any reason why he wants you to go, except that she has apparently spoken about her own life at last, and expressed a wish to see you. I'm sorry for you; it must be a terribly painful thing to see her again in this way, after having known her so well in India. He says that you know where she is. I thought I would tell you at once.'

Carteret was in a mood in which a man accepts the inevitable, and he would not have dreamed of refusing to visit Mrs. Charteris, however painful the ordeal might be to him. Yet the ordeal was a far more terrible thing than Wynnstay or indeed any living soul could have dreamed. But it had come at last, and Carteret never shrank for one moment.

He had in seven long years trained his resolution while he was trying to attain to some judgment upon himself that might make the madness of the past less horrible to him. His self-accusation never left his conscious moments, and now after all that he had endured, the dull worm of repentance turned at a word into a living remorse, and strained his failing strength beyond its breaking-point. There is no more foolish fallacy than that tears will bring relief. Carteret went home that night, after a day of work that he made unusually hard and long even for himself, and he lay with his head on the plain table of his sitting-room sobbing and helpless. Was it all useless? Penance he had inflicted upon himself with no kindly hand. No man could say that he had not in the few years in which he had earnestly striven to redeem the past, done all that a man could do with all his strength to help others on the path he had failed in himself. And was it all as nothing? Was the remembrance of the past to remain in burning letters over against his path and about his bed for ever?

He was wise enough even in the midst of his deepest grief and repentance to recognise that things would have been easier to bear if only she had not become insane. For upon his head thenceforward, without hope of change or further usefulness, was the soul of another that he had helped to damn.

And no one but he and she even dreamed of the secret that paralysed his life. Not one soul,—Charteris least of any.

A lesser man could have refused to go to this meeting without any man knowing or thinking less of him, but Carteret would have come at her whisper from the gates of death, though the old infatuation was long, long extinct. Some comfort had been his in the words of De Bernard, and in them he had gained a strength that he had before felt not once nor twice was slipping from his grasp. The truth of what Monseigneur prophesied was now to be proved. Were the meeting to be what he had forced himself to face, he could, he thought, abide it; if the old man of whose death Carteret had heard as of a thing decreed and written, could see him, he thought that he would be glad indeed to have spoken, and might even look on at the coming trial with grave confidence.

In a frame of mind that made prayer an impossibility, and faith a drifting anchor, he went, two days after Wynnstay had given him the message, to the large private asylum near Norwich in which Mrs. Charteris was restrained.

He found himself in a barely furnished room, talking with the doctor, who assured him with bland affability that there were several promising symptoms in the 'case' that he had come to visit. Carteret listened with difficulty, and soon the matron of the hospital was brought in to see him and the doctor glided away.

# OVERTRIED

To the woman he could speak with greater freedom, and he asked anxiously about Mrs. Charteris. The shrewd matron saw that he was not likely to be put off with a flattering commonplace, and told him the truth. The melancholia had lately become a form of religious mania, and Mrs. Charteris spent most of her days in the chapel of the asylum. The matron told him that such cases recovered themselves by a slow and almost unnoticeable series of sanities, but that the course of self-education was always liable to be wrecked by a shock, just as it might, on the other hand, be suddenly achieved by the same means. So far there had been no reason to suppose much change either way had taken place, and the doctors were watching the case with unusual interest for a decisive movement in either direction, for there had been no relapse for some time now. She warned him not to oppose her patient in any way, and left the room to bring her to him.

Carteret leaned against the window and shook with the suppressed agitation of the situation. He prayed in jets of the deepest fervour, and wiped away a very human sweat from his forehead as he still waited.

The door opened, and a slight figure in the deepest of grey gowns relieved with hardly a touch of white about the throat and wrists hesitated for a moment, and then seeing Carteret moved towards him without a touch of affectation.

In anguish he turned and took one step to her, and looked in amazement for the changes that he had so certainly expected to find in her. It was the same quiet, well-modelled face with great grey eyes and a tiresome wisp of hair that he nearly screamed to see her put back into place with the same movement as in old days. Quite unaffectedly she raised her eyes to his and said:

'It was good of you to come. They told me you were to see me to-day, and I wondered if you would have changed.

I think you have changed just as I would have liked you to change, and this dress pleases me so much, so very, very much.'

She turned to the window, and went on in a lower tone:

'I have been ill, you know, and of course I know what has been the matter. I don't think it has been at all sad; I even feel that if it had not been for this, I might never have known how wrong I have been. And now,' she said with a smile, 'I live the happiest life you can imagine. For they let me almost live in the chapel, and I sometimes wonder whether, when the time comes for me to go back to the world, I shall ever be allowed to be so free to spend my time with God again. I know well enough that a long time yet must elapse, for I can remember as in a dream that it was not so long ago since I was very ill,— you know what I mean,—and it hurt so horribly that I don't like to think of it. And do you know that it seemed to me, though I can't remember quite well, that it was just then that my old wicked self overcame me, and I used to despair. So it will be a long time yet before I come out, though I have had no bad time for a very long space now, and I feel that I have turned the corner.'

Carteret felt a wave of thankfulness glow through him to the very soul. This was the same woman, but purified till the innate simplicity and sweetness of her nature shone all the truer after her long ordeal. Half of the load that had for so long crushed down every waking thought seemed to float away in the presence of the soul that had borne her trial, as he most humbly saw, far more strongly and far more worthily than he himself.

She looked at him shyly, and said:

'Would you come with me to the chapel? I should like you to see the place where I have been so happy, and—I should like so much to say one prayer with you there—you won't refuse me that, will you?'

Carteret, with his heart too full to speak, turned with her, and together they walked across the quadrangle to the corner where two steps led up into the plain but handsome little chapel of the hospital. On the way a sharp, high, thin laugh, mirthless and unrestrained, came from across the open space. Mrs. Charteris said very simply: 'That is terrible, for I think that they never recover when they are like that. And we all had been so hoping that poor Margaret would be saved.'

Inside the chapel the two moved up a few steps toward the altar, and she whispered quietly: 'This is where I always kneel.'

And she put out her hand for the first time, and the two knelt down together.

In Carteret's mind there was no room for thought or reflection, phrase, attribution, or apostrophe save only one. Brokenly he muttered in utter gratitude and self-abasement, 'Thank God! Thank God!' There was a physical relapse, and he sobbed to himself with his face buried in his elbows. Then, remembering that it would be a bad thing perhaps for her, he steadied himself.

And at last he heard her speak in a quiet and steady little voice, and she said but one short sentence.

'And that I may take upon myself all his sin, his sorrow, and his punishment, by the everlasting grace and mercy of God and of His Son, Lord Christ.'

And Carteret bowed his head.

\*         \*         \*         \*         \*

Then after some minutes' silence she rose quietly and went out with him, saying, 'You know, you must not be very long here to-day.'

And the two went back to the room in which he had seen her first. Carteret felt exhausted, and in a dream as they retraced their way. At last the burden of his great repentance was lightened, and he could come to look forward to the years that yet remained to him with a steadiness that he had not known for even one hour since the news had reached him—among the first, for he was known to be a dear friend—of the awful trouble.

The reaction held him silent. Indeed he had said but a few words in all the time, for there seemed to be no need to speak, only to breathe out a great thankfulness for the utter goodness of God.

So they said but a word or two in the reception-room, and Mrs. Charteris touched the bell that they might know that her visitor was going.

They stood together in the middle of the room in silence, and he took her hand. She had kept her face down, and so they remained for just so long as one might count five, when she lifted up her head, and she laughed.

And the laugh grew hard and high, and her eyes grew hard and sightless, and the laugh became helpless, and she could only just manage to say to him in spite of it, 'Dickie, it was fun after all, wasn't it?'

And the nurse came in.

# A DEATHBED COMEDY

'How oft the jewel that we throw away
Becomes a gem when others pick it up!'

THE child was clearly sinking fast—much faster than the doctor had expected. He had gone on to another case some miles away, leaving instructions, but assuring Mrs. Gilchrist that there was no immediate danger. Lestrange had been sitting beside Miriam while her mother went away to her room for an hour's sleep. At about four o'clock in the afternoon the change occurred. Lestrange had seen death often enough to recognise that the end could not be far off, and almost under his eyes he saw the slow oncoming of the coma against which Miriam's tiny vitality would carry on but a forlorn struggle. All could be over before Thwaites could get back, even if he were sent for at once, and Lestrange made a movement to go and warn Mrs. Gilchrist.

But there was something in the child's eyes, fixed fully on him, which checked him. Her pain was unmistakable, but there was a look in her face which told another tale as clearly, and Lestrange's heart sank within him as he watched it. With a sudden instinct of the truth, he felt that if Miriam's mother were to be called, and of course remain to the end, the only happiness the child had ever known would be denied her in

36

these last few minutes of her life.

Lestrange knew well enough that Mrs. Gilchrist had built up a barrier of ice between herself and her only child. Brought up in the old and austere school of parental habit, Mrs. Gilchrist, with a dismal childhood of repression and lovelessness behind herself, had unconsciously improved upon her own mother's severity, and a long education in the need of duly hiding feelings and sympathies had totally alienated Miriam from her mother, though neither of them had up to that moment wholly realised the fact. Demonstration of affection was out of place at all times, and it had long been found unsafe by the child to let herself go in any direction in her mother's presence, for assuredly of that affection would her mother make a scorpion for to-morrow's daily portion of her 'education.' Of course, in her own childhood Mrs. Gilchrist had again and again with bitter cryings promised herself that if she should ever have a child herself, she would behave far differently, but, like all parents, this was soon forgotten in the earnest wish to discipline and train Miriam aright.

Miriam had grown up with the warmth of her nature repressed, and this had helped to deceive Lestrange. It was only now at the gate of death that he realised how entirely the love and trust of this small life had been surrendered to himself. But it was horribly clear now, and Lestrange's heart ached as he came to see how blind he had been. Courses of thought chased each other through his memory, and it must have been a strange moment in even the Recording Angel's experience, while the man and the child sat looking at each other with every veil torn down between them and the knowledge of quick-coming death crowning all. I think that the uppermost feeling in Lestrange's mind was a flood of utter shame for opportunities missed, for things left undone which it would have been so easy for him to do, and over all there flowed a wave of remorse for the sheer blindness on his part. He decided at once. This was no time to remember those conventions which Mrs. Gilchrist had forgotten for so long. That Mrs. Gilchrist loved the child in a way he knew vaguely enough, but the external severity of her manner had had its effect on Lestrange also, and he had not the faintest conception of the extent to which the suppressed devotion of that austere and narrow soul was centred on her only child. It seemed just then that Miriam herself was the only one to be thought of, and her mute appeal was beyond all mistake. Her mother had made her bed, and must lie on it.

To have called Mrs. Gilchrist in at this moment would have meant that never till the supreme moment would Miriam have been again at peace and happy, and Dick, who kept commandments unknown to Moses, found it written in his code that to destroy the contentment of the last hour of Miriam's life would be a cursed treachery to the small bandaged form beside him. She was watching him with hungry eyes. You could see waves of pain contract their iris, and, though always a reserved girl, her shyness slipped from her like a garment, and without disguise she let her dying gaze devour the only real friend she had ever known.

It was rather horrible for Dick, who could not feel that anything he had ever done had deserved this wealth of clean love; who could not pretend honestly to have returned it except in an occasional gust of pity for a small outcast who once or twice a year made him thankful that he had never married, lest he should perchance have married such a good woman as her mother. He wondered what he had ever done to bring him in such a harvest—he remembered that he had tied up her dog Brownie's leg when it was scratched by the cat, and in his mind there rose the contrast between these pinched white features on the pillow, and the swollen, red-eyed face with tear-stains on the cheeks which watched the almost miraculous skill with which he stanched the blood that dripped from a cut quite an eighth of an inch in depth. Mrs. Gilchrist, who saw that the whole thing was surgically a mere trifle, thought that Miriam should have been left to find out its little consequence as a part of her education. Dick, with the blind intuition often given to mere bachelors, had seen that the surgical aspect of the matter was not the important aspect, and as the sniffs of the really unhappy Miriam subsided, had one taste of the happiness that mere mothers must often feel. Another day Miriam and he had gone nutting. Dick's heart smote him as he remembered with what boredom he had set out with the grubby cotton frock and grimy sun-hat at his elbow. But he had not been bored, and Miriam had never forgotten that afternoon. It had never come again.

He bent over her and said, 'Dearie, will you be afraid?'

She seemed to pull herself back from dream-land with an effort almost unsuccessful and obviously painful, and put out one small hand.

'Can you listen a moment? Don't speak, just nod your head.'

Miriam's eyes grew brighter, and she nodded.

'Do you know that you are going off to sleep, a long, long sleep?'

A nod.

'Will you be afraid to go?'

The girl did not nod at once; her eyes filled with tears. Then she whispered painfully, and so low that Dick only just caught the words. 'Will it hurt very much? I don't want to leave you! I don't know what to do!'

The words were pronounced in a way that was hardly childish.

The pain was returning, and the child's strength was ebbing fast. The unknown horror of that final wrench which Miriam dimly and intuitively feared, and this lonely dread of losing touch with her only friend, were the only two feelings working in the tired little head.

Dick made up his mind. He rose quickly, and saying, 'I'll be back in one second,' went on tiptoe into the next room, where the operation was to have taken place. The table was still there. And the chloroform, which had not been used, was there too. Coming back, he sat down again by Miriam and lightly pressed his hand on her heart. The pulse was still steady, though very quick and faint.

'After all, if it does go wrong, all the better,' he muttered. 'Miriam, dear, I'm just going to show you how nice it will be; you needn't be a bit afraid. It doesn't hurt. You are going to sleep now for a few minutes, just as it will be soon.'

Miriam smiled painfully. 'Only a few minutes—promise?'

'I promise faithfully.'

Miriam paused, and her face grew anxious. There was no further possible concealment.

'And I'll be awake before mother comes?'

Dick nodded with a gulp.

'And you will be here when I wake up? Promise!'

A nod.

He lightly sprinkled some chloroform upon his handkerchief, and Miriam let him hold the heavy lime-spirit over her nostrils. The drug worked almost instantly on the child, and only a long drawn 'Oo—h!' of relief from pain escaped her lips. Then the wrinkles of her tightly set lips, that had fought against the ache for so many hours, relaxed, and with a smile her head nestled helplessly back among the pillows.

Dick took the handkerchief away and kept his hand on her pulse. It was only a slight anæsthesia, and after three or four minutes life, and with it pain, came back to the little body.

Her eyes opened dreamily, and her hand tightened upon his, as she saw he had kept his promise.

'Was it so very bad, Miriam?'

'Oh *no*! so nice and dreamy—and quiet fireworks.' She caught her breath as the pain surged back faster.

Soon, however, she was lying quietly, sinking back into the comatose state of the earlier part of the afternoon, almost unable to speak, much as she wished to. She managed to say, 'Will you take Brownie?' but with such an effort that Dick stopped her.

'Will you do something for me?'

Miriam nodded vigorously.

'When mother comes in again will you be very nice to her, and look at her only—her only, remember? Don't look at me, dear; remember that. I shan't be sitting next you then, and I want you to think of her all the time.'

'Till when?'

He winced. 'Till mother goes away.' Then he added earnestly: 'Now, will you promise me to do that? No, never mind why, dear; you will be pleasing me just as much as if you were talking to me, and I want you to do this, oh, *so* much!'

There was just the sound of a woman's skirt at the door, but neither heard it. Mrs. Gilchrist never uttered a sound till she had gone back to her room and had flung herself face downwards on her bed.

Miriam's eyes filled with tears, but she nodded bravely.

'I'll try,' she murmured. 'Really, but if I do look at you just once, you mustn't be very angry, will you?'

'O my God!' groaned Dick. Great deep-cut lines came out under his jaw, and his hand on the bed-rail quivered.

'Promise me too something.'

'Yes, of course.'

'Promise to be quite near me when I wake up again—afterwards? Promise again … and again; promise, oh, so hard!' Then as some dim recollection of the misunderstood shibboleth of a nurserymaid came into her head, 'Promise wishermadie.'

It was now his turn just to nod.

Miriam, happier now, soon relapsed into the listlessness that was at any rate a sign of comparative painlessness, but her fingers were still tightly clasped round Dick's forefinger, and so the two sat on in silence.

The minutes passed slowly. Outside, the leaden sky darkened slightly, and a few drops of rain pattered down now and again upon the bright laurels of the drive below.

There was no glory of a dying summer, no melancholy of a wind among the pines, nothing to tinge with sentiment the gasping out of a small life. Everything looked sordid in the dirty grey light. The watch in the old-fashioned watchstand of inlaid wood ticked on gently, and the silence seemed intensified by its tiny noise.

The rasping clang of an iron gate startled Dick as the rusty spring slammed it behind the slouching boy who had brought the milk in from the home farm, and had had his ears pulled by the cook, partly for whistling, but more as an outlet for her own feelings.

Dick had for once forgotten himself and his cynicism, but his habit of self-analysis now made him watch himself with a certain surprise. His own grovelling prayer to be of help to the child at any cost to himself came as a surprise. He had never considered before how much he had represented to her, or to what an extent he had been the colour of Miriam's short life. She had so often vanished from his mind for months that he never thought twice of the little woman's constancy to him.

He remembered that Mrs. Gilchrist had jestingly told him that at one time Miriam had rather shyly begun to add his name to a conventional catalogue in her prayers, and Dick smiled then to himself as he thought that the child had probably been quickly snubbed out of doing it by her mother. He was right enough in his surmise; but he did not know that the conventional silence after 'all women labouring of child, all sick persons' in the service in church on Sundays was from that time onwards filled in every week by the child by saying, over and over again, 'Mr. Lestrange' under her breath very quickly. Dick would have laughed if he had known the company in which his name was sent up to the Throne. The afternoon darkened, and the evening began to close in as dingy and colourless as the day.

Mrs. Gilchrist came in, and no trace of the agony she was in was visible in her face.

'The doctor had better be sent for,' said Dick rising, and Mrs. Gilchrist nodded. He went out of the room and, turning his head for one moment at the door, he looked at Miriam. He was being obeyed, though perhaps the child was even then afraid that she might never see him again before she fell asleep.

In the chair he had just left her mother sat down. Her dry, hot eyes noted a trifling discomfort in the child's pillow, and she set it right—God knows how glad to be able to do something for the child she had neglected for so long. Then, touched by the mockery of this, after a lifetime of misunderstanding and estrangement, a moan escaped her which she checked at once.

She started to find Miriam's bandaged hand gently touching hers. If she had not overheard Dick's orders it would have been the one thing needed to help out the tears that would not come. But now she only looked at it, and in that moment she trod the lowest depths of human repentance. This she knew was no instinctive clinging to a mother, no childish caress that would have come naturally now that Miriam was too far gone to speak. Mercilessly, Mrs. Gilchrist put the truth to herself and hugged its envenomed point with an inexplicable idea of making of her bitter humiliation the only atonement possible now.

In obedience to a request, and as an unlovely duty, prompted merely by the considerateness of a man who had won, without an effort, every fibre of her child's love, that touch had been painfully made. It thrilled her through and through till she could have screamed. It was an acted lie, and there rose up in her heart a hate of the man who had secured for her what, if she had only not overheard, would have been to the grave the dearest memory of her only child. Almost she hated the child herself, and she began to rock to and fro, laughing in a slow silly way till a look of wonder in even Miriam's tired eyes told her that she must pull herself together.

It was the bitterest hour that the woman ever spent: it was an hour that might in justice fall to the lot of many others.

As the child slipped away from under her eyes, helplessly drifting away from the awakened love of a mother repentant, away from the willing devotion of every remaining hour of her life, there was not one motion of affection now from Miriam that did not burn in upon Mrs. Gilchrist's tortured heart. All had been prompted by the casual stranger who had stooped carelessly to pick the treasure that she now knew at the eleventh hour should have been her own.

All was a fiction preconcerted, all a lie and a piece of acting arranged to hoodwink her.

It was hard; so cruelly hard that the bitter regrets for lost opportunities that had made her resting-time an hour ago a purgatory of reminiscences, faded beneath this bitter sense of injustice and impotence. Meanwhile the child's life was dying out, the life that had once been one with hers, that she had brought into the world, that she had then consistently turned over to the care of others.

The darkening rings round Miriam's eyes, the cold dew gathered on the lips and forehead, were a warning that the doctor would come too late, and still with pained and artificial insistence the child looked up at the woman who, she had always been told, was her mother.

Just then Dick softly re-entered the room. He made a motion of his head to show that the doctor had been sent for; Mrs. Gilchrist could not trust herself to speak, she motioned to him to leave them. In an instant Dick, recognising her right, turned to go, and then Miriam, who all the time had not taken her eyes from her mother for a moment, gave way. She turned her eyes towards him, and pulling all her strength together for one last effort, stiffly and painfully she said:

'I am sorry, mother, but Mr. Lestrange, you will be by me?'

'Yes, darling, I promise.' Dick left the room, and, as he went, he heard the muffled sound of a fall. He hastily looked back, but saw that Mrs. Gilchrist had fallen on her knees by the bedside, with her face buried in the clothes, away from where Miriam was lying. She had not fainted—far from it.

But as Lestrange began to descend the stairs at the end of the corridor, he heard the swish of a woman's skirts. Mrs. Gilchrist staggered towards him, feeling her way by the wall. She muttered hoarsely, 'I can't! I heard it all. May God forgive you!'

Lestrange stood like a pillar. 'Go back at once.' He swore frankly and without apology. 'That dying child is playing the game; haven't you the pluck to do the same?' and Mrs. Gilchrist went back to her Gehenna like a whipped dog.

He went downstairs and waited in the library below. The windows were open here and in Miriam's room just above, so that, sitting in the window seat, he could have heard if there were any need of help.

But there was no sound, and a warm, stuffy evening closed in. A blackbird clackered under the laurels.

He heard the postman's step as he crunched a newly mended stretch of the drive some long way down. He let himself through the window and went to meet him, treading on tiptoe across the gravel to gain the grass strip that ran under the laurel bank on one side.

Then he hurried off impatiently and met the man, who saluted him respectfully, and unslung the Manor postbag. He was turning away when he faced about and saluted again. 'Begging your pardon, sir, how is the little miss?'

'Doing badly, very badly, I am afraid, Andrews. There's no hope now.'

Andrews turned away stiffly without a word, and Lestrange liked him for it. There were two for himself, three for Mrs. Gilchrist, and—yes, one in a big sprawling hand for Miss Miriam Gilchrist.

A slight noise made him catch his breath: the Venetian blinds of Miriam's room were being gently let down.

\*　　　　\*　　　　\*　　　　\*　　　　\*

*Three years afterwards there was a scuffle on a frontier, and Dick was released to keep his promise—if he were allowed to. He hesitated.*

*'Bless me!' said St. Peter at the gate, 'of course your record is not much, but didn't you people on earth know that that was all that we asked for?'*

*For there was a small hand in Dick's by this time, and so they went nutting together again.*

# THURNLEY ABBEY

THREE years ago I was on my way out to the East, and as an extra day in London was of some importance, I took the Friday evening mail train to Brindisi instead of the usual Thursday morning Marseilles express. Many people shrink from the long forty-eight-hour train journey through Europe, and the subsequent rush across the Mediterranean on the nineteen-knot *Isis* or *Osiris*; but there is really very little discomfort on either the train or the mail-boat, and unless there is actually nothing for me to do, I always like to save the extra day and a half in London before I say good-bye to her for one of my longer tramps. This time—it was early, I remember, in the shipping season, probably about the beginning of September—there were few passengers, and I had a compartment in the P. and O. Indian express to myself all the way from Calais. All Sunday I watched the blue waves dimpling the Adriatic, and the pale rosemary along the cuttings; the plain white towns, with their flat roofs and their bold 'duomos,' and the grey-green gnarled olive orchards of Apulia. The journey was just like any other. We ate in the dining-car as often and as long as we decently could. We slept after luncheon; we dawdled the afternoon away with yellow-backed novels; sometimes we exchanged platitudes in the smoking-room, and it was there that I met Alastair Colvin.

Colvin was a man of middle height, with a resolute, well-cut jaw; his hair was turning grey; his moustache was sun-whitened, otherwise he was clean-shaven—obviously a gentleman, and obviously also a preoccupied man. He had no great wit. When spoken to, he made the usual remarks in the right way, and I dare say he refrained from banalities only because he spoke less than the rest of us; most of the time he buried himself in the Wagon-lit Company's time-table, but seemed unable to concentrate his attention on any one page of it. He found that I had been over the Siberian railway, and for a quarter of an hour he discussed it with me. Then he lost interest in it, and rose to go to his compartment. But he came back again very soon, and seemed glad to pick up the conversation again.

Of course this did not seem to me to be of any importance. Most travellers by train become a trifle infirm of purpose after thirty-six hours' rattling. But Colvin's restless way I noticed in somewhat marked contrast with the man's personal importance and dignity; especially ill suited was it to his finely made large hand with strong, broad, regular nails and its few lines. As I looked at his hand I noticed a long, deep, and recent scar of ragged shape. However, it is absurd to pretend that I thought anything was unusual. I went off at five o'clock on Sunday afternoon to sleep away the hour or two that had still to be got through before we arrived at Brindisi.

Once there, we few passengers transhipped our hand baggage, verified our berths—there were only a score of us in all—and then, after an aimless ramble of half an hour in Brindisi, we returned to dinner at the Hôtel International, not wholly surprised that the town had been the death of Virgil. If I remember rightly, there is a gaily painted hall at the International—I do not wish to advertise anything, but there is no other place in Brindisi at which to await the coming of the mails—and after dinner I was looking with awe at a trellis overgrown with blue vines, when Colvin moved across the room to my table. He picked up *Il Secolo*, but almost immediately gave up the pretence of reading it. He turned squarely to me and said:

'Would you do me a favour?'

One doesn't do favours to stray acquaintances on Continental expresses without knowing something more of them than I knew of Colvin. But I smiled in a noncommittal way, and asked him what he wanted. I wasn't wrong in part of my estimate of him; he said bluntly:

'Will you let me sleep in your cabin on the *Osiris*?' And he coloured a little as he said it.

Now, there is nothing more tiresome than having to put up with a stable-companion at sea, and I asked him rather pointedly:

'Surely there is room for all of us?' I thought that perhaps he had been partnered off with some mangy Levantine, and wanted to escape from him at all hazards.

Colvin, still somewhat confused, said: 'Yes; I am in a cabin by myself. But you would do me the greatest favour if you would allow me to share yours.'

This was all very well, but, besides the fact that I always sleep better when alone, there had been some recent thefts on board English liners, and I hesitated, frank and honest and self-conscious as Colvin was. Just then the mail-train came in with a clatter and a rush of escaping steam, and I asked him to see me again about it on the boat when we started. He answered me curtly—I suppose he saw the mistrust in my manner—'I am a member of White's.' I smiled to myself as he said it, but I remembered in a moment that the man—if he were really what he claimed to be, and I make no doubt that he was—must have been sorely put to it before he urged the fact as a guarantee of his respectability to a total stranger at a Brindisi hotel.

That evening, as we cleared the red and green harbour-lights of Brindisi, Colvin explained. This is his story in his own words.

'When I was travelling in India some years ago, I made the acquaintance of a youngish man in the Woods and Forests. We camped out together for a week, and I found him a pleasant companion. John Broughton was a light-hearted soul when off duty, but a steady and capable man in any of the small emergencies that continually arise in that department. He was liked and trusted by the natives, and though a trifle over-pleased with himself when he escaped to civilisation at Simla or Calcutta, Broughton's future was well assured in Government service, when a fair-sized estate was unexpectedly left to him, and he joyfully shook the dust of the Indian plains from his feet and returned to England. For five years he drifted about London. I saw him now and then. We dined together about every eighteen months, and I could trace pretty exactly the gradual sickening of Broughton with a merely idle life. He then set out on a couple of long voyages, returned as restless as before, and at last told me that he had decided to marry and settle down at his place, Thurnley Abbey, which had long been empty. He spoke about looking after the property and standing for his constituency in the usual way. Vivien Wilde, his *fiancée*, had, I suppose, begun to take him in hand. She was a pretty girl with a deal of fair hair and rather an exclusive manner; deeply religious in a narrow school, she was still kindly and high-spirited, and I thought that Broughton was in luck. He was quite happy and full of information about his future.

'Among other things, I asked him about Thurnley Abbey. He confessed that he hardly knew the place. The last tenant, a man called Clarke, had lived in one wing for fifteen years and seen no one. He had been a miser and a hermit. It was the rarest thing for a light to be seen at the Abbey after dark. Only the barest necessities of life were ordered, and the tenant himself received them at the side-door. His one half-caste manservant, after a month's stay in the house, had abruptly left without warning, and had returned to the Southern States. One thing Broughton complained bitterly about: Clarke had wilfully spread the rumour among the villagers that the Abbey was haunted, and had even condescended to play childish tricks with spirit-lamps and salt in order to scare trespassers away at night. He had been detected in the act of this tom-foolery, but the story spread, and no one, said Broughton, would venture near the house except in broad daylight. The hauntedness of Thurnley Abbey was now, he said with a grin, part of the gospel of the countryside, but he and his young wife were going to change all that. Would I propose myself any time I liked? I, of course, said I would, and equally, of course, intended to do nothing of the sort without a definite invitation.

'The house was put in thorough repair, though not a stick of the old furniture and tapestry were removed. Floors and ceilings were relaid: the roof was made watertight again, and the dust of half a century was scoured out. He showed me some photographs of the place. It was called an Abbey, though as a matter of fact it had been only the infirmary of the long-vanished Abbey of Closter some five miles away. The larger part of the building remained as it had been in pre-Reformation days, but a wing had been added in Jaco-bean times, and that part of the house had been kept in something like repair by Mr. Clarke. He had in both the ground and first floors set a heavy timber door, strongly barred with iron, in the passage between the earlier and the Jacobean parts of the house, and had entirely neglected the former. So there had been a good deal of work to be done.

'Broughton, whom I saw in London two or three times about this period, made a deal of fun over the positive refusal of the workmen to remain after sundown. Even after the electric light had been put into every room, nothing would induce them to remain, though, as Broughton observed, electric light was death on ghosts. The legend of the Abbey's ghosts had gone far and wide, and the men would take no risks. They went home in batches of five and six, and even during the daylight hours there was an inordinate amount of talking between one and another, if either happened to be out of sight of his companion. On the whole, though nothing of any sort or kind had been conjured up even by their heated imaginations during their five months' work upon the Abbey, the belief in the ghosts was rather strengthened than otherwise in Thurnley because of the men's confessed nervousness, and local tradition declared itself in favour of the ghost of an immured nun.

' "Good old nun!" said Broughton.

'I asked him whether in general he believed in the possibility of ghosts, and, rather to my surprise, he said that he couldn't say he entirely disbelieved in them. A man in India had told him one morning in camp that he believed that his mother was dead in England, as her vision had come to his tent the night before. He had not been alarmed, but had said nothing, and the figure vanished again. As a matter of fact, the next possible dak-walla brought on a telegram announcing the mother's death. "There the thing was," said Broughton. But at Thurnley he was practical enough. He roundly cursed the idiotic selfishness of Clarke, whose silly antics had caused all the inconvenience. At the same time, he couldn't refuse to sympathise to some extent with the ignorant workmen. "My own idea," said he, "is that if a ghost ever does come in one's way, one ought to speak to it."

'I agreed. Little as I knew of the ghost world and its conventions, I had always remembered that a spook was in honour bound to wait to be spoken to. It didn't seem much to do, and

I felt that the sound of one's own voice would at any rate reassure oneself as to one's wakefulness. But there are few ghosts outside Europe—few, that is, that a white man can see—and I had never been troubled with any. However, as I have said, I told Broughton that I agreed.

'So the wedding took place, and I went to it in a tall hat which I bought for the occasion, and the new Mrs. Broughton smiled very nicely at me afterwards. As it had to happen, I took the Orient Express that evening and was not in England again for nearly six months. Just before I came back I got a letter from Broughton. He asked if I could see him in London or come to Thurnley, as he thought I should be better able to help him than any one else he knew. His wife sent a nice message to me at the end, so I was reassured about at least one thing. I wrote from Budapest that I would come and see him at Thurnley two days after my arrival in London, and as I sauntered out of the Pannonia into the Kerepesi Utcza to post my letters, I wondered of what earthly service I could be to Broughton. I had been out with him after tiger on foot, and I could imagine few men better able at a pinch to manage their own business. However, I had nothing to do, so after dealing with some small accumulations of business during my absence, I packed a kit-bag and departed to Euston.

'I was met by Broughton's great Limousine at Thurnley Road station, and after a drive of nearly seven miles we echoed through the sleepy streets of Thurnley village, into which the main gates of the park thrust themselves, splendid with pillars and spread-eagles and tom-cats rampant atop of them. I never was a herald, but I know that the Broughtons have the right to supporters—Heaven knows why! From the gates a quadruple avenue of beech-trees led inwards for a quarter of a mile. Beneath them a neat strip of fine turf edged the road and ran back until the poison of the dead beech-leaves killed it under the trees. There were many wheel-tracks on the road, and a comfortable little pony trap jogged past me laden with a country parson and his wife and daughter. Evidently there was some garden party going on at the Abbey. The road dropped away to the right at the end of the avenue, and I could see the Abbey across a wide pasturage and a broad lawn thickly dotted with guests.

'The end of the building was plain. It must have been almost mercilessly austere when it was first built, but time had crumbled the edges and toned the stone down to an orange-lichened grey wherever it showed behind its curtain of magnolia, jasmine, and ivy. Farther on was the three-storied Jacobean house, tall and handsome. There had not been the slightest attempt to adapt the one to the other, but the kindly ivy had glossed over the touching-point. There was a tall flèche in the middle of the building, surmounting a small bell tower. Behind the house there rose the mountainous verdure of Spanish chestnuts all the way up the hill.

'Broughton had seen me coming from afar, and walked across from his other guests to welcome me before turning me over to the butler's care. This man was sandy-haired and rather inclined to be talkative. He could, however, answer hardly any questions about the house; he had, he said, only been there three weeks. Mindful of what Broughton had told me, I made no inquiries about ghosts, though the room into which I was shown might have justified anything. It was a very large low room with oak beams projecting from the white ceiling. Every inch of the walls, including the doors, was covered with tapestry, and a remarkably fine Italian fourpost bedstead, heavily draped, added to the darkness and dignity of the place. All the furniture was old, well made, and dark. Underfoot there was a plain green pile carpet, the only new thing about the room except the electric light fittings and the jugs and basins. Even the looking-glass on the dressing-table was an old pyramidal Venetian glass set in heavy repoussé frame of tarnished silver.

'After a few minutes' cleaning up, I went downstairs and out upon the lawn, where I greeted my hostess. The people gathered there were of the usual country type, all anxious to be pleased and roundly curious as to the new master of the Abbey. Rather to my surprise, and quite to my pleasure, I rediscovered Glenham, whom I had known well in the old days in Barotseland: he lived quite close, as, he remarked with a grin, I ought to have known. "But," he added, "I don't live in a place like this." He swept his hand to the long, low lines of the Abbey in obvious admiration, and then, to my intense interest, muttered beneath his breath, "Thank God!" He saw that I had overheard him, and turning to me said decidedly, "Yes, 'thank God' I said, and I meant. I wouldn't live at the Abbey for all Broughton's money."

' "But surely," I demurred, "you know that old Clarke was discovered in the very act of setting light to his bug-a-boos?"

'Glenham shrugged his shoulders. "Yes, I know about that. But there is something wrong with the place still. All I can say is that Broughton is a different man since he has lived here. I don't believe that he will remain much longer. But—you're staying here?—well, you'll hear all about it to-night. There's a big dinner, I understand." The conversation turned off to old reminiscences, and Glenham soon after had to go.

'Before I went to dress that evening I had twenty minutes' talk with Broughton in his library. There was no doubt that the man was altered, gravely altered. He was nervous and fidgety, and I found him looking at me only when my eye was off him. I naturally asked him what he wanted of me. I told him I would do anything I could, but that I couldn't conceive what he lacked that I could provide. He said with a lustreless smile that there was, however, something, and that he would tell me the following morning. It struck me that he was somehow ashamed of himself, and perhaps ashamed of the part he was asking me to play. However, I dismissed the subject from my mind and went up to dress in my palatial room. As I shut the door a draught blew out the Queen of Sheba from the wall, and I noticed that the tapestries were not fastened to the wall at the bottom. I have always held very practical views about spooks, and it has often seemed to me that the slow waving in firelight of loose tapestry upon a wall would account for ninety-nine per cent. of the stories one hears. Certainly the dignified undulation of this lady with her attendants and huntsmen—one of whom was untidily cutting the throat of a fallow deer upon the very steps on which King Solomon, a grey-faced Flemish nobleman with the order of the Golden Fleece, awaited his fair visitor—gave colour to my hypothesis.

'Nothing much happened at dinner. The people were very much like those of the garden party. A young woman next me seemed anxious to know what was being read in London. As she was far more familiar than I with the most recent magazines and literary supplements, I found salvation in being myself instructed in the tendencies of modern fiction. All true art, she said, was shot through and through with melancholy. How vulgar were the attempts at wit that marked so many modern books! From the beginning of literature it had always been tragedy that embodied the highest attainment of every age. To call such works morbid merely begged the question. No thoughtful man—she looked sternly at me through the steel rim of her glasses—could fail to agree with me. Of course, as one would, I immediately and properly said that I slept with Pett Ridge and Jacobs under my pillow at night, and that if "Jorrocks" weren't quite so large and cornery, I would add him to the company. She hadn't read any of them, so I was saved—for a time. But I remember grimly that she said that the dearest wish of her life was to be in some awful and soul-freezing situation of horror, and I remember that she dealt hardly with the hero of Nat Paynter's vampire story, between nibbles at her brown-bread ice. She was a cheerless soul, and I couldn't help thinking that if there were many such in the neighbourhood, it was not surprising that old Glenham had been stuffed with some nonsense or other about the Abbey. Yet nothing could well have been less creepy than the glitter of silver and glass, and the subdued lights and cackle of conversation all round the dinner-table.

'After the ladies had gone I found myself talking to the rural dean. He was a thin, earnest man, who at once turned the conversation to old Clarke's buffooneries. But, he said, Mr. Broughton had introduced such a new and cheerful spirit, not only into the Abbey, but, he might say, into the whole neighbourhood, that he had great hopes that the ignorant superstitions of the past were from henceforth destined to oblivion. Thereupon his other neighbour, a portly gentleman of independent means and position, audibly remarked "Amen," which damped the rural dean, and we talked of partridges past, partridges present, and pheasants to come. At the other end of the table Broughton sat with a couple of his friends, red-faced hunting men. Once I noticed that they were discussing me, but I paid no attention to it at the time. I remembered it a few hours later.

'By eleven all the guests were gone, and Broughton, his wife, and I were alone together under the fine plaster ceiling of the Jacobean drawing-room. Mrs. Broughton talked about one or two of the neighbours, and then, with a smile, said that she knew I would excuse her, shook hands with me, and went off to bed. I am not very good at analysing things, but I felt that she talked a little uncomfortably and with a suspicion of effort, smiled rather conventionally, and was obviously glad to go. These things seem trifling enough to repeat, but I had throughout the faint feeling that everything was not square. Under the circumstances, this was enough to set me wondering what on earth the service could be that I was to render—

wondering also whether the whole business were not some ill-advised jest in order to make me come down from London for a mere shooting-party.

'Broughton said little after she had gone. But he was evidently labouring to bring the conversation round to the so-called haunting of the Abbey. As soon as I saw this, of course I asked him directly about it. He then seemed at once to lose interest in the matter. There was no doubt about it: Broughton was somehow a changed man, and to my mind he had changed in no way for the better. Mrs. Broughton seemed no sufficient cause. He was clearly very fond of her, and she of him. I reminded him that he was going to tell me what I could do for him in the morning, pleaded my journey, lighted a candle, and went upstairs with him. At the end of the passage leading into the old house he grinned weakly and said, "Mind, if you see a ghost, do talk to it; you said you would." He stood irresolutely a moment and then turned away. At the door of his dressing-room he paused once more: "I'm here," he called out, "if you should want anything. Good night," and he shut his door.

'I went along the passage to my room, undressed, switched on a lamp beside my bed, read a few pages of the *Jungle Book*, and then, more than ready for sleep, turned the light off and went fast asleep.

'Three hours later I woke up. There was not a breath of wind outside. There was not even a flicker of light from the fire place. As I lay there, an ash tinkled slightly as it cooled, but there was hardly a gleam of the dullest red in the grate. An owl cried among the silent Spanish chestnuts on the slope outside. I idly reviewed the events of the day, hoping that I should fall off to sleep again before I reached dinner. But at the end I seemed as wakeful as ever. There was no help for it. I must read my *Jungle Book* again till I felt ready to go off, so I fumbled for the pear at the end of the cord that hung down inside the bed, and I switched on the bedside lamp. The sudden glory dazzled me for a moment. I felt under my pillow for my book with half-shut eyes. Then, growing used to the light, I happened to look down to the foot of my bed.

'I can never tell you really what happened then. Nothing I could ever confess in the most abject words could even faintly picture to you what I felt. I know that my heart stopped dead, and my throat shut automatically. In one instinctive movement I crouched back up against the head-boards of the bed, staring at the horror. The movement set my heart going again, and the sweat dripped from every pore. I am not a particularly religious man, but I had always believed that God would never allow any supernatural appearance to present itself to man in such a guise and in such circumstances that harm, either bodily or mental, could result to him. I can only tell you that at that moment both my life and my reason rocked unsteadily on their seats.'

The other *Osiris* passengers had gone to bed. Only he and I remained leaning over the starboard railing, which rattled uneasily now and then under the fierce vibration of the over-engined mail-boat. Far over, there were the lights of a few fishing-smacks riding out the night, and a great rush of white combing and seething water fell out and away from us overside.

At last Colvin went on:

'Leaning over the foot of my bed, looking at me, was a figure swathed in a rotten and tattered veiling. This shroud passed over the head, but left both eyes and the right side of the face bare. It then followed the line of the arm down to where the hand grasped the bed-end. The face was not entirely that of a skull, though the eyes and the flesh of the face were totally gone. There was a thin, dry skin drawn tightly over the features, and there was some skin left on the hand. One wisp of hair crossed the forehead. It was perfectly still. I looked at it, and it looked at me, and my brains turned dry and hot in my head. I had still got the pear of the electric lamp in my hand, and I played idly with it; only I dared not turn the light out again. I shut my eyes, only to open them in a hideous terror the same second. The thing had not moved. My heart was thumping, and the sweat cooled me as it evaporated. Another cinder tinkled in the grate, and a panel creaked in the wall.

'My reason failed me. For twenty minutes, or twenty seconds, I was able to think of nothing else but this awful figure, till there came, hurtling through the empty channels of my senses, the remembrance that Broughton and his friends had discussed me furtively at dinner. The dim possibility of its being a hoax stole gratefully into my unhappy mind, and once there, one's pluck came creeping back along a thousand tiny veins. My first sensation was one of blind unreasoning thankfulness that my brain was going to stand the trial. I am not a timid man, but the best of us needs some human handle to steady him in time of extremity, and in this faint but growing hope that after all it might be only a brutal hoax, I found the fulcrum that I needed. At last I moved.

'How I managed to do it I cannot tell you, but with one spring towards the foot of the bed I got within arm's-length and struck out one fearful blow with my fist at the thing. It crumbled under it, and my hand was cut to the bone. With the sickening revulsion after my terror, I dropped half-fainting across the end of the bed. So it was merely a foul trick after all. No doubt the trick had been played many a time before: no doubt Broughton and his friends had had some large bet among themselves as to what I should do when I discovered

THURNLEY ABBEY.

the gruesome thing. From my state of abject terror I found myself transported into an insensate anger. I shouted curses upon Broughton. I dived rather than climbed over the bed-end on to the sofa. I tore at the robed skeleton—how well the whole thing had been carried out, I thought—I broke the skull against the floor, and stamped upon its dry bones. I flung the head away under the bed, and rent the brittle bones of the trunk in pieces. I snapped the thin thigh-bones across my knee, and flung them in different directions. The shin-bones I set up against a stool and broke with my heel. I raged like a Berserker against the loathly thing, and stripped the ribs from the backbone and slung the breastbone against the cupboard. My fury increased as the work of destruction went on. I tore the frail rotten veil into twenty pieces, and the dust went up over everything, over the clean blotting-paper and the silver inkstand. At last my work was done. There was but a raffle of broken bones and strips of parchment and crumbling wool. Then, picking up a piece of the skull—it was the cheek and temple bone of the right side, I remember—I opened the door and went down the passage to Broughton's dressing-room. I remember still how my sweat-dripping pyjamas clung to me as I walked. At the door I kicked and entered.

'Broughton was in bed. He had already turned the light on and seemed shrunken and horrified. For a moment he could hardly pull himself together. Then I spoke. I don't know what I said. Only I know that from a heart full and over-full with hatred and contempt, spurred on by shame of my own recent cowardice, I let my tongue run on. He answered nothing. I was amazed at my own fluency. My hair still clung lankily to my wet temples, my hand was bleeding profusely, and I must have looked a strange sight. Broughton huddled himself up at the head of the bed just as I had. Still he made no answer, no defence. He seemed preoccupied with something besides my reproaches, and once or twice moistened his lips with his tongue. But he could say nothing though he moved his hands now and then, just as a baby who cannot speak moves its hands.

'At last the door into Mrs. Broughton's room opened and she came in, white and terrified. "What is it? What is it? Oh, in God's name! what is it?" she cried again and again, and then she went up to her husband and sat on the bed in her night-dress, and the two faced me. I told her what the matter was. I spared her husband not a word for her presence there. Yet he seemed hardly to understand. I told the pair that I had spoiled their cowardly joke for them. Broughton looked up.

' "I have smashed the foul thing into a hundred pieces," I said. Broughton licked his lips again and his mouth worked. "By God!" I shouted, "it would serve you right if I thrashed you within an inch of your life. I will take care that not a decent man or woman of my acquaintance ever speaks to you again. And there," I added, throwing the broken piece of the skull upon the floor beside his bed, "there is a souvenir for you, of your damned work to-night!"

'Broughton saw the bone, and in a moment it was his turn to frighten me. He squealed like a hare caught in a trap. He screamed and screamed till Mrs. Broughton, almost as bewildered as myself, held on to him and coaxed him like a child to be quiet. But Broughton—and as he moved I thought that ten minutes ago I perhaps looked as terribly ill as he did—thrust her from him, and scrambled out of the bed on to the floor, and still screaming put out his hand to the bone. It had blood on it from my hand. He paid no attention to me whatever. In truth I said nothing. This was a new turn indeed to the horrors of the evening. He rose from the floor with the bone in his hand, and stood silent. He seemed to be listening. "Time, time, perhaps," he muttered, and almost at the same moment fell at full length on the carpet, cutting his head against the fender. The bone flew from his hand and came to rest near the door. I picked Broughton up, haggard and broken, with blood over his face. He whispered hoarsely and quickly, "Listen, listen!" We listened.

'After ten seconds' utter quiet, I seemed to hear something. I could not be sure, but at last there was no doubt. There was a quiet sound as of one moving along the passage. Little regular steps came towards us over the hard oak flooring. Broughton moved to where his wife sat, white and speechless, on the bed, and pressed her face into his shoulder.

'Then, the last thing that I could see as he turned the light out, he fell forward with his own head pressed into the pillow of the bed. Something in their company, something in their cowardice, helped me, and I faced the open doorway of the room, which was outlined fairly clearly against the dimly lighted passage. I put out one hand and touched Mrs. Broughton's shoulder in the darkness. But at the last moment I too failed. I sank on my knees and put my face in the bed. Only we all heard. The footsteps came to the door, and there they stopped. The piece of bone was lying a yard inside the door. There was a rustle of moving stuff, and the thing was in the room. Mrs. Broughton was silent: I could hear Broughton's voice praying, muffled in the pillow: I was cursing my own cowardice. Then the steps moved out again on the oak boards of the passage, and I heard the sounds dying away. In a flash of remorse I went to the door and looked out. At the end of the corridor I thought I saw something that moved away. A moment later the passage was empty. I stood with my forehead against the jamb of the door almost physically sick.

' "You can turn the light on," I said, and there was an answering flare. There was no bone at my feet. Mrs. Broughton had fainted. Broughton was almost useless, and it took me ten minutes to bring her to. Broughton only said one thing worth remembering. For the most part he went on muttering prayers. But I was glad afterwards to recollect that he had said that thing. He said in a colourless voice, half as a question, half as a reproach, "You didn't speak to her."

'We spent the remainder of the night together. Mrs. Broughton actually fell off into a kind of sleep before dawn, but she suffered so horribly in her dreams that I shook her into consciousness again. Never was dawn so long in coming. Three or four times Broughton spoke to himself. Mrs. Broughton would then just tighten her hold on his arm, but she could say nothing. As for me, I can honestly say that I grew worse as the hours passed and the light strengthened. The two violent reactions had battered down my steadiness of view, and I felt that the foundations of my life had been built upon the sand. I said nothing, and after binding up my hand with a towel, I did not move. It was better so. They helped me and I helped them, and we all three knew that our reason had gone very near to ruin that night. At last, when the light came in pretty strongly, and the birds outside were chattering and singing, we felt that we must do something. Yet we never moved. You might have thought that we should particularly dislike being found as we were by the servants: yet nothing of that kind mattered a straw, and an overpowering listlessness bound us as we sat, until Chapman, Broughton's man, actually knocked and opened the door. None of us moved. Broughton, speaking hardly and stiffly, said, "Chapman, you can come back in five minutes." Chapman was a discreet man, but it would have made no difference to us if he had carried his news to the "room" at once.

'We looked at each other and I said I must go back. I meant to wait outside till Chapman returned. I simply dared not re-enter my bedroom alone. Broughton roused himself and said that he would come with me. Mrs. Broughton agreed to remain in her own room for five minutes if the blinds were drawn up and all the doors left open.

'So Broughton and I, leaning stiffly one against the other, went down to my room. By the morning light that filtered past the blinds we could see our way, and I released the blinds. There was nothing wrong in the room from end to end, except smears of my own blood on the end of the bed, on the sofa, and on the carpet where I had torn the thing to pieces.'

Colvin had finished his story. There was nothing to say. Seven bells stuttered out from the fo'c'sle, and the answering cry wailed through the darkness. I took him downstairs.

'Of course I am much better now, but it is a kindness of you to let me sleep in your cabin.'

# THE CRUSADER'S MASS

MILBANK of the *Daily Press* had been out in the direction of Sanna's Post on the day following the Kornspruit disaster, and was now retreating with General Colvile upon Bloemfontein.

But the work of the 19th Brigade in covering the collection of the wounded, and the operations of the mounted troops on the right to protect the withdrawal, drew him some distance to the south before Macdonald reached Bosman's Kop on the return journey.

He attached himself to three men of Rimington's Guides, who were reconnoitring a few miles out in the direction of a farm that flew a white flag. After making a hurried inspection of the house, and finding nothing except Van Zyl, a stolid Dutchman, who showed them with a grim smile that his house had been ransacked and pillaged by both sides, the guides turned back to the flank of Smith-Dorrien's brigade, while Milbank parted company with them, intending to work back upon Bloemfontein by himself, and hoping to strike the retreating column about four miles east of the capital, at or near Springfield.

But he had hardly gone a mile when an instinct for which he could hardly account made him wheel round under cover of a fold in the ground and halt; after a moment's hesitation he made a quick détour and returned to the farm he had just left.

He tied up his horse behind the kraal a hundred yards away, and stealthily approached the house, till through a side window he was able to command a view of the bare, dirty little room in which the Boer had received them a few minutes before.

'I'll have those papers, please.'

The window crashed in, and Milbank was inside. Van Zyl turned with an oath. Had he known that the correspondent was unarmed, he would have shown fight, but Milbank's right hand lay in an ominously bulging pocket, and the man was taking no risks. He stood aside from the grimy packet of despatches without a word, but his catlike brain was working, and he was almost ready to snatch them and make a bolt for it. Milbank's horse whinnied outside, and he saw the uselessness of it.

Milbank looked at the first of the papers and would have given much to have learned Dutch more thoroughly during the time of waiting at Modder River. He saw, however, that the papers explained the general plan of operations that had been begun so successfully at Ladybrand and Thaba 'Nchu. A little farther down the repetition of the name of Reddersburg made him examine the paragraphs more closely, and he suddenly realised the importance of his find.

The Boer stood sullenly aside. Milbank had placed himself between him and the door, and the Dutchman's little eyes ran nervously over this self-possessed intruder who seemed to belong to none of the corps with which Van Zyl had taken some pains to make himself acquainted in Bloemfontein.

Milbank turned to the second paper. It was a roughly drawn map of the country round Mester's Hoek and Reddersburg, and it contained dates and directions. Now, he knew well enough that Lord Roberts expected a counter-attack as soon as the Boers should have discovered that neither the Zand River nor Kroonstad was defensible, but the north-western approach to the capital that the British were holding was notoriously the easiest point of attack, and there Milbank knew that the Field-Marshal was more than ready for any advance. But this was a different thing, and he realised the importance of conveying at once to headquarters the news that the affair at the Waterworks was but part of a well-considered and brilliant counter-stroke. In brief, the intention of the Boers seemed to be to continue their advance towards Edenburg and cut the railway south of Kaffir River, holding both that place and Jagersfontein Road station until the bridges over both the Riet River and Van Zyl's spruit had been destroyed, their retreat being secured by the capture of Mester's Hoek and the Beyer's Berg.

This scheme entirely altered the military situation, though it was one that twenty-four hours' notice would be amply sufficient to frustrate, as Gatacre and Clements were both within easy striking distance of Reddersburg, a fact evidently unknown to the Boers.

But beyond this first realisation, the ruling pride of his profession touched him, and he flushed with excitement to think of the magnitude of the scoop that he had secured.

The third paper was a hastily written scrawl on a leaf torn from a note-book, apparently granting a commission, and signed 'pprinsloo.'

Milbank folded the packet up and put it in his pocket.

'You damned scoundrel, I know you! You were among the first to sign the oath of allegiance.' It was a shot in the dark, but it told. The Boer shifted uneasily. 'This—er—commission of yours will be——' He was watching the small blue eyes of the coffee-faced Dutchman as he faced the light from the window, and saw something that made him turn his head sharply.

'Friends of yours, I see,' said Milbank. 'You'll come outside.'

Two mounted figures appeared a mile and a half away, and moved cautiously forward, reconnoitring the house, near which the white square of calico hung motionless from the truck of the flagstaff.

Milbank happened to know the trick that had lost us already many men at one time and another, and determined to use his information as his only chance.

'Pull down that flag!'

The Boer started but did not move.

'I'll count five,' said Milbank, and his hand went back into his pocket. The flag dipped like a swerving bird before four was said, and the approaching burghers reined in their horses.

'Up with it again till I tell you to stop.'

And the white rag pointed its way up the pole until it hung three feet below the pulley at the top. 'Stop!' And the Boer, frightened as much by the knowledge of his captor as by the suspected revolver, tied it so.

The pair of horsemen vanished like magic into the veldt, for the sign of British occupation of a neutral house was well known—far even beyond the frontiers of the republics.

Milbank felt that not even so was he out of the wood. He had indeed scared off the scouts of the enemy, but he knew that Van Zyl would not have been given a commission without being supplied with a rifle and ammunition, and these he had neither time nor opportunity to find. Getting away would be the difficult thing, he knew. The two men eyed each other. Milbank recognised the necessity of acting at once. Ordering the man into the middle of the kraal, he bound the strap of his jacket round Van Zyl's eyes, and forbade him to move. Then he moved a few paces and waited, creeping back to his prisoner in time to press the cap of a fountain pen into his neck as he made a sudden movement to tear off the bandage, believing that Milbank was gone. Then the latter moved slowly and steadily towards his horse, swung himself into the saddle, and set off. It was impossible to conceal his intention any longer, and Van Zyl, after a moment's hesitation, heard the thud on the veldt of the retreating horse, tore off his bandage, and leaped into the house.

'Now, old lady, you've got to go for all you're worth!' And under Milbank's voice and spur the country-bred pony of thirteen hands tore across the veldt like a stumpy whirlwind.

'It's the most jumpy thing I've ever been in,' thought Milbank, expecting the first bullet every yard. But there must have been some delay in disinterring the rifle, for he was seven hundred yards or more from the house when the first shot touched the veldt ahead of him with a scream like a siren. Forty yards on another whipped into the dry sandy grass still nearer. 'God, he's a good shot!' muttered Milbank, wondering how far he was still from the left wing of Smith-Dorrien's brigade, and making a sharp détour to avoid giving the Boer a practically stationary target. Just as he was beginning to fear that——

\*         \*         \*         \*         \*

Milbank slowly recovered consciousness, to find himself in a heap on the veldt, his shoulder bruised, his back aching, and a bullet-hole in the front of his tunic, just in the ring of unfaded cloth that was usually protected by his belt.

He was in less pain than he expected to be, and indeed was thankful that his leg, which had been twisted under him when he fell, seemed all right and gave him no pain.

But he was losing a little blood, and found himself very weak. Quite calmly he decided to use one of his putties to bind himself up with; of course, he hadn't the first dressing with him—no correspondent ever has, after the first action.

He slewed round a little in his cramped and doubled-up position so as to move his body as little as possible, and reached for the string at his knee. There was something odd, he felt, in what he was doing, and the quaint thought came into his mind that it was like taking off some one else's putty.

At the thought that followed, the pupils of his eyes contracted to pin-points, and he stared vacantly at the string in his hand; then, like a man in a dream, he felt for and opened his pocket-knife, and deliberately struck it an inch into his leg above the knee.

It dropped bloodstained from his hand, and he watched the responsive red outflow matting the cut edges of the breeches in silence, a silence that was only broken by the whirling and blazing of wheels and wings within his head. He saw nothing in the darkness that encompassed him, nothing outside a two-foot circle of which the cut in his breeches was the centre.

There had not been a twinge of pain, and he knew well enough what that meant.

He said quite slowly, 'So my spine's broken!'

He played idly with the dry twigs of the sage-brush that pushed its thorns and sharp elbows deep and painlessly into his thigh.

'I've got a few hours yet,' he said; 'I must see about those papers.'

He hauled his dead half out from the bush, and lay more comfortably. Then, pulling the Boer despatches from his pocket, he wrote a note explaining the urgency of the news they contained, and especially ordering that any one who might find his body should take them instantly to headquarters even before reporting his death.

Outside the package he wrote in the largest letters he could: 'Most urgent: to be given to Lord Roberts at once.'

More than this he could not do, and he lay still and reconsidered his position. At any rate he had done his duty to the army. For his editor he then wrote out a short telegram in his notebook: 'Mortally wounded Lyons acting temporarily.'

71

Then he remembered that the cable people counted words of more than ten letters as two, and he altered the last word to 'interim,' wondering with a smile whether the censor would disallow it as being in a foreign language. Then he saw that he could save a word, and scratched out both the last words, and wrote, 'substitute.' He signed it and placed it between the leaves of the packet containing the despatches, and then leant back into the bush waiting, waiting.

He knew exactly the effect that would be caused by the news of his death among the other correspondents: he even felt that he could almost write the very words they would use in their letters home. Cartwright would note in cold blood that the unofficial work of a correspondent was at times of service to an army in the field, and would without doubt twist the affair into a 'further proof, if indeed any were still needed,' that the intelligence department should in time of war be recruited from civilians—an ever-present hobby of his; Britton would be full of inaccuracies as to the facts, but the story would have just that golden touch that no one else could apply, and that made his stuff worth precisely four times the amount paid by his shrewd editor at home; Emmelin would say nothing about it at all in his letters home, and would in Bloemfontein deprecate the wholly unnecessary prominence given to a press casualty; Farmer, whom no one trusted a yard, would write a dainty little paragraph about his own personal loss; Gregson would recall a similar incident in 1881.

Milbank's mind moved rapidly. He wondered whether the best of the whole corps, Roberts himself, would mention that his loss would be regretted? He felt that that would be all he could wish or hope for. Lyons, of course, would have to report his death formally to the paper. As he meditated, an idea came. Why shouldn't he write his own account? There wasn't much else to do—only one thing that he meant to put off to the very last.

So he set to work, and as he wrote his horse after a riderless gallop of three or four miles came back to him. She moved her head painfully, and Milbank saw that the bullet that had struck him had pierced the side of her neck, and made an exit near her windpipe.

She snorted and smelt her way up to him, and whinnied when she saw that he took no notice.

'Poor old lady!' said Milbank. 'If I could only make sure of your being found by our own side, I'd send you off with these. But the odds are that you would go galloping off straight into the arms of my friend over there; wouldn't you, you old idiot?'

She came up and shoved an impatient and insistent nose against his shoulder. Milbank smoothed the velvet skin with his pencil.

'No, it's no good, Kitsie; I've got to stop here for some time.'

He wrote quickly and easily; the Sanna's Post affair took him only half an hour, and he had had the story told him clearly enough by a man of 'Q' battery in outline. Then he briefly described the morning's work, and the retreat to Bosman's Kop, of which he had seen the start with many misgivings. He ended with the short comment: 'I was fired upon and wounded while riding away from Van Zyl's farm to the south of our late position.'

When he had finished his letter, he overhauled his pockets. Now that his public work was done, he set to work to put his own house in order before he died.

A bullet thee—e—e—eu—ued over his head near his mare, who stood a few yards away, pecking uncertainly at the dry sage-brush of the veldt. Milbank smiled: he remembered that the Boer, although he might by this time have established communication with his friends, was not at all likely to approach a man whom he believed to be armed with a Mauser pistol over the absolutely coverless veldt. Milbank had a small but quite sufficient patch of brush at his back, so that the only target offered was the horse, which of course could be well seen from the upper window of the farm. Evidently Van Zyl hoped to destroy the only means of escape for Milbank, of the extent of whose wound he could have no knowledge, and trusted to recover the papers by rushing him in the dark.

Milbank picked up a stone, and threw it at his horse. He missed her by a strange distance, but she moved away with a start, just as another bullet pecked up the dust near her. Would no one ever come?

He began to despair of ever getting the information in to Lord Roberts. He had a fair knowledge of projected movements on the line of communication, and realised to the full the importance of getting the two grimy documents to the Residency; also he knew well enough that unless help came by nightfall there was not the slightest chance of withholding them from the Boer, whose eyes, as he knew well enough, had been watching all the day. But the inertia that was paralysing more than his physical powers was attacking his energy, though his brain remained as clear as before—perhaps clearer: his conscience was at rest, he could do no more.

An extraordinary brilliancy of memory possessed him, and he lived in a rapidly changing panorama of incidents, facts, and perceptions, many of which had previously faded completely from his memory. He wondered idly if this could be the re-living of the past that so many who have been near the gates of death have described. Anyway, he stood aside, and watched the workings of his own brain as a spectator, and rarely had he known anything more intensely interesting.

The kaleidoscopic variety of his recollections was their only importance. A blot in a copybook was as important, neither more nor less, as a change of dynasty, and a wrinkle in the scalp of his Cape boy passed across the stage of his mind as deliberately as the pacing ritual of a Christmas mass in Rome. It seemed to him that he was unable to forget a detail of anything he had ever seen. Once he thought of recording his sensations up to the last moment, but gave up the idea out of sheer laziness, a fact that did not prevent him from actively recalling the exact words of another man who had done so,— or said that he had, for Milbank did not much believe that it could be a genuine account, so utterly willing was he himself to lie at rest and do nothing. It was the beginning of the end, he knew well enough, but he didn't very much care.

Such things as Merlin's disguise and the twin line out of Genoa, the tongue of a sick woodpecker, Grimm's law and the l.b.w. rule drifted in precise and orderly sequence through his brain without his seeing, or indeed much wishing to see, the connection. But the next vision, a pale face at Lord's glancing back quickly at him through a silver-grey veil, followed naturally enough, and he accepted it as a warning.

He recalled himself, moved one hand stiffly to his pocket, and pulled out a letter-case, one corner of which stuck tiresomely in the lining. It seemed to him a little unfair that at such a moment he should have to deal wearily with a spiteful little mischance.

He took a letter out, and after letting his eye fall over the first page, tore it up into very small pieces with his weakening fingers: then, recollecting, he sorted out with infinite fatigue and weariness the pieces that contained the name, and put them into his mouth.

It was all he could do, and he remembered wistfully that do what he might, the news could not be broken to her. She ought never to have been so much to him, though indeed he had nothing to reproach himself with except that he was humbly in love with another man's wife. And she was only a child, a disillusioned child of twenty. Not that the man in question cared, or had ever cared at all; only he knew of it. He used it at times to hurt his wife with. Milbank could well enough see him reading the news out to her casually from behind the newspaper to-morrow morning, and watching her face closely as he did so. He would be careful to do so while the servants were in the room.

Milbank remembered what she had said to him when he left England, and had always hoped that it might be for him, in case of accidents, the last of all human remembrances.

He wrote a note to Emmelin, whom he knew he could trust, to burn all letters and papers he could find, locked or unlocked up, except the *Daily Press* accounts; also he left him the curio number of the *Friend*, which he knew Emmelin coveted. He added: 'Do this even if you have to break the law. You might suggest afterwards, that the testamentary powers of a testator under martial law expressly include the case, and say it's Savigny or Montesquieu or Eldon—they won't know the difference. By the way, if you come across a half-written article on the matter, send it in to the *Friend*.'

The pen dropped. His thoughts flashed home, but he wilfully kept them from the woman who was going to be so desolate to-morrow.

The sunset was beginning, spreading wide in the western sky, and Milbank, lying huddled up and almost unable to move, faced it full. He could watch the gorgeous belts of incandescent colour, flecked with the light hurricane of sudden flakes, orange-crimson and gold, that flamed in his eyes. His fast-tiring gaze fixed dilated pupils on the molten horizon, which lighted with clear fire a face that bore no trace of fear.

It was all over for him. But still the world would do its daily work, and still the grey, orderly columns of the northern Abbey would upbear the dim vaultings in the ochreous half-lights of London; still, as he lay there and for a thousand years after, the lamp of repentance flickered and would flicker high upon the sea-turned wall of St. Mark's; and still the thin, high tinkle of the aerial bells of the Shwé Dagon would filter downwards to the moving crowd below—what matter if he were dead, he, Milbank of the *Daily Press*?

It couldn't last much longer. The heat of the sun parched his mouth, and he was now sorry that he had thrown his water-bottle away. The pain of his wound was but slight, and the loss of blood had ceased, but his power of movement seemed going fast in the upper part of his body as well. He cared very little now, and a drowsiness settled down over him.

Then a long-extinct memory of the 'Crusader's Mass' came quaintly into his head, and he felt beside him weakly on the veldt for the three necessary blades of grass.

And three brown, dry grass-bents, pricking up like thin bristles, he found by feeling on the ground. As he picked them, he realised that it was the last movement he would ever be able to make.

An aas-vogel vulture, that he had watched for some time, wheeled suddenly away from him. It was no weak, slow movement of his own that could so frighten the scavenger, but he was past all deductions now.

Painfully crossing his hands over his breast, helping one with the other, he managed to reach his mouth, and one by one he put the blades of grass between his lips.

'In Nomine Patris … et Filii … et Spiritus … Sancti.'

As he moved his teeth, the tiny morsel of paper that protected Her mingled on his tongue with the grass, and a feeling, first of incongruity and then of appreciation, swept through him. In one sense, perhaps in the right one, certainly in no poor one, he had been faithful unto the end. 'Je ne crains pas Dieu s'il sait tout.'

Then, with his Mass between his lips in the quickly fading light of the dying day, she, the only deep source of work and faith that life had held for him, brooded more and more deeply over his sinking consciousness. He knew that life would be a little—it could only be a little—more lonely and bitter for her henceforward, but his weakening senses allowed him little poignancy in his grief.

His ears were drumming with music now—deep-swelling chords that he recognised now and again, though they were not especially the sequences that had most deeply impressed him before; he could not imagine why they had not done so, for he did not doubt that he had heard them all before, somewhere; and always behind every change in this sweeping harmony of sounds a sweet fulfilling chord as of a heaven full of waters falling through rainbow light supplied the ground bass.

His tongue still moved the bitter grass and paper in his mouth, and, as he had wished, her words came again into his mind with a feeling of quiet triumph more than anything else: 'If you don't come back, I'll try to go through with it alone for the sake of the best man I ever knew.'

He waited with a little apprehension for the actual end—that last struggle of the heart against the grip that was to paralyse it, that was tightening upon its greatest vessels already: he knew that would hurt him a bit. Clear and magnificent the thundering 'Adeste fideles' was filling the heavens above, where one star tingled in the mauve chill of evening—he had always thought it the finest tune that man had ever written … 'Venite adoremus.' … It rolled and wailed in his ears, louder and still louder, and he smiled. 'Faithful?' And God in His utter mercy saved him from the end he mistrusted, for Van Zyl, in an hour's wary stalk, had come up to within three hundred yards, and a bullet crashed into Milbank's brain even as the words and music he loved were floating through his tired mind.

The Boer uttered a guttural cry of thanksgiving for the good God's exceeding favour, and leaped forward to rifle Milbank's pockets, finding the packet he sought in a moment. Then he gazed for one instant on the bullet-broken face of his victim, where even in the instantaneous shock of death there had been time for a weary flash as of disappointment after great hope, and he raised his hat almost in shame.

Then he crawled back to the farmhouse, unseen by the scouts who dotted the horizon on the flank of the still moving brigade.

# AN OUTPOST OF THE EMPIRE

' … A spy who was captured said that a white woman, who had been taken away by the rebels, was kept by them for a day or two, and then hanged. The same native said that the bodies of three white people would be found lying nine miles to the north.'

—*Pall Mall Gazette*, 1896.

*Margaret Daubeny, a woman of London, speaks very slowly, and without passion or self-pity.*

'THEY have broken the bones in my arm and wrist,
    They have blinded my eyes with a cleaning-rod,
And back to the tree a green cowhide twist
Ties up in the darkness and writhing mist
    A face that is scarce in the image of God.

'If the wind's not changed since they blinded me—
    It is cold to the blood in my sodden hair—
I am facing north to the old country, …
And the lowest star—could I only see!—
    Must be south on the roofs … at the end of the square.

# AN OUTPOST OF THE EMPIRE

'And your valse with its wailing burden tramps
    Across the trees on the twittering lawn,
And the long bright lines of your carriage-lamps
Pale in the silence where one horse champs …
    And I hang, O my sisters, I hang at dawn!

'Yes, dead in the morning, thank God, I lie!
    To where prayers have failed, perchance thanks may win—
For now there shall no man before I die
Have looked in his pity at what was I …
    I, Margaret, once of your kith and kin.

' "Of no mean city"—the deaf God's pen
    Writes fair and firm of the White Man's stay—
Yet I cried out once … but only then
To Him on the women who helped the men …
    And I think there was one who turned away.

*Margaret Daubeny is silent for a long time. Then she
speaks again—as one in a vision.*

'The Riders are out, set, silent, and grim,
    And north they press on my crimsoning trail.
For at noon they lighted on … Kitsie and Jim,
And the Measure they mete with is red to the brim.
    Though God is a-hunting, Man keeps the Tale.

'And these, as they lie round me, drunk with their feast,—
    Death is stroking their throats with his lean, white hand,
And grave as a Puritan, slow as a priest,
The price that is set upon one of her least
    By the Mother of Cities He shall demand.

# An Outpost of the Empire

*Margaret Daubeny remembers London.*

'O the long-wet wood of your shining ways!
    O the year-long break of your moving tide!
O the lonely life of your roaring maze!
O your tarnished sunsets, your ash-blue haze!
    O the hanging gems of your waterside!

'I was true, O my London, to your high creed,
    For I cried but once,—just a woman's moan
(O Woman, forgive me!) in utter need,—
And for that, for I am but a girl indeed,
    Let my silence for two long days atone.

> *After a long pause she speaks again, for the last time,*
> *always very slowly and without self-pity.*

'I have stood here long in the bitter night—
    O my sisters, your galop is nearly done!—
And Jim is waiting … Ah, God, for sight!—
For I feel on my cheek the first promise of light,
    And the welcome breath of the slow, sure sun.'

*Margaret Daubeny suffered again on that morning, and at the last was hanged before the rescue-party came up.*

*The manner of the vengeance which was taken upon the band of natives, men and women alike, who were guilty of her agony and death, was so dreadful that it is not spoken of in Rhodesia to this day.*

# 'AND OUR IGNORANCE IN ASKING'

THE principal Medical Officer was sitting with his assistant in a room in Thomas's farm, two miles south of the railway station at Belmont, making up the official list of the day's casualties. A candle burned steadily beside him, and now and again he held up to it the hurried notes sent in by the adjutants, by which he was checking the hospital lists.

He picked up a new one. 'Grenadier Guards,' he muttered, and his face lengthened as he looked down the paper. He ran his finger down by the side of the names.

'Twenty—forty—sixty—eighty—a hundred—hundred and twenty—thirty—three—six.'

Being human, he had already looked at the officers' casualties, and twice he had caught his breath sharply.

The sickening smell of iodoform reeked in the room, and a moan came from the tents in the garden. The assistant called over the names in a low voice.

'Elliot, Mackenzie, and Owen, all slight, in foot. Kane, killed——'

'Kane? Poor fellow, I remember him. Where?'

'Bronchial veins. Hopeless case; he died as we carried him back; secondary hæmorrhage.'

And the red list went on in the breathless room, with brief comments here and there, while outside under the poplar-trees, the impounded horses in the kraal pawed restlessly and whinnied at the smell of blood.

\*      \*      \*      \*      \*

'Doin' 'is duty? Huh, o' course 'e died doin' 'is duty. A fat lot of use that is to me, ain't it? Don't you go and put yoreself out, Mrs. Perkins, to come and tell me that.'

The atmosphere was obviously strained, but silence once more brooded in a small three-pair back in Ermine Row, where, in the midst of a litter of silk-wrapped wire, odds and ends of feathers and filosel, gimp, gold wire and chenille, a stout, heavily-breathing woman was staring at a somewhat younger one in a blue cloth skirt, a black cape, and a blackish bonnet with a bit of crape in it.

The hint, though broad, was ignored.

'Then you 'ave no children, pore dear,' resumed the comforter.

'Thenk Gawd!' was the uncompromising response. But Mrs. Perkins, after having obtained a footing in the room of the new widow, was not lightly to be deterred, and she felt that she owed a duty to the Row.

From the front, she looked as if she were sitting on the edge of her chair, but this was not the case. Her small, bright eyes were fixed on Mrs. Kane's face, while the latter impatiently twisted a garish leaf on to a stalk, keeping her eyes resolutely fastened upon her work. After a pause, in which her breathing was the only disturbing element, Mrs. Perkins returned to the attack.

'Then 'e was a good deal older than you, Sarah Kane, and 'e did used to beat you sometimes, didn't 'e, dear?'

Mrs. Perkins had some excuse for not expecting the outburst which followed. Wife-beating was not generally regarded as a delicate subject in the Row.

But Mrs. Kane leaped up, flaming with wrath. 'I'll thank yer to go away, Mrs. Perkins, before I spoil yer face fer yer. 'E never so much as lifted 'is 'and to me, and——' Mrs. Kane stopped contemptuously, opened the door with a crash, and stood waiting while her visitor drew her shawl round her with dignity, and prepared to go, feeling that even if she had not been a conspicuous success as a comforter, she had at any rate a good story of Sal's temper for the rest of the street.

Mrs. Kane, dry-eyed and tensely fingering the edge of the table, went on with a flushed face: 'And if 'e did, it was my fault—mind yer that, my fault every time.'

She followed her guest, the sight of whose back seemed to open the flood-gates of her temper, out on to the landing, and her shrill voice filled the well of the staircase. 'And if Mr. Perkins 'ad 'ad the pluck to comb yore 'air a bit, Mrs. Perkins, you'd be a sight better woman this day … an' yer can tell 'im I said so too … an' don't yer come here again a-spyin', Mrs. Perkins.'

The latter was some way down the first flight by this time, breathing a little heavily, and gripping the banisters with a knowing determination to get even with the vixen.

Sal returned with a beating heart to her artificial flowers, and the gaudy bits of silk grew into fearful shapes under her feverish fingers. As her temper cooled, her misery, forgotten for the moment, returned. She had just enough imagination to piece together the scene at Belmont, drawing for herself a harrowing and impossible picture, for the details of which she drew upon her recollection of an attempted suicide last summer in the same street. And poor Sal spared herself no agony that ignorance and a course of cheap fiction could suggest to her.

She allowed herself no relief in tears; she might yet have a visitor—for if you want privacy you might as well seek it in the Aquarium as in Ermine Row—and though she had no intention of admitting any one, she would have to answer the door.

The minutes passed into hours, and the flowers fell finished from her hands steadily and quickly. She did her work almost more for the solace of the half-attention that she was compelled to give to it, than for the scanty money it would bring.

As the light was fading, there came a knock at the door, and Sal, with her face set like a flint, rose and held it ajar.

'What is it?' she said shortly. 'I'm busy. If it's a track, yer can go away.'

'I'm Lady Evelyn Caryll, and if there is anything I could do——'

The quiet voice was drowned in the creak of the opening door, and Sal, still resentful, but accustomed to respect her betters by the unconscious influence of her husband's military training, stood in the entrance, feeling, however, almost at ease with the figure in quiet half-mourning, who had come to her in her misery. There was no impertinent curiosity in the eyes that looked down sympathetically into her own.

'I've heard of your trouble, and if I can do anything I hope you will let me know. I am working for the "Soldiers and Sailors," which has every right to help you now.'

'Thank yer, 'm. I won't trouble them. I can make my own living with the flowers, and I ain't got any children.'

Sal was obviously still on the defensive, but she moved back into the room with a bad grace, leaving the way clear for Lady Evelyn, who came forward with one hand in her muff, and played with a piece of silk on the table, keeping her eyes carefully averted from Mrs. Kane.

'I think I knew your husband—years ago before I married—he was Colonel Caryll's servant when he was in the third battalion, I think, and one never forgets a face in the regiment.'

Sal's face was a picture of mingled emotions.

'Are you Colonel Caryll's wife, 'm?' she asked irresolutely.

'Why, yes, so you see you mustn't mind my coming to see you.'

Sal wheeled round abruptly. 'Will you sit down, 'm?' As her visitor did so, she looked narrowly at her dress.

'Have you, 'm—er—lost 'im too?'

'No, he goes out next month with the other battalion.'

Then in Sal's sore mind it was slowly revealed that, essentially, Lady Evelyn had put on mourning for Private Kane, and her eyes filled with tears.

'You must thank Gawd, 'm, 'e wasn't at Belmont.'

'I had a brother there, and I hear that he is wounded—very slightly, I believe,' she added; 'but you see I have a little right to feel with you.'

'M'lady, I'm sorry for that. 'E was Captain Essington, I suppose?'

She was talking a little at random, while the great and comforting truth that war is no respecter of persons came to her for the first time. There was a moment's silence.

'I thought you were going to tell me to pray,' said poor Sal. 'I've turned them all out—I mean all the parsons. What's the use? I want my husband, I don't want anything else. And it's too late now, 'm, ain't it, 'm? It's no good praying for 'im now, 'm, no good at all!' Sal's voice was becoming unsteady. 'One man comes with a top hat, and 'e tells me that with Gawd all things were possible ... so I ... I turns 'im out as a fool. And I say it's a wicked thing to come and tell a woman what's lost 'er 'usband, dead and killed, that Gawd can send 'im back again all right.'

Lady Evelyn felt that she was on delicate ground. 'Perhaps he didn't quite mean that.'

'Well, 'm, I don't know what 'e meant, but it's what he *said*; anyway, 'tweren't any comfort. I want Kane, and I don't want nothing else. But 'e's a man, an' 'e couldn't understand, 'm, an' Gawd, bein' a man too, can't understand either, can 'E, 'm?"

Lady Evelyn flinched before this startling theological dogma, but felt that it was no time for doctrinal instruction. So, not without some inward thankfulness that there was no one else present, she suggested, with the timidity of the Anglican:

'But, remember the Virgin Mary.'

Then the last bitterness of the woman's grief was voiced in the sullen and envious response that was wrung from the heart of the childless.

'She 'ad a child!'

For a moment the hopelessness of any consolation that could reach Sal's lonely heart silenced her visitor. Then, moved by an impulse of which she would have thought herself incapable, she said the right word:

'But she lost him.'

In the silence that ensued, Lady Evelyn saw the birth of the only comfort that is real, the comfort that another helps us to make for ourselves. She was a wise woman, and moved across to Sal, saying in a kindly, businesslike way: 'Well, the chief thing now is for you to remember that if I can be of any use to you, I shall be glad to see you—you know where I live—92 Chester Square. And now, good-bye; you must let me help you for the sake of the regiment.'

'Good-bye, 'm—I mean my lady. Thank you kindly; I won't trouble you.'

And Sal, with wet eyes, watched her visitor descend.

She went back to her artificial flowers with a little less of her previous sense of friendlessness, but, after all, as she soon found herself arguing to herself, what was the good of expecting any comfort from any one? She knew that Lady Evelyn's husband was still with her, and that she had at least one child. And the relief of the breakdown of a few minutes before was paid for by a redoubled sense of loneliness, though the thought of St. Mary recurred to her again and again with curious insistence. Perhaps there was, after all, some consolation to be found in the religion she had always regarded as unpractical and suspicious.

The day had been foggy and frosty, but about five it cleared for a time, and Sal collected her flowers into a parcel, and set out to walk to a milliner near Cromwell Road, where her work was always taken. It was the first time she had been out since the news of her husband's death had reached her, and her loss was preached to her by every street lamp and corner in Westminster. She shut her eyes as she passed the Railway Inn, so keenly did she associate the gilt and enamelled glass with Kane; even the worst side of him was a sacred memory now.

She was chewing a bitter cud, indeed, as she turned into Eaton Square; she felt that her misery was greater than she could bear, and the sight of St. Peter's standing snug and respectable at the head of the square seemed only to bring home to her the isolation of her life. There was no under-standing there, and no one to whom she could bring the raw edges of her sorrow. Sullen and silent, she went on, hugging her grief, and beholden to no man.

It was a relief to her to be away from the Argus-eyed windows and doors of Ermine Row, and a sense of freedom from the stare of idle curiosity helped her to bend a little before the stress of her trouble. Lady Evelyn's remark had affected her more than she was willing to admit to herself, and her imagination was stirred by the remembrance of it.

Man was useless. Man had, too, in some indefinable way, coloured the invisible powers of the other world with his sex, and had even imprisoned the Mother herself in a halo of neutrality. But, in spite of all, Sal felt blindly that She would understand—that She must understand—once a woman, always—even on the steps of the Sapphire Throne, a phrase that had once caught Sal's fancy amazingly—always a woman.

Loss had been Her portion too, and Sal wondered in her misery whether the loss of a child was not perhaps as great a loss as even her own.

Jostled here and there on the pavement, without having the spirit to resent it much, the insignificant little figure made its way along, choosing the least frequented sides of the street. It was deadly cold, and Sal had been unwilling to put on her overcoat because it was of a kind of pepper and salt colour, and she would wear nothing that she could help that seemed unmindful of the dead man. Also she remembered in a sudden and distinct way, that she and her husband had quarrelled one Boxing Day while she was wearing the coat, and though she had worn it many times since without giving the matter another thought, she felt vaguely that it would be a kind of disloyalty to wear it just now, especially as she remembered the quarrel so distinctly, and the fact that she had had the last word with an insult that she had laughed over afterwards with real satisfaction. Now she remembered that Kane had not struck her for it, as she had quite expected at the time.

The setting sun was low over the end of Cromwell Road; a great ball of red across which grey and brown film wreaths, half smoke, half fog, passed above the thick lavender haze of the street below. Overhead it was the colour of quinine, and the gutters were packed kerb-high with morasses of freezing slush, through which the omnibuses drove their way shoulder-high above the scanty traffic.

Sal was in a state of nervous exaltation that she was unaccustomed to. Her feet were sopped and bitterly cold, her head burned, and the reaction from her three days of repressed misery was physically overwhelming her. The leafless trees outside Tattersall's within their iron railings intensified the dreariness of all around her. She began to sob bitterly and helplessly. Her own weakness frightened her, and she crept along the shops on the north side of the street to keep away from the rest of the world as far as she could.

It was the darkest hour of her trouble, for the blankness and emptiness of her future was forced upon her, and her straitened soul cried out in revolt against the injustice of her lot.

'A Reserve man too!' she muttered with a sob, as she passed the gabled gate of Trinity Church, too tired and wretched to go on. Blind with tears, she turned up the steps and into the Oratory, where she dropped motionless into a chair.

The dignity of the interior, which in the fading light had lost its tinsel garishness, and loomed over her silent and austere, was a solace in its permanence and peace. The noise of the street outside came dim and muffled, and the incense-laden air had an attraction it might not have had for a more refined pair of nostrils. Tired and soothed, she was content to let her sorrows relax themselves.

After all, she felt here that she was but one unit among a million, and the self-abasement caused by the sense of being in the presence of Infinite Power helped her in some odd way. Her eyes followed mechanically the obeisance of a woman who had risen from her knees and was going out. Perhaps she, too, had been praying like the others—and Sal realised that there were nearly a dozen women in the church, some as poorly dressed as herself—for some one in South Africa. Were they all in the same agony of ignorance?

She remembered the posters outside. The letters that had passed before her eyes almost meaninglessly at the time painted themselves on the darkening walls. 'Another Great Victory—Methuen crosses the Modder—Heavy British Losses.'

Sal realised that the army to which her husband had been attached was still moving on, and that the stern work of war

91

demanded as many lives now as it had five days before; in a fit of animal jealousy she found herself hoping that these too, each one of them, had lost their dearest—why should she be the only one?

Her eyes swept wearily round the shadowy walls until they lit on the crown of our Lady of Mercy in the side chapel to the right, and the remembrance of Lady Evelyn's words came to her again, fuller of meaning than before. A paste diamond glinted a steady shaft of green at her, so motionless was she, and she dimly made out the gold draperies of the figure below. Again the uncontrollable desire for sympathy overwhelmed her, and, moved by an impulse she hardly understood and could not control, she found herself on her knees before the low balustrade, sobbing her heart out to the Woman who had known sorrow too.

For a long time she said nothing; she only rested her hot forehead against the cool marble.

The unspoken prayer seethed to her lips, and she shivered with the stress of her petition, but she knew the folly of asking for what could not be given her; the silent figure overhead and her own invisibility in the gloom helped, not to words, but to the stripping of her soul.

She muttered brokenly: 'You understand—O m'Lady, *you* understand!'

She took her flowers and pushed them forward under the rails as far as she could reach. It was a silent offering, but it revealed her own misery to the full. She let herself slip down on the step, and hid her face in her hands.

She lay motionless for a long time, and then buried her hot brow in the elbow of her bent arm. Biting at the stuff of her dress, and half-choked, it came at last.

'Let me 'ave 'im back!—let me 'ave 'im back!'

Through her dulled brain fiery courses of thought flashed with a wisp of pain.

'If I could only 'ave 'im for a few days again—I wouldn't grumble then—I wouldn't, 'struth I wouldn't—just one man back—if you did a miricle just once, they—they wouldn't laugh at yer! You know what it is, 'm—tell 'Im to let me 'ave 'im back for just one day—only one day! 'E can't be so 'ard!'

Sal twisted herself on her hips, and raised her red throbbing eyes tearlessly to the tawdry figure over, which in the fast darkening church loomed out more and more gracious and beautiful.

Sal even thought without surprise that the statue did indeed bow itself down towards her just enough to be seen, and in the nervous exaltation of utter misery she went on in a quick and haggard undertone: 'Yer see, it wa'n't quite right between Kane and me when 'e went. I suppose it was my fault, but 'usbands are aggravating sometimes—and the neighbours made it worse than it might 'ave been——'

Sal felt the uselessness of explaining where all was known before, and fell back again on to the steps.

After a long pause, in which Sal abandoned herself utterly to the reaction of her strenuous and halting appeal to a God upon whom she felt that she had few claims if the description of Him by the Salvation Army orators of the Row were correct, a hand touched her on the shoulder, and a man's voice said in the darkness:

'Can I help you?'

'You?' There was a world of scorn in the tone. 'You? What use'd you be? Let me alone!'

A further attempt, meant well enough but miserably tactless and celibate, was cut short abruptly by Sal.

'Go away, for Gawd's sake!'

The steps moved on, and Sal was left still lying on the marble ascent of the altar. Syllables of any half-forgotten prayer of her childhood, chiefly irrelevant, moved her lips with a whisper, and behind them her one persistent petition lay, absorbing her deepest soul, and voiced, perhaps, none the less adequately because it took the form now of 'the grave as little as my bed,' and now of 'the voice that breathed o'er Eden,' and other irregular fragments of hymnology.

Sal would have seen as soon as any one that she was asking for what, in her daily life, she knew to be impossible, but it was no longer in her power to keep back the burden of her heart here in the darkness and silence, with the echoes of the world outside murmuring softly and distantly underneath the obscurity of the dome like the plash of light waves in a cavern.

It was warm, too, and Sal was soothed in the unaccustomed surroundings. Peace flowed quietly over her raw wounds, and she became half-ashamed of her late vindictiveness. She muttered: 'It's no good to me—I hope they'll keep their men.'

The dim candles burned low round the altars, and the red light of the Reservation grew brighter and truer in colour as the darkness of the evening deepened outside into a thick London fog. Sal could not now see even her own little oblation of gaudy flowers, but the gloom helped her to feel as she lay there in the silence that in some way there was a stable strength that lapped her own, and she was content to lie still in the hollow of it.

She was in no fool's paradise; she knew as clearly as before the lonely, poverty-stricken life that lay before her; she was no longer young, and any looks that might once have attracted Kane were long since gone; nor were the comforts that come to the refined and spiritually-minded for her. But sordid, broken, and hopeless as the future seemed, the relief of the temporary calm and the consciousness of self-surrender—which is the root and cause of all a woman's heaven or hell on earth—touched her aching brain with the restful feeling that at least she was now in other hands. If her petition was not to be granted, it could, she felt, be less intolerable than she thought it once, and she vaguely realised that her present comfort was one that stood always unchanged and ready for her if things became too much to bear.

At length, stiff and bruised from her long vigil, she crept out of the church into a black and spectral city of gauzy lights and strange sounds that swallowed her up instantly as she felt her way between the gates. But, though her heart was as sore and her common sense as merciless as ever, the peace of God, which is notoriously beyond all rules of logic, was in her, and a courage to abide the day, however long and wearisome it might be, lighted her narrow little soul as she went back empty-handed to her room.

\*　　　　\*　　　　\*　　　　\*　　　　\*

It was after the Modder fight, and the hospitals across the line from the ganger's hut were full indeed.

The P.M.O., worn out with the sleepless work of the past five days and nights, was again working over the long lists of casualties. This time there was hardly an anxious foreglance at the lists, even where he knew he had most cause to fear. Steadily with his assistant he plodded through the list. At last the Grenadiers' returns came up, and their comparative shortness reassured him a little.

'Essington, I see again, in the arm.'

'Very slight, sir; I met him going back to his mess, but I detained him.'

The list went on.

'Private Kane; slight, in the foot.'

'Kane?' The P.M.O. put out his hand for the list. 'I don't understand. Kane's dead and buried.'

'Oh, I meant to correct the return, sir; we only found it out this morning. It seems that Kane at Belmont threw his coat—with his identification ticket, of course, sewed on it—over the other man—Jameson, I suppose—who had had his own cut off him when they dressed him at the collecting-station, and I believe that Kane actually carried his own body to the grave, as one of the burying party on Wednesday.'

The P.M.O. was in no smiling mood, but his mouth relaxed a moment.

'Well have that telegraphed at once, please.'

And so the list went on, without another comment, to the end, under the stars that glinted whitely in the dark purple sky, while London, heart-sick and foul with fog, sat at breakfast with the newspaper it dared not open lying across the plate.

\*          \*          \*          \*          \*

Thus the Oratorians acquired a somewhat unruly disciple with robust if uninstructed faith, and the Church of England went without—they can hardly be said to have lost it—the presence of Mrs. Kane within their official fold.

# THE RECORDING ANGEL'S PEERAGE

EDGAR CARNEY was a man who was spoilt in early life by three things. First, he had more than a sufficiency of money; and he was a man who spent it with fair liberality upon his own purposes—like most of us. Secondly, though he came of a by no means plebeian stock, he spent his whole life in trying to make for himself intimacies which for other people in his class come naturally or not at all; and thirdly, he was the victim of a mean-spirited and invincible curiosity. He was jilted early in his life, and I do not think that he ever quite got out of his ears the tone of mingled amazement and disgust with which, some years later, a penniless girl refused his confident offer of his money and himself. So far as I know, he never made a third matrimonial attempt. Instead, he spent his time in a kind of eavesdropping existence which soon became notorious from one end to the other of the society in which he moved. At first he was known for his father's sake—a fine old gentleman who died too soon; then as a man who was to be tolerated for his money; and lastly, he found acceptance, if not a welcome, at most luncheon-tables, because he could be relied upon to give the latest version of pretty nearly every scandal in London. I do not know what the late Mr. Creevey was like, but I can fancy that at this period, and at his best, Mr. Carney bore some likeness to him. It would be a mistake to say that he was hailed with delight anywhere, but he was admitted because of his unfailing fund of well-peppered gossip. It is only fair to say that, malicious as much of it was, Carney's conversation was generally founded upon fact, though whether that is an excuse or an aggravation of his offence, it is hard to decide. He had, as I have said, plenty of money, and this no doubt smoothed his career, but it is hardly to the credit of those who received him that, from one end of London to the other, this almost universally mistrusted man was tolerated and even reckoned upon for a spicy, if not perhaps an edifying, hour's gossip at any moment. In one way or another he succeeded: there is no doubt about it that Mr. Carney's circle of acquaintances was enormous. Everybody disliked him, everybody said the rudest things about him behind his back, yet everybody went on asking him to dinner and accepting in return his own carefully calculated hospitality. It was the men chiefly that disliked Carney. Women, who are almost congenitally unable to detect a second-rate man when they see him, frequently defended him. He had a good deal of influence. Many of them, I honestly believe, were indebted to him for the opening to them of doors which, strange to say, were shut in Carney's own face. This is a mystery, but it is one which may be witnessed many times over by a close student of any London season. Others were attracted by his mere possession of money.

But after a time his position was strengthened in an ugly way. It gradually became rumoured that more than one woman had fallen helplessly into Carney's clutches because of the uncanny knowledge he had of every one's private life. People who had anything to conceal were unwilling to risk his enmity. In short, not to mince matters, Carney became known as a social blackmailer, and, as no one knew the exact limits of his extraordinary backstairs' information, his presence was acquiesced in quite as much from fear as from any other motive. Men did not care to run the risk of Carney's malevolence. Very few of us have such immaculate pasts that we should care to have them circulated in detail among our friends. And the feeling generally was that Carney was not only the sort of man who would be likely to have an inkling of our more speckly hours, but would also in retailing the story make use of his knowledge to obtain more.

Yet the man was elusive. It was difficult to pin him down, and there is no doubt that his reputation was vastly enhanced because few people really knew what the limits of the man's information were. In Carney's case, inquisitiveness had bred upon an originally nasty mind what was hardly less than a mania for prying into the seamy side of other people's lives. He had organised a special service for this purpose. He kept voluminous notebooks, he noted down every suggestion or hint that appeared in even the most verminous section of the public press, every word of gossip or scandal that was told him in the strictest confidence. From that he went on to the employment of detectives about matters that did not in the least concern him. He eventually allowed himself to bribe discharged servants and others who were able to recount to him the common slanders of the servants' quarters. The man became a common peril.

He had once or twice darkly threatened that before he died he would publish all he knew. It was never supposed that he really intended to do so, but the mere threat gave him the advantage he desired. He knew that he was unpopular: apparently he never wished to be otherwise. But he also knew that he was feared by almost every man and woman whom he met, and this sense of power acting upon an abnormal brain was for him an almost irresistible temptation.

In person he was of middle size, with brown hair slightly flecked with grey, and his sandy moustaches grew abruptly and vulgarly out of his skin. He had steady and colourless eyes, and said only what he wished to say. He had never been caught out in any definite act unbecoming a gentleman. There is no doubt that the committee of the Carlton would have been only too glad to get rid of him if they could. He had been originally elected a member because, while a young man, he had stood as Conservative candidate for an almost hopeless bye-election. He had not been returned. He never had expected to be returned, and his political aspirations vanished from that moment. But this service to the party, which had been carefully calculated on his side, enabled him to obtain election at the Carlton—a privilege which he coveted for many reasons—and in the end he became one of the most familiar figures in Pall Mall.

One evening Robert Leighton and Carstairs were dining together at the Carlton. They had finished dinner, and were drinking their coffee, when Carney made his way up to their table. Both men disliked him intensely, and Carstairs took no pains to conceal his own aversion. Leighton was more civil. Carney, after a word or two of meaningless conversation, said that he was busy correcting the proof of his book.

Leighton's face changed slightly as he said:

'What book do you mean?'

'Oh,' said Carney, between two pulls at his cigar—he was one of those tiresome people who kiss rather than draw at their cigars—'I mean my monumental work upon the manners and morals of London at the present day. I have got a splendid name for it. I am going to call it *The Recording Angel's Peerage*.'

Leighton looked at him steadily for a moment, and even Carstairs allowed himself to glance quickly at his figure.

'You have had the proofs in?' said Leighton.

'Yes,' said Carney, 'the first half came in last week.' He thrummed with his fingers on his front teeth. 'I tell you, it will be amusing reading for some people.'

'What are you going to publish it at?' said Leighton.

'It won't be published at all,' said Carney. 'In fact,' he added, 'I'm inclined to think that, if I wanted it, I could make a lot more money in sending proofs to certain people and asking them what they will give me not to publish it.'

At this moment Carstairs said quite, quite clearly:

'Dirty swine!'

Carney's eyes narrowed to slits. He turned and spoke directly to Carstairs. 'Very few people in London will speak to me after the book is published, but I can dispense with your acquaintance even sooner.'

Carney went away, and Carstairs broke out.

'I can't understand, Leighton, why you allow that scum of a beast to talk to you!'

'Well,' said Leighton, 'I have my reasons; they wouldn't interest you at all.'

'Blackmail, too!' said Carstairs, cocking one eyebrow up.

'Yes,' said Leighton vaguely; 'blackmail, I suppose, of a sort—of a sort.'

'Poor devil!' said Carstairs. 'Well, let's go and see these Swedish people at the Alhambra.'

Next morning at breakfast Robert Leighton happened to let slip some mention of this incident to Noreen, his young and businesslike little wife. Full of indignation, she orated with an eggspoon in her hand upon the iniquity of Carney and all his works.

'Can nothing be done to stop this wretched man? Why don't you men do something? Mother used to know him ages ago, and I remember her telling some one once that if only duelling were still possible in England, the man would have been killed twenty times over. Surely something can be done.'

Leighton held his peace. He saw the difficulty of acting. Indeed, he knew a great deal more about it than Noreen. But the latter would not be appeased. She said:

'You know him better than most people?'

'I suppose I do,' admitted Robert.

'More shame to you!' parentheticised Noreen. She went on in a breath: 'Well then, can't you get him to stop? Anyway, to put off the publication of his wretched book that every one talks about, is dreadfully frightened about, and knows nothing about really. What is this book, then?' said she, determined to get to the bottom of the matter.

Leighton tried to put her off with some pretence to ignorance. But she insisted on being told, and some threat she let fall made Leighton think that she had better hear anything from himself and not from another.

'Well,' he said reluctantly, 'it is a pretty full record of the misdoings of society. I've never seen the book myself, but Carney once explained to me his method. It's in the form of a peerage, and the peccadilloes of every man and woman that you and I know and our forebears knew are put down. The sins of commission and the sins of omission are both there, and the results are logically stated. For example,' he said, 'you won't find Lord Cherborough or poor old Kilbury or Fiennes Stotterton there. Of course, we all of us know the scandal in those three cases, but this old brute has apparently put down relentlessly a thousand other cases which are probably untrue, and of each of which only a very small circle of people has at the present time the slightest inkling. Of course one might expect that George Billiter wouldn't find a place in this wretched book, but I am told that he has had the effrontery, by means of omissions like that, to throw discredit upon about a quarter of the women you and I know. So far as I can make out, this man Carney has spent his life in examining the dirty linen of what they are pleased to call the upper classes, and has actually dared, in the case of many women still living, to omit any children about whose parentage there has ever been a scandal.' Looking at his wife rather closely, Robert went on:

'Of course, it is only his dirty mind. I dare say that half the things he says aren't true——'

Mrs. Leighton interrupted with shining eyes:

'Do you mean to say that that foul old man is going to publish in black and white a kind of backstairs' record of all the things that no one ever speaks of? Why don't you men kill him? The man's vermin!'

Leighton answered rather gloomily: 'The worst is that some people must talk about them, or Carney would never find them out. You know that as well as I do. But, so far as I can make out, he isn't going to publish it in the ordinary sense of the word. You won't be able to go into a shop and buy it for a guinea. Carney is as rich as be-damned, and doesn't need the money. All he wants is the *réclame*. He wants to make a big sensation once in his life, and upon my soul,' added Leighton, 'I think he'll do it. I don't know whether five copies of the book will ever be printed, but there it will be in the background as a threat, and Carney's blackmailings will in future be more insistent than ever.'

Mrs. Leighton's subsequent remarks were intemperate. She ranged up and down the full gamut of feminine expostulation, but her husband could only repeat:

'What's the use? We can't kill the man, and as the book isn't going to be published for every one to buy, I don't see how we can stop it.'

Mrs. Leighton ended up with a remark that her husband remembered afterwards. She said:

'Of course, it doesn't affect us, but if my name were mentioned in that book, rightly or wrongly, I would not only kill Carney with my own hands, but I should think that I had done the world a service in getting rid of such an unclean beast!'

A few days later Carney came to call on the Leightons. Mrs. Leighton was dangerously pleasant and lured him on to speak of what he regarded as the work of his life. But he seemed reticent, and she could not get much out of him. It seemed clear that the man intended to use this mysterious volume simply as a threat. Sometimes Mrs. Leighton almost doubted whether it had ever really been written. Her curiosity was piqued, and when Carney invited her to come to tea in the Albany at any time she liked, she immediately closed with the invitation. She suggested the following Thursday, and to cut a long story short, at four o'clock on the next Thursday afternoon, Mrs. Leighton found herself, with her husband, in Carney's rooms in the Albany. They had come somewhat earlier than Carney had invited them, and, before he had time to put away his work, Mrs. Leighton saw upon his desk the long galley-proofs of this detested work. She pretended not to have noticed them, and Carney, perhaps in order to conceal them the more effectually, left them lying on his desk as he rose to welcome his visitors. Carney had an interesting collection of Oriental objects, a considerable knowledge of Eastern art, and, at one time while Carney and her husband were intent upon some curious pieces of very early Chinese bronze, sparsely ornamented with *champlevé* enamel, Mrs. Leighton went up to the table, and easily sifting between her fingers the long proofs, stole that which was headed 'Viscount Lyminge'. At any rate, she meant to know what this ghoul was going to write about her own family. She hurriedly crumpled the slip into her sleeve and rejoined the other two.

That evening, when she went upstairs to dress for dinner, she took out the slip, and smoothing it out on her dressing-table, she began to examine in detail what Carney had written. On the whole there was not much, she thought. There was an ill-natured reference to her uncle's questionable exploits while at Oxford, and another to her aunt's plebeian parentage. Lady Lyminge, it must be confessed, had with her American dollars somewhat gilded the tarnished coronet of the earldom. She was described as 'the daughter of Josiah Hickson, originally pork-butcher in Ontario, subsequently the head and managing director of Hickson's Canning Factory, of Chicago, Illinois, U.S.A.' The escapade of Lady Lyminge's brother with a chorus-girl in New York was set out impartially, and the question of the latter's guilt was discussed in the words of the judge's summing-up. But there was no word said against Lady Lyminge personally. Noreen's two younger uncles escaped almost as easily. Her elder aunt, Mrs. Deans, was referred to as having had some unnecessary connection with the Howlett financial crisis, and then Mrs. Leighton turned mechanically, but without a trace of anxiety, to the record of her own parents. For the moment she breathed a sigh of relief. The facts and dates of her father's and her mother's birth, marriage, and residence were put down without malice or insinuation. Noreen ran her eye over the entry, and for the moment paid no special attention to the bald list of their children. Indeed, she discovered for the first time that her father had been in Brazil in '65. Then she read on, and she put her finger beside each entry to check it. It looked as harmless as Debrett. After all, the later Burleighs had, every one of them, been respectable to the verge of dullness. There was not a word of criticism. But still something seemed to be wrong, though at first she hardly saw what it was. Then at last, hardly believing that it could be so, at first inclined to put it down to some stupid oversight on Mr. Carney's part, she realised with a chill of horror that her own name had been omitted from the list of her father's children.

It was some time before Noreen was able to understand the real significance of what she had just discovered. Never for one moment did the faintest suspicion of disloyalty cross her mind. But it gradually dawned upon her that this devilish omission was entirely deliberate, and must reflect some foully false scandal of which she had never before heard. Never in her lifetime had she dreamt that the things she had so often heard of others, and indeed had often herself discussed, could by any possibility come into her own home circle. She knew how lightly she had from time to time listened to and repeated idle gossip without caring very much whether there were truth in it or not. Unless there was something to mark the story out from the ordinary tittle-tattle of a London drawing-room, she rarely remembered it, and, like the rest of the world, she never allowed it to make the least difference in the way in which she regarded the subject of it. It came lightly and it went lightly. But this was quite another thing.

Everything appeared to her in a strange and horrible light. The very furniture and pictures in her boudoir took on an appearance of unfriendliness, her untidy bureau was a stranger's desk to her, as she sat there motionless with the accusing strip of paper in her hand. Once she sought refuge in the idea that the omission of her name was due to mere forgetfulness. But she hurriedly looked again at the proof, and she saw that some trifling correction had been made by Mr. Carney both in the date of the birth of her youngest brother, and ten lines lower some equally unimportant addition had been made in the record of her cousin. The thing was deliberate and brutal, and Noreen's soul, forgetting her loathing and disgust of Carney, went out in a flood of sympathy to her mother. It seemed a horrible thing that for all those years there had been a tag of scandal to be borne even by her. To Noreen it mattered very little that she herself was immediately concerned in the tale. Only with the idea before her of her mother's trouble should this miserable book be published, did she turn over and over again in her mind all and any means of preventing its publication.

It was an act of wanton and heartless brutality thus to record for later generations a story which, if it had any foundation whatever, could only be the light banter of twenty-five years ago. Yet, as she thought the matter through and through, Noreen began to realise how helpless she and her mother were. She felt that against them there was suddenly raised up a hard and inexorable brutality that knew neither justice nor mercy. Her powerlessness to do anything faced her whichever way she looked. Yet was it conceivable that Carney really intended to circulate this volume of libels among his friends, and dare them to take action against him? After long thought, during which Noreen's brain ran hotly over every aspect of the wretched affair, she pulled herself together, locked the proof slip in a drawer of her writing-table, dressed and went down to the drawing-room. She felt in a state of half-insane despair. There was nothing to guide her. Such a catastrophe as this had occurred to no one else she had ever known. Such a calamity was among the unthinkable contingencies of the somewhat kindly circle of people among whom Mrs. Leighton easily found and chose her friends. Yet something, she knew, had to be done, and what was more, had to be done quickly. Leighton came in late for dinner. He had dressed hurriedly, and excused his unpunctuality on account of staying late for bridge at the club—an excuse that he backed up with a more than usually copious apology when he saw, as he thought, that Noreen did not take it with a good grace. But she smiled at him and they went down to dinner. No one was dining with them, and the conversation kept itself, so far as Noreen was concerned, to pleasant conventionalities and platitudes. Leighton was in more than usually high spirits, and perhaps hardly noticed that Noreen ate little and spoke little all through the meal. He had a new story to tell about the approaching Goodwood week parties, one of them about a woman of whose character neither Noreen nor the rest of the world had any doubt. She listened with a sudden restless antagonism that rather surprised her husband. When taxed with it, she explained listlessly that after all, whether it were true or not, it was the wretched woman's own business and no one else's, and Leighton cheerfully passed on to other matters. For coffee the two went into Robert's library, and, when they were there alone and beyond all possibility of interruption, Noreen spoke. She was standing by the fireplace with her heels on the low fender, a favourite trick of hers.

'Robert——'

There was a pause.

'Well, dear,' said Leighton, as he reached across for his coffee, 'what is the matter?'

'Robert—I want to talk to you about Mr. Carney's book.'

Although Noreen could not see it, Leighton's face grew somewhat troubled.

'Do you think it is a good thing for all that beast's private mud-scrapings for the last half-century, whether they are true or whether they are false, to be published?'

'Why, no,' said Leighton, rather intently; 'I think that nothing could well be worse. But we don't know what he has said. We don't know what he has included, or what he has left out. His bark is probably much worse than his bite, and anyway, I don't see what could be done even if I could tell you who is to do it.'

'Have you ever read any of this book, Robert?'

'Not a line. I believe that he has only allowed it out of his sight to a compositor whom he has employed privately. I believe the man sets the book up in a back room in Carney's own house.'

'You've never read a line of it, then?'

'No,' said Robert, 'never, though I dare say I should recognise many stories that I have heard if I ever see the book.'

'Well, I've seen as much as I want to see of it,' said Noreen slowly and hardly.

Leighton sat still, silent and expectant, as if he knew what was coming.

'You've seen that book?'

'Yes,' said Noreen; 'I stole the Lyminge proof-sheets this afternoon.' Robert sat still and made no comment. Noreen turned to the mantelpiece and picked at the enamel of a cigarette-case. She went on with a catch in her throat: 'Carney says in it that I am illegitimate.'

There was a long silence. Robert Leighton, avoiding Noreen's eye, looked hard into the empty fireplace. Then, as if he remembered what it would be natural for him to do, he said:

'What do you mean?'

'Carney says in it that I am illegitimate,' repeated Noreen mercilessly.

Leighton leaned forward.

'Impossible!'

'But it is possible, and it is the fact,' answered Noreen. 'I have got the proof-sheet upstairs.'

Leighton got up and proceeded to pace the room. Noreen barely paid any attention to him. She had turned, and her gaze was fixed on the electric lamp on his writing-table. After a bit she said in a colourless tone:

'What are you going to do about it?'

Leighton paused at the very end of the room, and then said with some difficulty:

'Of course, my dear, something must be done at once. The thing is absolutely absurd—ridiculous—preposterous! Something must be done about it at once. I will—I will see Carney. I will see him to-morrow.'

Noreen was so intent upon the world of misery and shame that her hour's meditation before dinner had called up before her eyes, that she barely noticed at the time the tinge of uncertainty in Leighton's voice which she afterwards remembered. But she did notice that Leighton took the news with a calmness that seemed to her extraordinary, and then she said decisively:

'I want you to understand that that book will have to be

destroyed before a copy gets into any one else's hands, and I shall rely upon you, Robert, to make sure to-morrow morning that this is done—at any cost whatever, either to yourself or to me: remember, at any cost.'

Leighton murmured his acquiescence, but resumed his walk up and down the room. He felt that he had somehow done the wrong thing. He should have blustered, he should have stormed, he should even have accused Noreen of hastiness, he should have refused to believe in the possibility of such a thing before the actual printed slip was put before his eyes. Watching Noreen make her way out of the room, he realised that he had made a mess of the whole thing. As a matter of fact, Robert Leighton knew that there was some old and vague story, though he had for many years deliberately put aside all remembrance and all knowledge of it. It was the reason that he was civil to Carney when Carstairs cut him. But Leighton was not actor enough, when suddenly and unexpectedly pressed, to pretend even for the sake of the wife of whom he was so fond that the old scandal was a mere malicious invention of Carney himself. He went back to his chair, and was lost in the deepest thought. He could remember little about the details, much as he tried to recall them, except that, long before he fell in love with Noreen Burleigh, some partner over the whist-table had, as a matter of idle moment, even with a cigar between his teeth and even as he considered his cards and the state of the game, said absently something about Mrs. Burleigh which Robert Leighton had remembered only vaguely until that moment. Yet there could be no doubt of it: in one sickening moment an old dead scandal suddenly reared its head again upon his very hearth.

He considered what course he had better take. He was a man constitutionally averse to a scene of any kind. He was of a common type. Probably every scene that has ever been necessitated has been essentially due to the unwillingness of some man or other to face a situation in time with rapidity and firmness. There is this much to be said for Leighton. He did not know, and he did not wish to know, more of the story than his whist partner, ten years ago, had told him. He did not believe the story then, and his long acquaintance with his mother-in-law had merely succeeded in persuading him more than ever that, in whatever other direction her faults might lie, she was at any rate free from that particular one. To a man of his character, Noreen's demand was singularly baffling. It necessitated a personal interview with Carney, and by Noreen's own confession she had only arrived at this miserable information by what was very little short of theft. Carney would be justified in refusing to discuss the matter; if Leighton knew his man at all, Carney certainly would refuse, besides letting him know, and possibly letting the rest of the world know also, what he thought of the honesty and manners of his wife.

Moreover, there was just that one chance in a thousand which no sensible man of the world ever entirely forgets, except in the case of his own blood relations, that Carney might have better ground for this outrageous insult than Leighton knew. Suppose that Carney, instead of resenting Noreen's petty theft, justified his insinuation? This would precipitate in a moment the much dreaded scene, and for the life of him Leighton did not know what he was going to do afterwards, either to silence Carney or to appease Noreen. The only comfort he could lay to his soul was that only half a dozen copies of the book were to be printed, and that, so far as he remembered, Carney had said that he did not intend any one of them to be circulated until many years after his own death. But he knew well enough that Carney had played the game of social blackmail all his life with such success that he was not to be depended on for a moment.

He did not see Noreen again that evening, and next morning they avoided the matter by common consent until

# The Recording Angel's Peerage

Robert was leaving the house between eleven and twelve. Noreen then, with a quiet determination that he had never known in her face before, said to him:

'Remember, I expect you to see Mr. Carney to-day, and to take any and every necessary step to destroy that book of his.'

Robert promised that he would, went to his club, saw Carney in the distance, did not say a word, and was compelled, about four o'clock, ignominiously to confess his cowardice when questioned by Noreen. It is the way of all weak people, but when a man is weak the unfortunate results of his indecision are far greater to other people than those of a woman's irresolution, which is apt to recoil chiefly upon herself.

Noreen then made up her mind that she must go at once to see her mother. Mrs. Burleigh, since her husband's death, had lived in a house in Eaton Place. She maintained a quiet existence, did a good deal of unostentatious and painstaking work for local charities, and in general made friends with a very different circle from that which had in other days graced their large house in Portland Place. Noreen found that her mother was at home, and went up unannounced to the drawing-room.

There were, as there are in most Eaton Place houses, two drawing-rooms, divided one from the other by folding doors. Noreen heard her mother speaking to some one in the inner room, and sat down for a moment to wait till the visitor should have gone. She knew that her mother particularly disliked to be interrupted whenever she was in the inner drawing-room. Noreen, a prey to her own grave thoughts, paid little attention to anything else. She took up a copy of the *Tatler* and idly let her eyes run over the illustrations. So absorbed was she in her own trouble that it was with a kind of surprise that she roused herself to realise that she had been listening for the last minute to her mother's voice plainly in distress. She could not distinguish the words, but there was no mistaking the tone.

Noreen put the *Tatler* down and listened in blank amazement. She had always known her mother as a quiet, self-controlled, somewhat princess-like person, but that shaken voice was, beyond all doubt, her mother's. Quiet as it was, Noreen, with a touch of that telepathic sympathy that rarely fails between mother and daughter, realised with a thrill of horror that her mother was in some terrible emergency. A second later, and even before she heard the voice of her mother's visitor, she also realised, with a chill at the heart, that that visitor was no other than Edgar Carney.

\*             \*             \*             \*             \*

No coherent story has ever before been told about the next five minutes. Mrs. Leighton and her mother betrayed no nervousness under the cross-questionings to which they were subjected, both in public and in private, but there was a good deal of surprise shown at the manner of Carney's death, though few regretted it.

All that was clearly known to the world was that Edgar Carney died that afternoon in Mrs. Burleigh's house in Eaton Place. He was found at the bottom of the stairs with an ugly fracture on the back of his head. The servant who rushed up from the basement on hearing the noise found him unconscious, and he died before the doctors came. Mrs. Burleigh betrayed the utmost concern, and every possible attention was given to him in her own drawing-room. Except for a few minutes, there were servants in or out of the room the whole of the time between Carney's fall and the arrival of the doctors. Carney was an oldish man of uncertain health, and he died without regaining consciousness. There was a question about the nature of the wound on his head. At the inquest the matter was mentioned, but it seemed useless to follow it up. It was admitted that the two ladies were the only persons in the drawing-room during his visit, and no suspicion could be cast upon the manservant who rushed up on hearing the fall. Carney was a man without friends, and his executors, partly in order to save themselves trouble, and partly also from a sense of public duty, destroyed all his papers and distributed, or, to be exact, made 'pie' of the many galleys of type which they found set up in a back room in his house. One of the executors, as a mere matter of curiosity, noticed that from among the proof-sheets on Carney's table that dealing with Mrs. Burleigh's family was missing. Being a very wise man, he did not even mention the fact to his co-executor, but with his own hands he destroyed the whole set of proofs.

There is no doubt about it that the West End of London breathed more freely when the news arrived that Carney and all his collections were gone together, and no one felt inclined to inquire very deeply into the matter. Carney, as I have said, had no friends, and his next-of-kin, who knew that they would have had nothing if Carney had had time to make a will, were not inclined to trouble themselves over anything except the realisation for the best price of the many curios and works of art that their unknown and cordially disliked cousin had collected during his life. In short, Carney and all his works vanished as if they had never been, his pictures were sold in King Street, and the executors finally wound up the estate.

\*　　　　\*　　　　\*　　　　\*　　　　\*

But one thing did happen that afternoon. Mrs. Leighton remained with her mother while Carney was lying unconscious on the sofa. There was not in her heart the slightest pang of remorse for what she had done. She had discovered that her mother was pleading for mercy, that she must have heard before of this odious scandal. Perhaps her affection for her mother increased tenfold in that terrible second. What

Noreen did not understand was the way in which, after she had made her presence known, Mrs. Burleigh again and again tried to intercede between Carney and herself. It was a mad and hectic interview, and in Noreen's determination and pluck Anne Burleigh could scarcely recognise her own daughter. On the other hand, Noreen, had she been able to view the matter coolly, would have guessed Carney had some curious power beyond even that which his bare knowledge of her mother's wretched secret gave him.

He played with Mrs. Burleigh as a cat plays with a mouse. At last, growing angry, he refused absolutely and point-blank to cancel his book or any leaf in it. He said, moreover, that he had changed his mind, and that instead of reserving its valuable information, as he termed it, for the enjoyment of others after his death, he was going to make amends for much that he had suffered in the past—and with this he looked straight at Mrs. Burleigh—by letting the connoisseur in human frailty have the advantage of his researches during his own lifetime. He died because he misunderstood Noreen Leighton, because he forgot that even a woman's curios might include one of a deadly character, and thirdly, he died because he allowed himself to make use, to Anne Burleigh and of Anne Burleigh, of the one word for which, as he should have known, no mercy can be shown even in non-duelling London, and of which no retractation is valid.

But when the man was dead and the doctor was gone and the two women found themselves alone again in the drawing-room, the mother turned to her daughter, and looked long at her with eyes in which horror sat enthroned. Then she turned to the window and said, quite slowly and almost monotonously:

'Noreen, Noreen, can't you understand?'

But Noreen never did, and lives to-day an unrepentant and even cheerful murderess in our midst.

# MRS. RIVERS'S

# JOURNAL

I

'*May 19th*. Two or three people to dinner and a play. Dennis, Mr. and Mrs. Richmond, Lady Alresford, and Colonel Wyke. D. saw me home after. I think something must be the matter. D. was very much upset last night, I'm sure. It all happened very suddenly, as he had been as delightful as ever all the evening. I can't think what it is. It was about midnight when he said something to himself, as he was looking out of the window, and changed completely.'

Later in the day Mrs. Rivers added, almost in another hand, these notes:

'D. called here this afternoon. At first he was very silent, and I asked him what the matter was. He said that it was not my fault in any way, and that he would explain some day. Meanwhile he asked me not to worry. But I'm sure something is very wrong, and if it is not my fault I'm half afraid that it may be on my behalf that Dennis is so upset. But he won't say anything, and I can't think that there is anything really to be feared. He only stayed half an hour, and went away saying that he would like to see me to-morrow morning. I thought it was a pity that he should come too often to the house, and said that I would meet him in the National Gallery at twelve o'clock. I wonder what it all means.'

Mrs. Rivers, whose locked journal is here quoted, was in herself a very ordinary kind of pretty woman. So far as the world knew, she was a widow, and a rich widow. Her husband had died about four years before this date, and it is unlikely that he was very seriously mourned. Colonel Rivers—his title was really a Volunteer distinction, but the man deserved no little credit for the way in which he worked up his battalion— was an inordinately jealous man, and though no one believed he had the least reason for suspecting his wife's acquaintance with Captain Dennis Cardyne, there is no doubt that, shortly before he died, it became almost a monomania with him, it may even have been a symptom of the trouble from which he must even then have been suffering acutely. Cardyne, a remarkably straight and loyal friend, with no brains, but a good sense of humour and principles which were at least as correct as those of his fellow-officers, was surprised one day by being peremptorily forbidden the house by Colonel Rivers. Human nature being what it is, it is possible that Cardyne then felt that the least impediment which friendship or loyalty could impose was removed, and there is no doubt that a general feeling of sympathy and affection for Mrs. Rivers took on quite another colouring by this idiotic proceeding on the part of Mrs. Rivers's husband. Cardyne's eyes were opened for the first time to the life that Mrs. Rivers must have led since her marriage four years before, though indeed she had previously taken some pains that he should quite understand her unhappiness at home. But Cardyne, who knew and liked the Colonel—in the patronising way that the most junior of regular officers will regard a volunteer—unconsciously discounted a good deal, knowing that most women like to think that their husbands misunderstand them. Hitherto he had neither disbelieved nor believed what Mrs. Rivers was insinuating. Now, however, his pity was aroused, though nothing in his conduct showed it at the moment.

I do not suggest for a moment that Mrs. Rivers was either a very interesting or a very virtuous person. But she had the little fluffy pleading ways by which many men are strangely attracted, and even if Cardyne had made any advances, her respect for conventionality, which was far more sacred to her than she quite realised, fully supplied the place of morality during the few months that elapsed between Colonel Rivers's explosion of jealousy and his sudden death.

There were not many people, except the very nearest of kin, who were aware of a curious clause which Colonel Rivers had inserted in his will about the time that he forbade Dennis Cardyne to come to the house. Personal references of an unpleasant kind are not copied into the volumes in Somerset House, which contain the wills to which probate has been granted. A proviso in the will that Mrs. Rivers, in the event of her marrying again, was to forfeit one-half of the somewhat large fortune bequeathed to her by her husband was public property, but only to those who were chiefly concerned it was allowed to be known that in the event of her marrying Captain Dennis Cardyne—whose name was preceded by an epithet—she was to forfeit every penny.

When Mrs. Rivers heard the terms of her husband's will, she lost the last tinge of respect she had ever had for her departed helpmeet. The prohibition certainly achieved its end, but it was not long before Cardyne and Mrs. Rivers settled down to a hole-and-corner flirtation, which probably brought far more terror than pleasure into the latter's life. Cardyne assured me that there was never anything more, and I am accustomed to believe that Dennis Cardyne speaks the truth. But the world thought otherwise and found many excuses for them. Mrs. Rivers could always justify to herself what she was doing by a remembrance of her husband's insane and ungenerous jealousy; but the fact remained that, however much this sufficed to quiet her own conscience, Mrs. Rivers was, to the very marrow of her, a common little thing, utterly afraid of the world's opinion, and quite unable to carry through the unconventionality of her affection for Cardyne without a burden of misery. And they did the silliest of things. After all, if a man will see a woman home from the play night after night and stay till two in the morning, he must be ready for a howl or two from the brute world. We have all done it, and done it most platonically, but at least we knew that it wasn't over wise.

I used to meet her at one time. She was always to be found in houses of a certain type. Her friends were women who took their views of life from one another, or from Society weekly papers. In the wake of Royalty they did no doubt achieve a certain amount of serviceable work for others, and at least it could be said of them that none of them seemed likely to scandalise the susceptibilities of their comfortable, if somewhat narrow, circle. Never twice would you meet a clever man, or a brilliant woman, at these feasts.

If you will take the names of those who were present at Mrs. Rivers's small dinner-party on March 18th, you will see exactly what I mean. Colonel Wyke was an old friend of her husband's. He had a little place in the country in which he grew begonias very well, and was, I believe, writing the history of the parish, from such printed material as he could find in the library of the county town. Lady Alresford lent her name to every charity organisation without discrimination or inquiry. She was a president of a rescue home in London, which probably did much harm to conventional morality. Mr. and Mrs. Richmond were a quiet, and somewhat colourless, little couple of considerable wealth, but without any real interest or purpose in life except that, if the truth must be told, of gossiping about their neighbours. I have never known Richmond at a loss for an inaccurate version of any scandal in London.

I have set out the circumstances in which Mrs. Rivers lived at greater length than may be thought necessary. But I am inclined to think that it was very largely the facts of her surroundings, and the influence unconsciously exerted by her friends, that eventually led Mrs. Rivers into the most awful trouble. As I have said, I am a somewhat silent person, and I meditate more perhaps than talkative folk upon the reversals and eccentricities of fate. I think I could safely affirm that though I did not then know the real relations that existed between Mrs. Rivers and Cardyne—who, by the way, for all his density, was head and shoulders above this crowd—I still could never have dreamed that fate would have whetted her heaviest shaft to bring down such poor and uninteresting game as this. But, as a matter of fact, I did not know that Mrs. Rivers was nothing more than a close friend of Cardyne's. On the face of it I thought that Cardyne could never be very long attracted by any one possessed of so little interest as Mrs. Rivers; but, against that, I admitted that Cardyne's constancy was quite in keeping with his general simple loyalty; and, on the other hand, I was not sure that Mrs. Rivers might not be more interesting in that relation than she might have seemed likely to be to a mere outsider like myself. She might have been possessed, like many other women, of the two entirely distinct and mutually exclusive natures that Browning thanks God for.

I came to know Cardyne pretty well in those months, and if any feeling of anger should be caused by the story I am going to tell with the help of Mrs. Rivers's journal, it is only fair to say that Cardyne did all he could. It is a grim tale.

\*     \*     \*     \*     \*

Cardyne, as he had promised, went to the National Gallery at twelve o'clock on the 20th of May. It was a Friday, and in consequence there were very few present except the young ladies in brown holland over-alls, who were painting copies of deceased masters in the intervals of conversation. But in the central room there was one industrious figure labouring away at a really important copy of the Bronzino at the other end of the room. Mrs. Rivers was sitting in a chair opposite the Michael Angelo,—a picture, by the way, which she would certainly have relegated to a housemaid's bedroom had she possessed it herself.

Cardyne was punctual. But it was clear from the moment he entered the gallery that the interview was going to be unpleasant. He walked listlessly, and with a white face, up to where Mrs. Rivers was sitting.

She was really alarmed at the sight of him, and, putting out a hand, said to him:

'Good gracious, Dennis, don't frighten me like this!'

Cardyne sat down and said:

'You've got to listen, Mary. It is a matter that concerns you.'

Mrs. Rivers grew rather white, and said:

'Nobody knows, surely? Nobody would believe. We are perfectly safe if we deny it absolutely?'

Cardyne shook his head.

'Listen,' he said wearily; 'did you see the posters of the *Star* as you came along?'

Mrs. Rivers thought that he was going mad.

'Yes,' she said; 'there was a speech by Roosevelt and a West End murder, but what has that got to do with us?'

Dennis put his hand in front of his eyes for a moment, and then said:

'Everything—at least the murder has.'

Mrs. Rivers grew rather cross.

'For Heaven's sake tell me what you mean!' she said; 'I don't understand anything. What can this murder have to do with you and me?'

Cardyne said, in a dull and rather monotonous voice:

'A man called Harkness was murdered on the night of the 18th of May. He lived at No. 43 Addistone Place.'

Mrs. Rivers began a remark, but Cardyne impatiently stopped her.

'That house, as you know, is exactly opposite yours. The old man was found murdered yesterday, the police were making inquiries all day, the newspapers have just got hold of it, and an arrest has been made. They have taken into custody a maidservant called Craik, who had apparently one of the best of reasons for hating Harkness.'

Cardyne broke off. Mrs. Rivers breathed again.

'But what in the name of Heaven has all this to do with me or you?'

Cardyne paused for thirty seconds before he answered:

'The maidservant is innocent.' His sentences fell slowly and heavily. 'The murder was committed by the manservant.'

Mrs. Rivers was not a person of very quick imagination, but she vaguely felt that there was something horrible impending over her, and, after an indrawn breath, she said quickly:

'Where did you see it from?'

Dennis turned round and looked at her straight in the eyes and did not say a word. Mrs. Rivers felt the whole gallery swinging and swirling round her. She seemed to be dropping through space, and the only certain things were Dennis Cardyne's two straight grey eyes fixed in mingled despair and misery upon her own. A moment later the girl at the other end of the room looked up with a start, and went quickly across the gallery to ask if she could be of any use. Mrs. Rivers, in a high falsetto that was almost a scream, had said, 'What are you going to do?' and fallen forward out of her chair. She pulled herself together as the girl came up, and muttered a conventional excuse, but she hardly knows how it was that she got home and found herself lying on her own bed, vaguely conscious that Cardyne had just left the room after giving her the strictest instructions as to what she was to do to keep well, and assuring her that there might not be the slightest risk or trouble of any kind. And he added that he would return about six o'clock in the evening, and tell her all there was to be known.

## II

I heard this story some time afterwards, but I remember, as if it were yesterday, the remark which some one made to me about Mrs. Rivers during the season of 1904.

'The woman's going mad. She goes to every lighted candle she can scrape up an invitation to, and last week, to my certain knowledge, she—she, poor dear!—went to two Primrose League dances.'

Rightly enough this feverish activity was regarded as a sign and portent, for Mrs. Rivers was one of those people who thought that her social position was best secured by kicking down her ladders below her. I confess that a night or two later I was amazed indeed at finding her at my poor old friend Miss Frankie's evening party. Miss Frankie was the kindest and dullest soul in London. She was also the only real conscientious Christian I have ever known. She refrained from malicious criticism of those around her. This perhaps made her duller than ever, and I will admit that there was a curious species of mental exercise associated with visits to her house. As a rule, one found the earnest district visitor sitting next one at dinner, or it might be some well-intentioned faddist with elastic-sided boots bent on the reformation of the butterflies of society, or the House of Lords. But among those who really understood things, there were many who used to put up with the eccentricities of a night out at Miss Frankie's if only because of the genuine pleasure that it obviously gave to the little lady to entertain her old friends. I twice met San Iguelo the painter there, and for the first time began to like the man, if only for going. Now this was particularly, I fancy, the social level from which Mrs. Rivers had herself risen; but precisely therefore was it the social level which she took particular pains now to ignore. A year ago Mrs. Rivers would have regarded an evening with Miss Frankie as an evening worse than wasted.

That night, I was sitting in a corner of the room. I was talking to a young artist who had not yet risen in the world, and probably never will; still, she had a sense of humour, and knew Mrs. Rivers by sight. She watched her entrance and, without a touch of malice, she turned to me and said:

'What on earth has made Mrs. Rivers honour us with her presence to-night?'

I did not know, and said so, but I watched Mrs. Rivers for some minutes. Of course it was Mrs. Rivers, but I doubt if any one who knew her in a merely casual way would have been quite sure. I am perfectly certain that the woman was painted. Now Mrs. Rivers never painted in old days. Moreover, she never stopped talking, which was also unlike her. (The woman had her good points, you see.) However, there she was. Once, our eyes met, and probably neither of us liked to define the uneasiness that I am sure we both felt.

She had a way of leaving her mouth open and allowing the tip of a very pink tongue to fill one corner of it. I knew it well in the old days. Somebody must have told her that it was arch. It was a touch of vulgarity of just that sort of which no one could very well break her after she had once started climbing the society ladder, and in time it grew to be a trick. At one moment, when Miss Frankie was occupied with a newcomer, Mrs. Rivers's face fell into a mask that convinced me that the woman was ill. As soon as her forced vivacity left her, the whole face fell away on to the bones, the eyes became unnaturally bright, and there was a quick, hunted look about them. She was evidently quite oblivious for the moment, and I saw her tongue go up into the corner of her mouth. It was a small matter, but the contrast between the expression of her face and this silly little affectation no one could fail to notice.

She stayed for half an hour and went on somewhere, I suppose to a dance. She was alone, and as I happened to be at the foot of the stairs as she came down, I thought it was only civil, as I was myself hatted and coated for going away, to ask if she had her servant there to call the carriage. It was all rather awkward. I moved across the floor to her with the conventional offer so obviously on my lips and even in my gait, that I could not well be stopped going on with my part, even though at the last moment, almost after she might have recognised me, she shut her eyes and said in a tone of broken helplessness: 'O my God, have mercy upon me!' She opened her eyes again a moment afterwards, saw me with a start, recovered herself, and pressed me almost hysterically to be dropped somewhere by her, she did not seem to care where. But I refused. I did not much want to be dropped by Mrs. Rivers, and I am quite sure that my humble diggings did not lie anywhere on the route to her next engagement that evening.

A few days after that I met Cardyne, and with the usual fatuity of any one who tries with all his might to keep off a subject, I said to him that I had seen Mrs. Rivers, and that she seemed to me to be strangely upset and unlike herself. He looked at me rather hard for a moment and said:

'Oh, I know all about that: she is worried about her people.'

Now that is absurd, for nobody ever is worried to that extent about her people, or at least she doesn't say, 'O my God, have mercy upon me!' if she is. However, it was no business of mine, and I went on in my humble way of life, though from time to time I heard some notice taken of Mrs. Rivers's hysterical behaviour during that season.

*         *         *         *         *

Cardyne told me afterwards that at the moment when I had noticed Mrs. Rivers's behaviour, she was almost determined to make the sacrifice by which alone, as it was now too clear, could the unfortunate maidservant at No. 43 be cleared from the charge against her. The excitement caused by the murder had died down somewhat since the middle of May when it had taken place, but every one was looking forward with gladiatorial interest to the trial. It was appointed to begin on the 30th June at the Old Bailey, and though, as I have said, from a legal point of view the case looked very black against Martha Craik, the servant, it was still felt that something more was needed before the jury would accept as proved a crime which for some reasons a woman seemed hardly likely to carry out. Cardyne told me that, of course, his first duty was to reassure Mrs. Rivers. This he did at first with such effect that the woman regarded the likelihood of any serious issue to the trial as most improbable, and eagerly hugged to herself the relief which her lover thus held out to her.

'On Thursday afternoon,' said Cardyne to me, 'after our meeting in the National Gallery, the unhappy woman had so convinced herself that there was nothing really to fear, that she went down on her knees in her own drawing-room beside the tea-table and made me kneel with her.' Cardyne's face, as he said this, almost made me smile, though it was hardly an occasion for mirth. 'She rose, gave me tea, and all the time asked me to see in it the kindness and tenderness of God, and hoped it would be a warning to me.' Of what, I really hardly think either Cardyne or myself knew. 'But at any rate,' said Cardyne, 'I had cheered her up for the time being. But I lied like a trooper.'

As a matter of fact, the case against Craik grew blacker and blacker every day. She was the only servant who slept alone in the house, and all the others were ready to swear, with unanimity, that neither they nor their stable-companions had left their rooms all night. To this I ought to have attached little importance, as servants, when frightened, are always ready to swear that they did not sleep a wink all night. But it made a very great impression on the public.

The knife with which the murder was done was found in rather a curious way. The police inspector was asking some questions of the manservant in the passage outside Mr. Harkness's bedroom door. Another servant came by, and both men took a step inwards to allow room for him to pass. The manservant, whose name was Steele, in taking a sharp pace up to the wall, actually cut his boot upon the knife, which was stuck upright in the floor, blade outwards, between the jamb of the door and the wainscoting, where it had escaped notice. It was an ordinary kitchen table-knife, worn and very sharp, and the fact that Steele cut his boot upon it was taken as proof beyond all hesitation or question that Steele at least was totally ignorant of everything connected with the crime. But Steele was the man whom Cardyne had seen in Harkness's room.

To return to Mrs. Rivers. Cardyne found that it was impossible to conceal from her much longer the fact that things were going badly indeed against Craik. One afternoon, about a fortnight before the trial opened, he found it his terrible duty to make Mrs. Rivers see that unless his evidence was forthcoming, an innocent woman might be condemned to death. For a long time Mrs. Rivers had understood that all was not well. Perhaps if all had been well she would have had just the same nervous breakdown. The woman was at her tether's end, and there is no doubt that in spite of her hysterical attempts to distract her thoughts, she was coming to realise what the position was.

Here are some extracts from her diary at different times:—

'*June 20th.* All going as well as possible. D. tells me that he still thinks there may be no real reason for alarm. He hears at the club that the verdict at the inquest is thought unreasonable by people in town.'

(Let every woman remember that there is no more worthless authority for any statement than that a man has heard it at his club. As a rule, it is worth no more than her maid's opinion as she does her hair that evening.)

'*July 1st.* Lady Garrison came across this afternoon and upset me a good deal. D. never told me about the door of 43 having been chained all night. Will see him about this to-morrow.

'*June 10th.* [This was about the time when I saw Mrs. Rivers.] Worse and worse. Of course everything must go right, but I would give five years of my life to be over the next two months. All must be right. D. tells me so. The suspense is awful.

'*July 14th.* Sampson gave me warning this morning. I was horribly frightened when he actually told me, and I'm rather afraid that he noticed it. He says he is going to his brother in Canada, and of course he has always told me that he would go as soon as he could. He said nothing to make me uneasy, spoke very respectfully, and offered to suit his convenience to mine at any time. I don't know what to do. I must ask D. Perhaps it would be better if he left at once?'

\*         \*         \*         \*         \*

I am sure it passed through that wretched woman's brain that if her butler could, so to speak, be made to look as if he had bolted from the country a week before the trial took place, some suspicion would be aroused which might, perhaps, cause a postponement of the sentence, if the worst came to the worst. More than that, she was, of course, anxious to get rid thus easily of some one who, for all her precautions, might have known about Cardyne's visit, and finally, in the event of her having to go through a great nervous strain at the time of the trial, she hardly knew whether it would be better to have a new butler who might simply look upon her with unpleasant inquisitiveness as an hysterical subject, or the old one who, for all his discretion and sympathy, could hardly fail to see that something very new, very odd, and very wrong was going on in her life.

It was clear, in fact, that Mrs. Rivers was slowly realising that there was actually a probability of the trial resulting in the conviction of Craik, and when, a fortnight later, Cardyne took his courage in his hands and went to Addistone Terrace to break the news to her of Craik's conviction and sentence to death, I fancy she knew all before he opened his lips. Cardyne never intentionally told me much about that interview. Indirectly he let me know a good deal, and I am perfectly sure that any feeling of repugnance or horror that he ever felt against Mrs. Rivers was that afternoon changed into the deepest and most heartfelt pity. It was one of those interviews from which both parties emerge old and broken. Mrs. Rivers apparently saw what was going to be urged by Cardyne, rattled off his arguments one after the other, with horrible fluency, and then, while he sat in white silence on the sofa, flung at him:

'And you've come to tell me that as things have gone wrong, I'm to sacrifice my honour and my reputation for that wretched woman's life!'

All Cardyne could say was simply, 'I have.'

At this Mrs. Rivers leant against the mantelpiece and spoke clearly and monotonously for half a minute, as if she had been long conning the lesson, and drew out before Cardyne's dazed understanding a dramatic but unconvincing picture of what a woman's reputation means to her. She declaimed with pathos that, like any other woman, she would rather die than be disgraced in the eyes of the world. Poor Cardyne's one interruption was not a happy one, yet it is one which, from a man's standpoint, had a touch of nobility. He said:

'But it isn't a question of *your* dying.'

When Mrs. Rivers said that she would rather die than suffer dishonour, his involuntary ejaculation told her plainly enough that, up to that moment, he had not conceived it possible that any woman could be so vile as to sacrifice the life of an innocent woman for her own social ambitions.

There was a silence of a quarter of a minute. Mrs. Rivers fidgeted with the fire-screen. Then she said:

'So you intend to betray me?'

At this poor Cardyne was more hopelessly bewildered than ever.

'Good God, no!' he said; 'of course I can only do what you decide. The matter is entirely in your hands; but surely——'

Mrs. Rivers stopped him with a gesture.

'I absolutely forbid you to say a word. I will decide the matter, and I will let you know; but, understand me, except with my express permission, I rely upon your honour to keep the secret for ever, if I wish it.'

This at least Cardyne could understand, and he gave the promise with unquestionable earnestness. But he was to realise that a man placed in such a position, with honour tearing him in two opposite ways, is condemned to the worst anguish which the devil knows how to inflict.

However, he had given his word—a quite unnecessary proceeding, if only Mrs. Rivers had known it—and it only remained for him to try and make her see the matter from the point of view from which he himself regarded it. He could not bring himself to believe that she would refuse. This continual appeal resulted in almost daily scenes. Cardyne, with the best of intentions, was not a tactful person, and in season and out of season he presented the case to Mrs. Rivers from a standpoint she never understood, and never could have understood. She in turn, driven to bay like an animal, wholly failed to see that in this matter Cardyne's secrecy might be trusted to his death, and shook with terror as the date for the execution drew on. These two wretched souls, during the last fortnight in July, fought out this dreary fight between themselves, until poor Cardyne came to wonder how it was that he had ever in the wildest moment of infatuation cared for such a woman as Mrs. Rivers daily proved herself to be.

All this while Mrs. Rivers was steadily going out to dinners and dances, and in the afternoons she attended more regularly than any one the committee meetings presided over by Royalty with which her name had been so long and honourably connected.

III

It is strange in the light of after events to remember Cardyne's life among us during the days which followed the trial of Martha Craik. I have never supposed, nor do I now suppose, that Cardyne had in him many of the necessary constituents of an actor, but I am perfectly sure that there were few among us, his friends, who noticed at that time anything in him except perhaps a certain absent-mindedness and irritability. Perhaps the man's simple nature was its own salvation. To his mind there could be no two views as to his own personal duty. He was clearly bound to adopt Mrs. Rivers's decision in this matter, just as on a doubtful field of battle he would not have dreamed of disobeying his colonel's most desperate order. What must have made it doubly hard for him, however, was the feeling that though he was thus bound he was obliged to use every fair argument in his power to make Mrs. Rivers see that she had adopted a course which, to him, and I believe to any man, was almost unthinkable. Here his plain, blunt tactlessness served him poorly indeed. One afternoon, after an hour's conversation—if any discussion between a man and a woman of such a topic can rightly be called conversation—it happened that he blurted out what, in his simple soul, he had imagined Mrs. Rivers had understood from the beginning. To her incessant argument that death was better than dishonour he opposed, as if it were the most natural thing in the world, the remark: 'But there is not the least reason why we should survive. Provided this woman's life is saved you will have done everything that is necessary, and I think you would be right. I will gladly die with you.'

Upon Mrs. Rivers's fevered brain and throbbing conscience this last suggestion had at least the effect of making the woman and the man understand each other at last. Disregarding, forgetting all that she had said, the haggard, red-eyed woman, dressed as it chanced in the most becoming of biscuit-coloured cloth gowns, turned upon Cardyne with a scream.

'Die!' she echoed. 'Do you mean that I ought to get that woman off and then kill myself? Good God, what a brute you are!'

And then Cardyne understood what manner of woman wretched Mrs. Rivers was. Perhaps a clever man might have availed himself of her reaction, which set in the next day and which was necessarily great, but poor Cardyne had had neither the capacity nor the inclination to conceal from Mrs. Rivers, as he had left the house the previous day, that he detested and despised her. He never went back till the afternoon before the day set for Craik's execution.

Now and then, during the course of the next day, Mrs. Rivers saw things with Cardyne's eyes. So far, however, from this leading to any permanent change of her intentions, it merely made her suspect in abject cowardly terror that those considerations might, as the fatal day approached, prove too much for Cardyne, and that on his own initiative he would blurt out the story. The days went on. Mrs. Rivers still clung to the hope that though Craik had been sentenced to death, something would be done, something must happen to prevent the execution. What was God in His heaven for if not for this? She had a blind hope that somehow or other a wholly innocent person could not be allowed by God to suffer capital punishment in these days of modern civilisation.

There had been a time in these miserable weeks when she attempted to persuade Cardyne that what he had seen would not, after all, make much difference to the fate of Martha Craik. But upon this point he was as clear as the ablest of barristers. He had seen the manservant in the house opposite, stripped to the skin, with a knife in his hand, moving about in Mr. Harkness's room at midnight. Cardyne was the only man in England who knew why it was that so barbarous a murder could have taken place without the murderer receiving even a splash or smear upon his or her clothes. Mere proof of the presence of a naked man moving about in the house that night would beyond all question have saved the unhappy maidservant.

Martha Craik had been sentenced to be hanged at eight o'clock on Monday morning, July 30th.

Cardyne spent Sunday afternoon with Mrs. Rivers.

Sunday evening he spent in his own rooms. He did not leave them for three months. I suppose if ever a man had an excuse for intentional and continuous self-intoxication, Cardyne was that man. He had done his best. He had used every argument, entreaty, and exhortation he knew of. He had failed completely, and his sense of honour bound him with a band of iron. Few men will dare to criticise him. He would have killed himself if he had been sober, I think.

Mrs. Rivers was in a state that night which clearly bordered on insanity. Twice over she wrote out a confession. Once she actually rang the bell and gave the letter, which was addressed to Cardyne, into her servant's hands, but she was at the door calling for it again before he had reached the bottom of the stairs. About one o'clock she got into a dressing-gown, and with dry, hot eyes and scorching brain she watched the small hours of the morning go by. She was up in her room alone. The servants had long gone to bed.

Daylight came, small, thin, and blue, between the crack of the curtains. Six o'clock. Mrs. Rivers was kneeling by the side of her bed with her face buried in the quilt. One hand dropped beside her, the other was stretched out and clutched a prettily designed Italian crucifix.

She had prayed at intervals all night long, and had even denounced the injustice of God that no mercy or comfort was extended to her in what she even then called her hour of trial. You will have grossly misunderstood the nature of Mrs. Rivers if you think that this was mere blasphemy. It was the solemn conviction in that poor little mind that God was treating her very hardly in not deadening the last appeals of her conscience against her own wickedness.

Dry-eyed and with aching brain she watched, with her chin on the quilt like a dog, the daylight grow. Seven o'clock. There was a clock on a church near which gave the chimes with astonishing clearness in the morning air. The milk-carts had ceased to rattle through the street. Vans took up their daily work, and the foot-passengers hurried by, sometimes with a low murmur of conversation, under the bright, ashy sky of a London July morning. She still knelt there unmoved. She could not have moved, I think, if she had wished; anyway she told herself that physically she could not do anything now, much as she wanted to. It was now too late.

In the curious half-light of her curtained room she could

distinguish things pretty well, and one of the three slants of light fell upon herself. There was a glass between the windows, and as the light increased she could see herself in it. Even then she had time to pity the drawn and haggard misery which was stamped upon the face that met her own.

\*　　　　\*　　　　\*　　　　\*　　　　\*

The first chime of eight o'clock struck from the church clock. With a shudder Mrs. Rivers drew her face down again and buried it in the side of the bed, convulsively clutching the crucifix. The four quarters tinkled out, and then the hour struck.

There was a light knock at the door.

Mrs. Rivers did not answer. With her face buried in the side of the bed, she was still trying to pray, but she heard it and she listened.

There was a step across the room, and some one was clearly standing at her side. She moved her eyes enough to look downwards, and she saw, three feet away from her, the end of a common skirt and two coarse boots. They did not belong either to her maid or to any one else in the house. With a sudden icy hand at her heart, she turned back with shut eyes to the position she had occupied for so long. At last she let her eyes open. She fixed them horribly upon the reflection in the glass. And she has known little or nothing since.

\*　　　　\*　　　　\*　　　　\*　　　　\*

Sometimes in sheer defence of Cardyne himself, I think that he *must* have lied to me about their relations. Sometimes I feel sure he did lie.

# SKIN
# FOR SKIN

## I

'HERE'S another of them!'

President Carmichael, of the upland Georgian Republic, threw across to me an important-looking document from the Police Department, and looked moodily into the fire.

He betrayed himself at first sight. There was no mistaking that bull-necked, short-cropped head, round as a ball and overweighted by the mass of jaw and fleshy chin which hung from it. He had won to his position by thirty years of the hardest work, and if report were true, he had left undone few of those things which—to judge from a standpoint a little in advance of that of the primitive republic over which he presided—he ought not to have done.

I glanced at the report. It was a terse and urgent communication. The police had had their previous information corroborated; there existed a plot for the assassination of the President, and the actual day on which the attempt was to be made was about the only thing that had escaped the vigilance of the Department.

Carmichael ran his fingers round his chin and debated aloud:

'If one could only believe the police—if they had not

136

consistently muddled everything for the last four years, one might so far give in to them as to be ill for the next fortnight.' He glanced to me: I doubt whether there was another man to whom he would have admitted as much, but, on peculiar terms, we thoroughly understood each other. At least, I thought I did at this time, afterwards I was not quite so sure.

He went on: 'But they are always finding these mare's nests, and it would be disastrous with the elections coming on to show the white feather—simply disastrous. I can't stand the way they shirk responsibility! They say that they know this man Castro, or they say they do. I sent down and told them to arrest him on some charge, trumped-up if necessary; but the man's own record is probably quite enough. They answered that their information was confidential, and that any betrayal of their knowledge before the day—which, remember, they don't know—would merely shift the duty of assassination on to some one else, whom they do not know and therefore cannot watch. They are deliciously logical, these detectives. But there is something, perhaps, in what they say. Meanwhile, what in the devil's name am I to do?'

Carmichael was no coward. He was a strong, unscrupulous man without a trace of weakness, except a rough good-nature to those who did not stand in his way and whom he happened to like. I knew and in a vague way admired him. I wanted nothing from him, and when at last he realised this, he changed a good deal for the better. From that moment he became a different man, and though I saw him only two or three times in the year, and I didn't suppose he ever made a friend in his life except for the purpose of using him, yet I cannot remember ever having discussed the things that really count for something in this world as freely with any other man, as I did with this hard-wood stub of unscrupulous capacity.

Whatever else he was not, President Carmichael was a man. I had no actual fear that he would be killed; but there really seemed to be some project afoot against his life, though I had been guilty of a passing speculation, when the matter was first mentioned, whether the whole thing were not a shrewdly devised contrivance of his own for the purpose of securing his re-election two months later. But though the man was fully capable of such a dodge, he was—to me at least—no liar, and when I approached the matter he assured me, with a laugh and a word of regret that he had not thought of it himself, and that these warnings were genuine enough. If so, I could understand the difficulty he was in. Re-election meant for him the success of his policy, and from another point of view, which must have had more than equal weight with him, it meant his personal fortune also.

'I tell you what I would do,' I said. 'I have half a dozen suits of Bikanir chain armour hanging up in my house. They would be of no more use than brown paper against a Krag-Jorgensen bullet, but they don't assassinate presidents at long range, and it would do a good deal more than turn a knife; I would not mind being potted at with a cheap revolver in it. Moreover, they always go for the stomach, as the larger target, being shaky when the actual moment arrives. We can double the shirt there.'

I had hardly been serious in making the suggestion, but as I spoke the sense of the proposal became obvious. But Carmichael hesitated.

'Footy little things, those steel shirts!'

'Well, you have never been in Rajputana. Come home with me now, and see if you can drive a hunting-knife through one. I will bet you ten pounds to a hat you can't.'

The President, characteristically enough, pressed a bell and ordered a carriage at once.

'I may as well come and see them; there's no time like the present. Besides, it is dark, and I shan't be seen. Lord, what a contemptible business it all is!'

He resumed his gaze into the fire. 'Silvester's money is what makes it hard for me, but I'll carry it through, by God I will!' He betrayed a very rare emotion as he turned to me. 'There is nothing I would not do: I believe there is no crime I would not commit,' he added without the vestige of a smile, 'to win this election. I have waited for it, I have worked for it, I deserve it, and the country needs it—desperately.'

I remembered that there were people who did not share his views, but after all, it was no business of mine who was chosen by the great and corrupt electorate of Georgia as their figurehead, and I contented myself with smiling at the earnest, concentrated gaze of Carmichael's eyes, which contrasted strongly with his coarse face and stunted, thick figure. They impressed me as they had impressed many in the course of his stubborn climb to the presidency.

'I am a poor man,' he said reflectively, 'a very poor man.' And, though he would have been believed by few, this was literally true.

The carriage was announced. We drove off together through the late winter afternoon with the fast trot of the orderlies behind us. It was so common a thing for him to do, that really no notice was taken, and we drew up at my house without attracting the attention of more than a couple of half-caste boys who whistled and went on as we entered the house. The carriage moved on, with orders to return in twenty minutes.

Once inside, I took down a couple of the mail-shirts from the wall of the staircase, and I was struck by his keen examination of the workmanship. I spread one on the carpet, and the President went down on his hands and knees. 'Good work this,' he muttered; 'every link annealed, and blue-stone of the best. Might turn a revolver-bullet after all.' He put his hand up for the knife I had brought him, without taking his eyes off the shirt. Professionally he was delighted with so good a piece of work, and asked me more questions than I could answer about the steel-workers of Rajputana. He struck, several times, towards the end with all his strength, but he could not break a link. Then he laid it on his knee, and struck again, wincing with the pain of the bruise as he did. But it held well enough, and he stood up.

'I'll take this. You might add the helmet, and,' pointing to the mace, 'that spiky thing. You see, if any one asks, you have made a present of the whole set to me,' he added, a little uncomfortably.

He waited till the carriage was reannounced, and spent the time in discussing the approaching election. He could never carry off the obsession of the moment.

I wrapped up the shirt in brown paper, he took it, and I followed him down the steps with the helmet in my hand and the mace under my arm. He moved across the pavement with the red light of the sunset in his eyes.

Upon my word, almost before I could shout or even realise it, a figure with a knife in its hand had glided across the flagstones, with the silence and rapidity of a snake, and was behind Carmichael's shoulder. Then I yelled, and he turned, only to receive the stroke over his shoulder. There was a soft thud, and the President was on the sidewalk with his hat rolling wobbily from his head into the gutter. The brown-paper parcel dropped on the asphalt, and at the same moment a policeman threw himself upon the assassin. The latter, overbalancing, fell upon his back with the detective upon him, but struck out wildly with his knife at his captor's back. He saw that he was wasting his strength, and moving his arm slowly inwards tried to thrust the blade at short-arm distance into the man's flank. I was within striking distance then, and saw that there was nothing to do but disable him with the mace I was carrying. I never dreamed of the power of these short weapons. I let out heavily, and the bones of his arm and wrist splintered like macaroni stems in a red mash of flesh, and I remember the huge blue spark which flashed out where one of the spikes caught the stone pavement. The man screamed shrilly and gave no further trouble.

Carmichael was lying in a waste of trickling blood, but raised himself without a word. The blow that would a moment sooner have cut down through the jugular between the shoulder and the neck had glanced down his ribs as he turned, laying bare a red matted slit in the coat, waistcoat, and shirt. If the blow had spent itself so, the damage was limited, and I anxiously examined the wound. The President's heavy and somewhat vulgar watch-chain had caught the point of the knife at the last moment and saved his life. He was, however, bleeding profusely, and fell forward into my arms without a word. I took him home and delivered him to the hospital staff—about the only entirely qualified and uncorrupt body in Georgia. Perhaps it would have been better if he had died then and there.

II

After the attempted assassination I was called away on business, and had to leave the capital for some weeks. I gave in a sworn statement of the incident. It was unnecessary to do more then, as the prisoner, the very Castro of whom Carmichael had been warned, was still in hospital when I returned, and his trial had of course been postponed. I sent round to the Presidency, and received at once a request that I would go to the President that evening; he was well enough to transact business and see people, though when I arrived at the house I was asked by the doctor in attendance not to stay very long.

To me there was always something half pathetic in the contrast between the long, deep-carpeted corridors with their opulent electric flambeaux, the central marble-pillared hall with the inevitable group of palms in the middle, and the gorgeous gold and onyx staircase at the end on the one hand, and on the other the brutal little figure of my vulgarian friend the President, who never looked more like a stud-groom than when he was coming down the stairs on some official occasion, with the green, yellow, and white Presidential riband across his waistcoat.

I was conducted upstairs under the huge gilt representation of the arms of the republic, bedecked all round with state flags, to the President's own room.

He was weak and did not rise from his chair as I came in, but otherwise he seemed hardly the worse for his desperately narrow escape. I could not help noticing the touch of refinement which his convalescence, and probably also his enforced temperance, had added to his appearance. Moreover, I had rarely seen the look of genuine welcome in his face which was upon it as he shook hands with me.

It was an unusual symptom in him, I thought, that he spoke of other things than the one topic which I had foreseen would be occupying his mind. He dismissed my reference to his wound by saying that the doctors had from the beginning been satisfied with his progress; it had been nothing but the healing of a flesh-wound. He had, he said, gone back into harness, and attended to the more important affairs himself; but there was little of real importance just then. He asked me—almost, as I thought, to keep the conversation from drifting towards his trouble—about my own business with more interest than I had ever known him show before. But I stumbled on the trouble at last.

'Well,' I said as I got up to go, 'there's one good thing in all this. It has made your re-election certain. I suppose you have seen the papers?'

Carmichael did not answer for a moment. He was playing with a paper-knife, and a hopeless look came into his eyes.

'Re-election? Oh yes, perhaps!'

Then I guessed how the trouble took him.

'You mean the prerogative of mercy?'

He glanced up at me for an instant and went on playing with the paper-knife.

'Yes.'

For a minute we were silent. I had not quite understood that this too must come upon him, with his other duties, as soon as he took up his work again. The position closed in like a vice.

'It's a pity you didn't take two months' rest.'

'No use. The man's been in hospital ever since, and his trial can't begin before the end of next week. They had to amputate his arm at the elbow.' He grinned and looked up. 'You must have struck almighty hard. Of course it won't take long. The result is a foregone conclusion; he comes under the Act of 1901. I drafted it myself, after M'Kinley's death.' There was a long pause. Carmichael shaded his face with his stumpy fingers. 'But he can't be hanged for about three weeks.' He spoke in a dull voice.

I began to gather up the threads. 'Three weeks?' I said. 'Why, that is three days before the election comes off.' Carmichael nodded. There was a pause. Other aspects of the case thronged in upon my imagination, and I began to see that for a far more delicately balanced judgment than Carmichael's, the rights of the case were indeed complicated.

'What are you going to do?' On the whole, he had rarely gone out of his way to meet a difficulty in his life before he came to it, that I could not but realise his present anxiety and agitation.

He shrugged his shoulders and muttered an oath.

Soon after, I went away, my mind filled with the question, which took on a new complication every twenty minutes. But I comforted myself again, that the matter was no affair of mine, and that the President had never been given to morbid introspection. That did not prevent me from combing out the various motives and counter-motives in an academic spirit, which I flattered myself was entirely outside the capacity and beneath the consideration of my distinguished friend.

In four days' time I received another invitation to go to the Presidency. By this time the man in the street seemed to have realised something of the position. It was obviously indecent to discuss the matter in the papers before the trial and sentence of Castro, but the near approach of the elections invested the affair with an importance that the mere technical want of a death-sentence could not restrain on men's lips. In fact, there was no conceivable defence possible for Castro. It was generally known that it was premeditated.

There was but one decision. If the President, whose return to apparently perfect health had produced an inevitable reaction after the wave of sympathy, did not exercise the prerogative of mercy, it was clear enough that the reaction would be turned into a storm of abuse, and Silvester's success was certain. If, on the other hand, Carmichael pardoned the prisoner, the vote in his favour would in many districts be almost unanimous, and Silvester's chances were gone. One may call this sheer melodrama, but in a republic like Georgia, where the climate, the fewness and the Spanish descent of the inhabitants all conspire to defeat academic considerations, the government of the country is a mere matter of melodrama, and no one had owed more to a judicious use of transpontine methods in the past than Carmichael himself. Of the result of his action in this matter there was admittedly no doubt, and Silvester openly cursed the luck which had placed in his rival's hand the very weapon which he needed. It was felt on all sides that Carmichael had really had a very narrow escape. It was impossible, therefore, to start the rumour that the President had arranged the whole thing.

I went to the Presidency, and found Carmichael in the same room and in the same frame of mind—the doctors had not been satisfied with his general convalescence, though the wound had closed at once, and left no cause for anxiety.

This time there was no beating about the bush. The door had hardly closed behind the servant before Carmichael said with an oath:

'What in the name of God am I to do?'

I asked him how matters stood, and he told me. He had seen a good many of the higher officials of the republic, and in a guarded way they had all of them let him know the view that was taken of the matter by the world in general and by themselves in particular. They had told him nothing new. He had worked the whole situation out during his illness with unerring foresight. His political agent had come to him with absolute conviction that the President would play the trump card which fate had dealt out to him, and make a splendid exhibition of magnanimity, three days before the election. Till then, he urgently advised him to keep his own counsel. He knew the value of a violent reaction, and every word he used sank deep into the mind of the man who had taught him all he knew about the running of elections. To the agent the issue was simple, and, said Carmichael, 'I didn't discuss the matter.'

The law officers of the republic had, with equal confidence, assumed that the President would not degrade the high position in which he was placed, and stultify the urgently needed 1900 law by making political gain of his position. He had never interfered politically with the administration of justice before—this was, as I knew, true—and there was no single thing which could be urged in the case of a scoundrel like Castro, caught red-handed in the act. 'They, too,' said Carmichael, 'went away in full confidence that I should see the matter as they did.'

'Silvester has been here. He practically said that my past record made my action at this juncture a matter about which there could not be two opinions. He even admitted that in my place he would abuse his position exactly as I would. But he was silly when he clumsily dropped a hint at the end of his conversation that if this Castro were reprieved, there would be another attempt—to his certain knowledge—within a week.'

The man was changed. He had never before been worried by anything except the possible failure of his schemes. Their abstract morality had been a matter of complete indifference to him. It is true that in his description of the various arguments which had been used to him, he had in no way referred to any motives but the most practical, but there was an underlying note in his narrative which made me realise that I had not wholly summed him up hitherto. If he had decided to settle the matter on lines of self-interest alone, he would never have sent for me. I do not for one moment wish to convey that my own standard of right was in the least better or other than his own, but in the course of conversations with him I had so often found myself almost artificially upholding the opposite opinion to his own, that he had come to regard me as an exponent of a morality he respected, but avoided.

I put to him a plain question, plump out.

'Do you, or do you not, believe that your own re-election is necessary for the good of the country?'

He turned to me, and with a face moved almost to greatness he said, 'In the name of the God I have forgotten so often, I do.'

There was a pause. The soft scurry of the electric fan alone broke the silence.

'You don't know,' he went on. 'There are four distinct things that must be carried through. No one else understands them. No one else could work with the foreign agents. Two are games of bluff, and we can't afford to change captains till we have run the cargo; one is a delicate bit of diplomacy which

Silvester would turn to his own personal gain, and one thing is'—he shrugged his shoulders—'a deliberate and careful lie which will secure to Georgia most favoured treatment with two European countries. And then, there's the secret-service money. If I go, the things are lost, lost, lost! It isn't only that Silvester is incapable, he is out of sympathy with the actual needs of the country; moreover, if the opportunity is missed, it can never come back.'

This was an additional complication. I held my tongue.

'If I could only get Silvester to believe that I am right, and intrust me with the job of carrying through even two of them, I wouldn't mind, but he wouldn't do it. Why should he?

'Then the Archbishop has been here. He put on all his purples and crosses and chains and laces, and harangued me as if I were a congregation. He knew well enough that in adjuring me to show Christian forgiveness he was imploring me to do the best for myself. He told me that I should follow the example of our Saviour. He knows well enough that I haven't been inside a church for twenty years. He wants his cardinal's hat, and thought that the good God had given him the chance of his life.' Carmichael's tired eyes sought mine. He threw out his hand with a hopeless gesture. 'Come now,' he said, 'what do you think Christ would have done if He had been me now?'

I could say nothing. There was something that rose above mere grotesque incongruity in the idea of this bullet-headed, self-seeking politician, who had always throughout his life trodden down his ladders and despised only the unsuccessful, whose strong intellect was his god, whose dependence upon no man was his boast—retiring from his own dilemma to see how the Galilean would comport Himself under the same cir-cumstances.

'The man's life is in my hands as certainly as if I were God,' said Carmichael, with characteristic abruptness.

Still there was nothing to be said. 'For the sake of Heaven,' said the President sharply, 'say something!'

'There is nothing to be said. I can only ask questions. Do you believe in a God? If so, I suppose you ought to do the obvious duty attaching to your position, and allow a wise law to take its course, trusting that somehow the balance of benefit to the country will be secured to it by Him. If you do not, it is your clear duty to secure your own election, presuming always that your patriotism is genuine and unselfish.'

He took up a paper-weight and balanced it in his hand. 'I think,' he said, 'that there is a proverb about giving bread in the form of stones. Have you nothing more to say?'

'Barring suicide,' I said flippantly, and in execrable taste, 'I don't see that there is anything else to be suggested.'

He looked at me in a way that suddenly convinced me that I had not been the first to put the idea into his mind. The thing was serious indeed, and I never felt more helpless in my life. This was a man I had never met before, long as I had known him.

'You are to blame for all this!' he broke out. 'Why the devil didn't you kill him when you had the chance! The man was there, caught in the act, and trying to assassinate a detective as well. You contented yourself with smashing his wrist. I would have reduced his skull to pulp and got done with it!'

It was true. It would have been better, and had I known the difficulties which would be caused by Castro's life, I would have killed him on the spot, without the slightest compunction. Was I, then, a good adviser in the present *impasse*?

The doctor came in, and I took advantage of the fact to say good-bye. I had been of no use whatever, and I felt humiliated.

\*            \*            \*            \*            \*

A week passed, the trial took place, and Castro was automatically sentenced to death. There was no possible defence. I gave my evidence, and was not even cross-examined. The President did not appear.

No sooner had the sentence of death been pronounced than the newspapers of the republic took up the question of the exercise of the President's prerogative of mercy with unleashed vigour, and the whole of the dreary arguments, sordid, opportunist, or sentimental, were paraded in every print. There was less doubt than ever that the re-election of the President depended wholly upon his action in the matter. The Opposition journals screamed against the prostitution of the prerogative for political and party purposes—in the bastard Spanish, the alliteration was even more effective than in English; the Church papers drew sentimental but unconvincing pictures of the holy imperative by which the head of a Christian state was bound. For eight days the question was fought with increasing earnestness. On the ninth, it was quietly but officially announced that the President had seen no reason to interfere with the course of justice, and that the execution of Castro would consequently take place on the day appointed—the fourteenth, I think. There was a low growl among the good electors of Georgia, fanned by the pulpit and the press, and a week later ex-President Carmichael walked out of the Presidency into the darkness, a ruined and unsuccessful man.

I took him to my own house till he could find some means of livelihood, and as he eventually left my roof, I could have asked a man whom I had always regarded as an interesting, but sordid-minded agnostic, for his blessing.

# BETWEEN THEE AND HIM ALONE

LUCAS ANDERSEN, a spare, blue-eyed Norwegian, had been commandeered early in November 1899 for service on the western frontier with his brother Oscar.

It was no quarrel of theirs, but after long and earnest consultation they had decided that their sin would be as the sin of the men of Succoth if they withheld their hand when the chosen people of the Almighty went forth to protect their coasts from the invader. So with Fourie's commando they had travelled down from the Transvaal, and at each station the children were waiting with coffee, and the old men were gathered, half in enthusiasm, half in vainglory, to see these apparently endless trainloads of armed men sweeping down to the south. The day had at last come, the day for which their predikants had long taught them to look forward, as to an appointed time when the long-suffering sons of God would in their turn rend the ungodly who had for so long schemed and plotted within their gates. Of the result of the war there could be no doubt; more than one predikant had dared to use from the pulpit the awful words that if the English obtained but one victory, he for one would abjure God and Christianity alike.

The march of the burghers towards the front was, in this aspect, more like the Crusaders' progresses than the mobilisation of a modern force. There was, however, in their midst a strong contingent, as yet unconscious of their own numbers and above all unwilling that their real feelings should be suspected, to whom this religious mask was but a tedious farce. It was, however, one that had at any cost to be played out to the end, that there should not be at the very moment when victory seemed about to crown their workings, the risk of losing the stake for which they played. Still, the doctrine of the chosen and favoured people was one that might be pressed by the victorious peasants one step further, and those who had been wholly responsible for the long and subtle policy that had at last resulted as they had hoped, in war, might then find themselves shut out from the enjoyment of the very substantial profits.

Night after night, as the force moved across the veldt from Jagersfontein Road to Winkelhoek by easy stages, prayer-meetings and debates occupied the two hours that intervened between an early dinner and bedtime. And no voices were so loud, so determined, and so well up in their Bibles as those of the small knot of men who were determined to move heaven and earth to ensure the instant invasion of Cape Colony even to the Hex River. They saw rightly enough that upon such immediate action hung the issue of the campaign, but they also knew well that the project would meet with stern denunciation from an influential body of the older men. It was all the more necessary that they should build up reputations for un-impeachable piety beforehand if they were to have the least success in forcing their policy upon the combined commandos among whom they were perhaps represented more strongly than they themselves had at that time any idea.

Life on commando was by no means comfortable, though the burghers were in most cases used to the annual rough concentrations which were given the name of rifle meetings.

Latterly, they were also held under cover of religion, the periodical *nachtmaalen* being but thinly disguised occasions for organising and inciting the country burghers to the dreams of an united and greater Holland. Rough as the accommodation was, the food was sufficient, and a certain amount of extra consideration was allowed to the brothers, who were well able to pay their way, and had a certain number of comforts that they had brought with them. Among these was a great sleeping-bag of sheep-skin carefully sewn on three sides, with a huge L. A. worked in blue worsted on it in the Italian style of calligraphy. Augusta had spent many hours over this great monogrammatic achievement, and Lucas remembered well the flush of delight with which she had given to him the results of many hours of secret work known only to her husband and the invaluable Sannie. The three lived together, and it had been no easy task to keep from his knowledge the long and industrious working of the gift.

Lucas was very fond of his sister-in-law. He was fond of few people, and there were many who found him unco guid and inclined to testify out of season a little too much. The theology of his fathers, sour, uncharitable, and self-sufficient, had taken deep and bitter root in the nature of a man who had for years lived the life of a hermit. But his younger brother and his wife had come out from Norway with their little capital, and, still glowing with a honeymoon elation, had transformed into a home the dull five-roomed house in which Lucas had lived with his Bible and his sovereign's picture, careless alike of the opinion of his neighbours and of his worldly success,—of which, however, he had had his full share.

Three years before, Augusta had given birth to a child—Wilhelmina—whose existence had wrapped the brothers together in a manner it would have been difficult for either to explain. At first Lucas doubted whether his overtures—clumsy and stiff enough, but as a matter of fact quite understood of the child—would not provoke jealousy, but one night—one blessed night, as he called it without a tinge of affectation— he had overheard the child's small petition to her God that she might be friends with her uncle Lucas, and—so far as the girl was concerned—the last crust of ice was melted from his frozen heart. The child's affection taught him the unsuspected depth of his love for his brother, and the roughness of their present life gave opportunities for not a few unnoticed acts of self-denial on the part of the elder man that meant perhaps more from him than from others. A lonely life for many years had not inculcated unselfishness, and Lucas had sometimes to prompt himself by a recollection of the grief of his niece and of his sister-in-law when the time came for parting from the little farm at Krugersdorp.

Round his very gates the excitement of the Raid had effervesced and died out four years before. Lucas had then taken up an attitude of stolid indifference—or what seemed to be indifference—as to the result of Jameson's wild attempt. But the fact that the result had entirely justified his unconcern did not wholly remove a certain mistrust of his loyalty from the minds of the burghers of Krugersdorp. He had been commandeered before others of his nationality, in order to discover his attitude on this wider question, and it was somewhat of a surprise to the field-cornet that the brothers had responded at once with three fine horses and an unusually large contribution to the messing of the commando.

The responsibility of having by his example induced Oscar to come out on commando weighed heavily on Lucas's mind. For once the will of his God seemed to him to be uncertain, and he spent many anxious nights and hours of self-examination in the attempt to justify his exercise of the influence that his unquestioned leadership gave him. For he knew well enough that in deciding for himself he was deciding for his brother also, and the fourfold responsibility—for the child's bungled message of intercession to the strange God who made the crops grow and the locusts eat them rang in his ears from the night in which he had left them—proved a heavy burden as the prospect of an immediate action became more and more certain.

The methods that the burghers had already adopted made his doubt the greater. He had come out himself because it seemed the will of God that he should serve in His army against the invader of the people of His choice, but the same deep-seated religious conviction that would have carried him alone against ten thousand rifles up to the frontier fence, told him with equal decision that it was an accursed thing to carry the war one yard beyond it into the enemy's country. Yet the thing was being done on both sides, Natal and the Old Colony alike. That it was the inevitable and obvious course— one that the most rudimentary knowledge of military tactics demanded—he neither could nor would see. Was the Lord to go back on His spoken word? Was a man after all to save himself by his own great strength? What of Midian, of the Egyptians, of the Canaanites?—could they not rest in the Lord's promise and abide the issue? President Kruger's action bewildered him: it was true that he had forbidden the closer investment of Mafeking even in the face of Cronje's most urgent and even insubordinate remonstrances, but weeks had passed and still there was no withdrawal from the territory of the neighbour. Only one of the Dopper congregation of the Transvaal could have understood to the full the sacredness of the frontier fence in the eyes of the Scandinavian bigot. His neighbour's landmark, just or unjust, was his own inviolable boundary, and the voice from Gerizim was loud in the ears of this sour Puritan, who found his own unflinching Calvinism echoed to the last horror by the predikants of his adopted country.

At one of the meetings for evening debate the subject, 'Gideon's Triumph over Midian,' had taken a local colour, and Lucas, goaded into speech by the innuendo of the Hollanders, rose, and, thrusting aside the quiet remonstrances of his brother, denounced the policy that Piet Cronje from the north was forcing upon the republican armies. A field-cornet, who had asked a man standing near him a hurried question before interrupting, rose and reminded Andersen that the strategic advantage of this slight invasion of the enemy's territory rendered it necessary, and further, that on commando a burgher could not be permitted to criticise his superior's orders or policy.

The reproof was the one thing needed to set free the flood of long pent-up protest that had been seething in the troubled mind of the Norwegian. Lucas still remained in silence till the impromptu chairman had finished his remarks, and then, advancing a step into the circle of light cast by the single lamp tied to a wagon-wheel, and hardly repressing his emotion enough to make himself understood in a language that in moments of extreme excitement seemed suddenly unfamiliar, spoke again.

'I will not have the commands of God filtered to me through the brains of any man! Is the Lord's arm shortened that He cannot save? Who are we to say that His eternal purposes are helped or hindered by the curve of a kopje or the sweep of a river? What is it to Him that we are but a body of untrained peasants who know nothing of the arts and crafts of war? Is not uprightness of more value than all the science of the enemies of God? I say again, that rather than follow those who are even now persuading us to commit trespass, I for one would send back all those Hollanders who have come forward in these days of trial to help us, if their advice is to cause the people of God to fall away.'

He sat down amid a whispered babel that was afraid to

declare itself, and before more harm could be done the debate was hastily adjourned.

*         *         *         *         *

Two anxious meetings were held in different parts of the camp that evening.

The leaders of the expedition, few of whom had been actually present at the debate, were gathered between two wagons beneath the buck-sail discussing this criticism of their orders with some impartiality. Some of them were either themselves inclined to agree with Andersen, or were very well aware that a strong and by no means negligible party in the force, elsewhere as well as there, were becoming seriously dissatisfied with the presumed intentions of General Cronje. It was indeed of the nature of a test which a large number of Boers were unwilling, either from fear, conviction, or policy, to have applied to themselves. To announce that a serious invasion of the Colony was to be attempted would, now that the question had been thus openly broached, have been a dangerous thing; on the other hand, it was being borne in upon the majority of those in any position of authority, that to refuse to take advantage of the golden opportunity that was now presenting itself would be an act of such negligence or Quixotism—as some of the small party called it, to the disgust of the older section present—that, speaking humanly, the success or failure of the entire war would be irrevocably hazarded. The krijsraad lasted till midnight without arriving at any conclusion. The feeling, if anything, intensified rather against than for Cronje's proposal the more the matter was discussed, and the members of the council separated about midnight on the understanding that at least nothing would be done until there had been time to refer the whole question once more to the President. The last to be left were the minister and a Hollander named Van Cloete—the man to whom the field-cornet at the debate had referred the question raised by Andersen. A change came over the meeting as soon as these two found themselves alone with the new commandant, a man called Viljoen, who was reputed to enjoy the personal confidence of the President and most of the leading members of the Executive Council of the Transvaal. He was a taciturn man, and was regarded by both parties in the camp as having a deciding voice in such a matter as that which was now under discussion, probably for no better reason than that he had carefully refrained from expressing an opinion upon any point since he had assumed the command.

But when the three men found themselves alone there was a distinct change in the tone of the discussion.

'This fool Andersen must be stopped before he has done any more harm.' Viljoen nodded a guarded assent, and the Hollander went on:

'It will be all over the frontier by to-morrow, and God knows where it will stop. These men only wanted a spokesman, and now they have one.'

'The moment,' suggested the minister, 'offers a chance that is not likely to be repeated. Naauwpoort is defenceless, and——'

'You're wrong there,' said Viljoen. 'We have a telegram from De Aar—I thought you saw it—giving the text of a cable sent by a correspondent to a London paper who had been over the fortifications. He reports that it is a second Plevna.'

Grobelaar, the predikant, smiled. 'We are a little inclined to underrate the intelligence of our friends the rooineks. You remember that Schoepers was going to strike hard through Colesberg and Arundel a fortnight ago? Well, he believed that information and kept off. But I hear that the real truth was that the commandant of Naauwpoort was playing a game of what they call "bluff," and that the telegram we had so carefully reported to us was a put-up thing between him and the correspondent, as they had some reason to suspect that there was a little—leakage, shall we say—in the instrument-room at De Aar. The telegram never went further than Kaapstad. Wasn't meant to.' The predikant resumed his pipe, and there was a moment's silence. The commandant was obviously impressed.

'How do you find out all these things? Our scouts seem to think that they haven't earned their rations if they haven't brought in some mare's nest bigger than the previous day's. I don't believe a word of all this talk of Buller and twenty-five thousand men at De Aar, but one after another they all come in and swear to the same story—too much the same story for my taste! How do you manage to get news?'

The predikant shrugged his shoulders. 'Who can tell? One thing in one way, and another in another. But my informants make no mistakes; why should they? It is our policy to observe, and to observe, and to keep on observing—and our practice too,' he added. 'There is no truth in all this nonsense about Buller and the twenty-five thousand men. Methuen comes with ten thousand, perhaps a little more.'

'We are wasting time,' said the commandant. 'I shall report to the President by the earliest runner to-morrow. You,' he added, turning to Van Cloete, 'might ask Andersen if he has any letters for home—or Oscar Andersen might want to send one to his wife. So pretty, is she not, Van Cloete?' and the discoloured teeth of the Boer showed themselves through his unkempt moustache in a horse-laugh, at which the Hollander stiffened with anger.

Grobelaar interposed. 'I too shall have a letter for Krugersdorp to-morrow. I'll have it ready by dawn. Meanwhile, do I understand that our previous arrangements hold good?'

No one seemed able to answer the question, and Van Cloete moved off in the darkness to the other small knot of men at the other end of the camp, who were smoking their pipes in the darkness and impatiently awaiting him.

He slipped down beside them, and whispered the result, or rather the lack of result, of the krijsraad.

'There is nothing more to be done, not yet at all events. We must communicate with Cronje and report the trouble that Andersen is making. More we can't do. The President himself can do nothing if this is a real feeling among the burghers. But the cause is lost unless we do make this invasion, and for myself, I would stick at nothing to keep them to it. It means just the failure of all our hopes if the blow is not struck before these reinforcements land. God! what fools these Boers are! Everything is lost, everything, I tell you, if this scheme is abandoned. What was the use of forcing the situation if Kruger did not intend to make full use of the opportunity that three weeks' sail from England offered him? Did the fool really think that he could meet these English on equal terms? Upon my soul, I sometimes think that he is ass enough for even that! I tell you, it means everything—everything! I know Schreiner well enough; he'll play a double game with us unless we force his hand by appearing at the Hex River. And every mile of veldt that we go south means so many thousand more fighting men and rifles for us, so many thousand more wagons, sheep, oxen, horses, and afterwards so many more miles for the rooibaatches to reconquer, with the railway in coils on the veldt and the wells—undrinkable. It's madness, madness! And not even to cross the fence ten miles and hold the line is sheer delirium!'

'You be careful, Van Cloete: all you say is true enough, but you should have thought of that before you joined in the matter. You knew the Boer well enough, or you ought to have known him. Didn't you see that this trouble would arise at once? Natal was different. Laing's Nek and Majuba were scenes of Boer successes, and they took place on land they have claimed from the English. But here—'

'Here!' echoed the Hollander. 'Almighty! I have it! Do you remember Waterboer?'

He explained the history of the cession of the strip of the Free State, that contained the Kimberley diamond-fields, to the English. And the story of how England forced the Free State to cede the diamond-fields, a tale somewhat questionable at the best of times, did not lose in the telling.

The false evidence that had been honestly enough brought forward on Waterboer's assurance, and had deceived the arbitrator, was quoted as the perjured treachery of the British Government, whose title to the land was in equity entirely null and void.

It hardly satisfied some, but the majority of the commando were willing enough to accept as sufficient the story that Van Cloete told them as to the ownership of the strip of land that embraced so many of the finest positions for defence that lay on the western frontier. The men were indeed only too glad to secure an excuse, however flimsy, for the occupation of points the value of which was well enough appreciated by almost every man in the force. But beyond the old limits of the Free State, no persuasion or argument on the part of Van Cloete or predikant Grobelaar could induce them to go south or west. It is true that a certain number of the less religious burghers were detached quietly for the ostensible purpose of strengthening the force round Kimberley, though really to make a raid into Central Griqualand, but it was found so necessary to conceal the real object of the expedition from the men of the commandos under Prinsloo in the south-western part of the Free State, that a strong warning was sent north to Cronje on his way from Mafeking, to the effect that an offensive campaign was impossible except within very narrow limits.

It at once altered the whole aspect of the war: Delarey saw more clearly than Cronje the enormous difficulty that the religious prejudices of the burghers created, and explained to his chief that the Boers were fighting with one hand tied behind them, and that it was practically an impossibility to hold their frontiers with any hope of success unless the defensive measures included heavy and immediate operations of an unmistakably offensive character. Cronje, a slow-witted and thick-headed general, but a born leader of men, saw at last the full meaning of this refusal of the burghers to carry the war into the enemy's country, and his wrath against Andersen, whom he regarded as primarily responsible for stirring up this untimely and disastrous feeling, knew no bounds. His first action was an attempt to induce the President to overrule the decisions that the commandants in the south had come to, but this resulted in nothing. He was the last man to succeed in any such effort after his ill-advised and intemperate protest from outside Mafeking against the veto imposed by Kruger on any attempt to carry the town by assault. Kruger knew better than any that it would be useless even for him to endeavour to override a religious scruple that was grounded in the Scriptures, however inconvenient it might be for his present purposes, and he had no reason to trust to the discretion of the general. A curt answer was received that no invasion was to be made into any territory that had not belonged in old days to the burghers, such as Griqualand or Natal. The text from the Bible with which the despatch ended was an additional insult in the eyes of Cronje, as he and the President had at one time been on terms that had opened the former's eyes considerably as to the meaning of these repeated appeals to the authority of the Holy Book.

The project of the Hollander section was now at a standstill, and Van Cloete seriously debated with his colleagues whether it might not be possible to bring extra pressure to bear upon

Kruger from Europe. The position was maddening for men who had finally cast their lot in with a nation which had lying at its feet what was not only an excellent chance, but almost the certainty, of success, yet was persuaded by the ranting folly of a few fanatics to throw it away. News kept coming in that made the situation more and more tantalising. It was rumoured, not once nor twice, but with growing insistence, that the small isolated camps of the British along the line of railway between Stormberg and Orange River were really defenceless, that the only guns at the disposal of Milner were a few of obsolete pattern that belonged to the Volunteer Artillery of Capetown and were now massed at Orange River bridge, the only point that could offer the least resistance. It was reported that the entire garrison of Naauwpoort was a half-battalion with two hundred mounted infantry, that Stormberg was in a similar condition, and that at De Aar, where one and a half million pounds' worth of stores was lying detrained upon the veldt, the Yorkshire Light Infantry and a three-pounder without a carriage, were the only defenders. The armoured train ran, it is true, between the points, but only the youngest attached much importance to that.

And day after day the thousands of troops that England was pouring out were coming nearer, and the golden opportunity was being wasted.

Lucas and his brother had by this time subsided into the position of private burghers on commando, and had steadily refused to be drawn into any further action. He had made his protest, and it had been effective. There was nothing more to do, and he was unwilling to argue further about an abandoned plan. And he was ready after some delay to accept the reasoning of Grobelaar, who proved to him, Bible in hand, that it became the duty of the burghers to act as the instrument of God in restoring the ancient landmarks of the state. So far Andersen was willing to go. He acquiesced in the holding of the railway, and thence-forward almost dismissed the matter from his mind. Certainly he was quite unaware of the momentous and far-reaching nature of the issues raised by the speech he had made in the debate. That it had been the cause of an appeal to the President he had no notion, nor did Van Cloete, who was continually in the company of the two brothers, enlighten him.

The Hollander used to spend hours with the younger man, sometimes fishing or dredging the dams for tortoises, of which the burghers made very fair soup, sometimes helping him with his letters home, for Oscar was a poor performer with a pen. Van Cloete was the postal officer and censor of the commando, a post that he filled to general satisfaction. Indeed, he was a most popular man in the camp, though the highest officials of the army, Cronje alone excepted, had a most wholesome mistrust of his influence and of his personal character, which, it appeared, had not enjoyed a high reputation in Holland.

The days passed without any further incident of note, till it was reported that Methuen had at last been given orders to start, and had crossed the Great River. News of the fights at Belmont and Rooilaagte came in, and the sound of the guns had been heard on most days. But nothing definite was known. Many on commando were, however, convinced that the republican forces had been severely worsted in spite of the excellent telegrams that were forthcoming after each retirement. Lucas's commando retreated with the Boer forces, keeping well to the east, though at the Modder River battle Viljoen's men had actually taken a small part in the engagement, on the extreme left flank of the Boer line.

A pause was made after this fight, and the republicans took advantage of the lull in hostilities to secure the heights of Spytfontein.

But there then ensued a severe difference of opinion between Cronje and Delarey: the latter held out firmly against the trenches being dug on the summits of the kopjes. He contended warmly that all the experience of the campaign pointed to the abandonment of the old theories of defence, and to the entrenchment of the foot of the hills. This, and Delarey's second contention that the proper position to be defended was not Spytfontein at all, but the southern position of Magersfontein, angered the general beyond words. At first he abruptly refused to listen to such a foolish scheme, but eventually found that he could not so ignore the reiterated protests of a man who had had experience in the present war, and who was looked upon by many as a tactician of great capacity. Every endeavour to bear down opposition was met with a cool request that the matter should be referred to a proper krijsraad, and the short, burly general employed in vain the bellowing insolence that had passed for strength hitherto. Delarey was firm, and the appearance of Steyn, the Free State President, was accepted by both as a means of escape with dignity from a quarrel that had become a source of paralysis.

After patiently hearing both sides, Steyn unhesitatingly gave his verdict for the plan advocated by Delarey, and Cronje flung himself out of the council.

It was the evil luck of Lucas that he happened to be within Cronje's hearing at this moment, and was with a shrug of the shoulders expressing to his brother—he would never have spoken so openly to any one else—his relief that Steyn had come in to arbitrate upon a matter that was causing a deadlock at this most important juncture. He added that in his opinion Delarey's proposal was obviously the better in view of the almost successful issue of the Modder fight.

Cronje sent for this plain-speaking critic, and then and there threatened, with a burst of ungovernable rage, that he would have him shot if he uttered another word of criticism. A bystander had mentioned Andersen's name, but the Boer general did not realise till he had finished his abuse, that this was the man who had caused all the trouble ten days before. A suspicion of this came into his mind as he paused. He asked him abruptly whether it had been he who had preached the refusal to carry out the orders—Andersen had no idea that he had arrested a movement as far advanced as that—to invade the territory of the British.

For a moment Andersen stood in bewilderment, and when about to answer, was stopped by Van Cloete, who saw that Cronje had said too much already. The latter was induced to go away, still almost beside himself with anger and mortification, and Lucas went back to his trench with a feeling of unrest, to find his brother almost in tears at a continued absence of news from Krugersdorp.

After the departure of Steyn, the supreme command was again vested in Cronje, who so far declined to accept the decision of the President that he caused additional trenches to be dug on the heights of Magersfontein, though after Steyn's decision he could not refuse to allow the main works to be made in front of the ridge, along the line that Delarey indicated, some hundred or two hundred yards in advance of the actual foot of the kopjes. But as Cronje detailed several hundreds for the upper trenches, there was no time to carry the line of earthworks along the full length of the line to the east, and on the afternoon of the 10th, while Methuen was engaged in searching every nook and corner of the ridge with shell, Delarey compelled Cronje to agree that an advanced post must be made in the centre of the line, and that the defenders of the post must hold on in the event of an attack under cover of night, until there should be time for the Boers along the line of trenches to come up in relief of this, the weak spot in the defences. Belmont had taught them the need for such a picket, and the decision was not an unreasonable one, though it was perfectly well known to all the members of the krijsraad that the post thus formed was a post of extreme danger, and there was a pause when the question of manning it could no longer be postponed. It was eventually left to the Transvaalers, and Van Cloete before leaving for Pretoria suggested that Viljoen's commando should be told to detach a sufficient number to hold it.

There is no need now to relate again the issue of that day's battle. It was as unexpected by the Boers as by the British, but the fortunes of the Scandinavian commando, which was almost annihilated by the guns of 'G' battery, closely affect the event of the story that is now being told. One of the earliest to fall was Oscar, killed outright by half a dozen shrapnel bullets. Within five minutes it was clear that the position was untenable, and the Scandinavian survivors, under a man named Flygare, who displayed intrepid courage up to the last, evacuated the position, only to find themselves between a cross fire, and, in the majority of cases, compelled to surrender. Lucas himself escaped back into the Boer lines with two of the horses under a heavy fire. Still the Boers had won the day.

Bitterly as he grieved for his brother's death, and greatly as he shrank from the duty of sending news of it to his sister-in-law, not the slightest suspicion of the good faith of his superior officers entered his mind, though three or four of the few Scandinavians who had made their way back into the trenches loudly accused the men for whom they had been fighting of having left them to their fate.

There was a distribution of letters that evening for all who chose to go to headquarters for them, and Lucas, partly to distract his mind, partly because the continued silence of Augusta was causing him grave anxiety, went to the post-wagon himself to ask for any letters there might be for either of the brothers. In the past they had been content to await the distribution by Van Cloete, but the commando post had now been merged in the burgher field post.

There was one letter, for himself. He went back to his bivouac, and sat down to read it with a heavy heart: he saw from the envelope that it was from Augusta. It ran:—

'MY DEAR BROTHER,—I cannot tell you the grief and shame with which I am writing, but it is your fault as much as mine, why have I had no letter from you for so long, again and again I have written, and some at least have reached you for Mr. Van Cloete has told me that he has given them to you but you have never answered me by even a line. And Oscar has not written for six weeks, and Wilhelmina asked for you so often, over and over again just before she died. Poor child her one cry was for her uncle, and I wrote again and again but you never sent me a word I can never see you again and I have left the old home. You will not care perhaps you have been at the bottom of Oscar's wickedness, for I could never have believed it of him. O Lucas why could you not keep him in the straight path? You will never see me again—Mr. Van Cloete has been so kind and he has told me everything, and I have waited so long and no help came, and they have taken away all I had and I was a pauper in the camps, and the child died of fever and now there is nothing else for me to do, and Mr. Van Cloete has been my only friend, but try to forgive me though it is too late, I can't write more Goodbye,

AUGUSTA.'

Lucas read the letter with chilled heart and almost madness in the brain. He saw more and more as the piteous disjointed sentences followed each other. The wholly miserable truth unfolded itself before him, pitifully unmistakable. Oscar was killed; Augusta gone; Wilhelmina— his little Wilhelmina, was dead, dead in the belief that her uncle was careless and brutal. He alone was left, he—and— Van Cloete!

Van Cloete was in Pretoria now; he would guess that Lucas knew, and would see to it that Lucas too was removed.

Slowly, like a man in his sleep, Lucas, straight, stiff, unswerving, moved out across the trenches in the dark to where his brother had been killed. Men shouted to him to be careful, as the rooineks were still holding their position, but he neither turned nor answered. Only when the gruff and sudden challenge of a hidden sentry among the British outposts checked him, did he mechanically throw up his arms and allow himself to be disarmed and led in to be tied to the wheel of a wagon till dawn.

He was taken back into Modder River on the following day, and closely cross-examined by the provost-marshal, who, however, could make so little of the man that he detained him till the case could be gone into more carefully. But at the request of Major Shervington he was separated from the other prisoners, and remained under a special sentry till the evening.

Then he was sent for, and cross-examined by the general, with whom was Shervington. When he knew that the latter was present, Lucas for the first time betrayed some interest, and a curious expression came over his face at the sight of the man whom above all others the rebel hated and the Boer feared. Not a word was, however, said by him, till the general had asked a few questions and received no answer.

Andersen, after declining to explain his surrender in any way, was about to be sent down to the Cape in the usual way, when Shervington said, 'If you'll allow me, sir, I should like to have a moment's talk with this man.'

The two were therefore left together, and Shervington remarked, 'I got a message from you?'

Lucas bowed, and watched the major narrowly.

'Of course, you are asking for an unheard-of thing, and I wished to ask you myself what grounds you had for supposing such a thing to be possible for a moment?'

'I had very small hopes.'

'You were not in any red-cross corps or ambulance?' Lucas shook his head, and Shervington's eyes grew clearer. 'You admit, in fact, that you were up to yesterday fighting against us?'

'Yes.'

'Then what possible hope could you have had that we should treat you otherwise than as a prisoner of war?'

'I am prepared for that. In any case, I could not have stayed on in the burghers' camp.'

'Why?'

Lucas would make no answer.

'And you say that you are willing to place at our disposal your personal knowledge of the country?'

'Yes.'

'And of the disposition of the Boer forces in this part of the country?'

'No.'

'You will tell us nothing that you have learned about their strength or armament?'

'Nothing.'

'Then how can you expect us to place the slightest trust in your good faith?' There was a moment's silence. 'I will go and see the general.'

And Shervington, leaving his papers on the table, went out of the room. He went straight to the general, and asked him if he might use Lucas if he thought fit. The latter demurred.

'How can you know anything about the man? You are running a fearful risk, and I can't allow it.'

'He's going through a pretty severe test at this moment, though he doesn't know it. May I report again, sir?'

'Well, you know your own business best, but there must be a very good reason shown me before I can even consider it.'

Shervington went back to the room, exchanging a silent question and answer with a man who seemed to have nothing much to do. He had, however, kept a close eye on Lucas Andersen through a crack of the door.

The interview was apparently satisfactory, and Lucas became a member of the Guides. The immediate result was that two of them, without one instant's warning, were arrested, and the corps knew them no more. There was a short shrift in those days, when the net was once drawn round a wretched man in the pay of the enemy.

But not a single caution was relaxed, and, though there was little to show it, the surveillance under which the Scandinavian lived was unwearied and minute. But his detection and exposure of the spies had of course put things in a new light. Lucas adhered to his avowed determination to betray nothing of such information of Boer strategy as he possessed—and probably never knew how much that unshaken determination helped him to obtain the confidence of Shervington and the position he asked for.

The war dragged its interminable length along, and the months rolled into the years: the defence degenerated into mere brigandage, and the Guides were at last broken up to serve with twenty different corps. By this time Lucas, who had been time after time exposed to the hottest fire without shrinking, and had become a marked man among the enemy with a heavy price upon his head, was regarded as one of the most valuable men in the service, for his local knowledge was good, and his integrity beyond question. Shervington understood but half, and that was but a guess; the remainder he never attempted to find out.

But he still looked with interest on the man who had so abundantly justified his hazardous experiment, and it was with a real feeling of regret that he eventually allowed his most valued, if also his most silent, man to leave him to accompany

Carruthers's Horse into the Lydenburg district in chase of Viljoen. But he knew Carruthers, and was aware that a good man was not wasted upon him. A word or two passed between the two men as the troop started, and Shervington's last words were of unbounded praise for Andersen. 'But I fancy there's a strain of madness in him.'

'All the better,' laughed Carruthers. 'I wish there was a bit in some others of my men.' And he appointed Lucas second in command of the maxim. Never had his officer known a gun kept with such minute care, and Lucas, whom a last-joined recruit might have laughed at with impunity, was chaffed a good deal about his 'infant.'

But after months of trekking the man changed; the dull, painstaking look gave place to another of almost painful excitement. It was rumoured that the Boers of whom the force was in pursuit were actually those of his old commando. They were on outpost duty, just where Andersen's knowledge of the country continually called him, and he spent night after night on his knees, silent and shaking with the stress of religious emotion.

Carruthers found him more instant and reliable than ever, though the wearisome chase of a desperate body of brigands through an almost impassable country was telling severely on the bodies and spirits of the whole force.

When the end came, it came, as it always did, with astounding suddenness. It was nearly three weeks since the column had started, and there had been some reason to believe that Viljoen had managed to double back between Carruthers and the parallel column to the west before the former reached a point beyond which the retreating Boers would fall into the hands of a third force that had been drawing in from the north. The scouts of the force were making their way cautiously round the spur of a lofty table-headed berg, when Lucas, who had chosen to work higher than the others, and in consequence had a wider view, signalled to the rest to stop. Carruthers himself made his way with his adjutant up to the gully from which Lucas was gazing out across the veldt with a set and strained look, that his colonel noted as unusual in the usually dour and self-controlled Calvinist. But Carruthers could see nothing, though his sight was as good as that of the Scandinavian. Lucas's first words explained this well enough.

'You see that kloof, sir?' and Carruthers nodded. 'If you will look carefully to the right—'

'That's a flight of locusts, Andersen; the top's straight.'

'Yes, yes. But farther to the right, sir, the colour—the colour——'

Carruthers, being partly colour-blind, shook his head, and Andersen almost impatiently called the attention of his adjutant to a patch of mauve in the ultramarine distance forty miles away.

'That's true,' said the adjutant. 'How near do you suppose the column that is making that dust is from us?'

'Twelve miles, sir, and heading straight for us; I've noted it by a grass stalk for three minutes. There are thirty wagons, I should say.' And the guide saluted and retired a pace.

'This is luck! We've got them this time—"What though the spicy breezes blow soft o'er"—unless,' the adjutant added, breaking off his most unmelodious noise, 'they're the other column to the north?'

Lucas's face hardened as he heard the well-known tune. So Van Cloete would escape him after all, and live in comfort in Ceylon. Was this to be the end of all his silent work? Was the weapon of God, as Lucas called himself in his starlight communings, to be turned aside after all?

'That we'll soon see,' said Carruthers.

The force was rapidly disposed around the trap of kopjes that Carruthers's force held. One officer with Lucas and the maxim was some distance to the right front to where a cleft offered good cover, and in utter silence the approach of the convoy was awaited.

'That can't be the Boers,' said the officer in charge of the maxim; 'they'd never come straight into our arms like that. Why, they must guess that we're here.'

'They think that we're round by Aasvogel Kop, sir.'

'How do you know?'

'I told them,' was the quiet answer.

Lucas Andersen had become a proverb for his extraordinary sources of information, but this made even the subaltern open his eyes. However, there had long ceased to be any question of Lucas's loyalty, so he said no more, and he was never able afterwards to find out what the Scandinavian actually meant by his cryptic remark.

The loosely thrown line of horsemen, some hundred and fifty in number, were drawing nearer, riding easily in the blazing sunlight with long stirrups, their rifles carried across the saddle, and the creaking wagons following. The scene was one of the most perfect peace. Not a sign was to be seen of the ambushed English, and the troopers almost held their breath in keen anxiety that the commando should not escape them.

The main body of the Boers had passed well within the jaws of the ambush when the inevitable happened, and a careless finger pressed too hard upon a trigger.

In an instant, without a moment's confusion, the Boers were off their horses, and taking cover even where there seemed a moment before to be none. But the storm from three sides that broke out at once should have shown the merest fool among them that it was useless to hold out. Acting on their usual plan, the Boers opened a heavy fire upon the maxim, and the cover for the crew proved insufficient from the point that the commando had reached. The officer in charge fell at once, severely wounded, and the only other man besides Lucas was killed out right. But as quietly as on parade the guide adjusted a new bandolier and re-found the range.

The firing from Carruthers's men had meanwhile been incessant, and the response of the Boers weakened. There was not the slightest chance of escape, and their commandant sullenly put up a white flag.

Instantly there was a cease-fire from the English, and an answering white flag was raised from the spot on which the colonel was standing.

Carruthers was standing with two of his staff in the centre of the position, and commanded both wings of the line. The maxim was four or five hundred yards away on his right, concealed to the axles from him by a fold in the ground, and entirely hidden from his men. There was the usual necessary delay to make sure that the white flag did not cover some act of treachery, but this time there was no doubt. The Boers piled their arms reluctantly where they stood, and advanced a little way from them.

The picture upon which Carruthers looked down was one of peace, that extraordinary peace that South Africa always suggests. Away to the right a farm nestled in a clump of greener veldt, with poplars and a kraal of aloes below the half-empty dam, which gave a note of red to the scene. A wire fence of five strands ran across the open up to the corner of the kraal from behind the kopje on the left, and beyond it climbed lightly up the hill behind and vanished over the crest. Through it the half-dozen tracks through the veldt that go by the name of a road out there swerved out of the way of a donga, and climbed up to where Carruthers was placed. For the rest, there were only the rising and falling curves of the high veldt, dusty, pasture-less, and brown, with the sun beating down in the dead silence. Not a man was to be seen on the British side, and the sound of the rifles gave place to an utter silence, in which the hoarse commands of the Boer commandant could be clearly heard.

Carruthers's heart beat high with excitement as he saw a man detailed by the commandant to approach the British lines with a white flag.

The man started out to cross the four hundred yards that intervened with a quick, almost a jaunty, step.

Lucas with his maxim leaned forward over the breech, watching the messenger, and the face of the man altered. His eyes became set, and the blood surged through his head with a bursting current of fire. Then he laughed twice quietly, though he could see nothing in front of him but the foresight and the moving figure.

A shot rang out, and Carruthers started with an oath: he thought that a magazine had gone off by mistake, but the eye of his adjutant noted the curl of red dust that leaped up at the feet of the messenger. Another and another followed, and then their source was made clear by the drumming stutter of a flight of bullets. The Boer cried out and started to run back, then he ran forward, preceded everywhere by an intermittent volley from the maxim.

Carruthers was speechless: he still thought that there must be some mistake on the part of the officer in charge, but the truth was soon beyond doubt.

Shrieking and dodging from side to side, the wretched man dashed forwards to the British lines, and the dust kicked and eddied always at his feet. Carruthers saw it all now, and his face aged ten years. His adjutant hiccupped in horror beside him.

'Look! He's playing with the poor devil!' And it was clear that Lucas had the man at his mercy at any moment, and that he was pursuing him with the maxim as a cat plays with a mouse. The adjutant set off to run to the gun, shouting like a maniac, but Carruthers by intuition did a wiser thing. Leaping up to a rock, from which he could well command the maxim, he poured shot after shot with steady aim at the minute target afforded by his own gunner's helmet.

On either side the truth seemed to be understood, and the Boers stood as stupefied as the British while the horrid sight went on before them. In vain the man doubled and ran, in vain he screamed for mercy; the bullets drummed round him, just missing him right and left.

One shot of Carruthers's had struck Lucas through the point of the shoulder, but it did not even distract his attention. But Van Cloete was nearing the English position, and the Scandinavian thought fit to stop the play.

The first seriously aimed shot brought him down with a last scream. He never moved or spoke again, but Lucas was not yet satisfied. A thrashing arch of lead spanned the distance, and hardly a bullet now pecked up the dust: even when from that distance the madman could see the body of his enemy turning under the blows to a mere streaming red heap, he still kept on with his maxim steaming and shaking like a live thing.

Suddenly one of Carruthers's bullets stopped the stream by crushing a cartridge in the band, and the deathly silence that settled down upon the scene was broken only by the hoarse, high shriek of the adjutant, who was still running to the gun.

Lucas made no attempt to resist the men who came up and disarmed him. He was weak from the wound he had received from Carruthers, and he found too on trying to walk that a later ricochet bullet had shattered his shin-bone.

Late that night Carruthers, after a useless discussion with his adjutant, who had received too great a shock to be of much use, sent for Lucas, gave him a seat, and dismissed the guard to wait outside the door.

'Do you plead madness?' The Scandinavian shook his head.

BETWEEN THEE AND HIM ALONE.

'Have you anything to say?'

'Nothing.'

Carruthers rested his chin on his hand, and looked fixedly at Andersen. He was convinced that the man was momentarily mad, but he had not therefore the least hesitation in doing what he thought to be his duty in putting him to death for an offence for which not even that excuse could be in his eyes sufficient. Still, the man's perfect civility and calm troubled him.

'Is there anything that you wish said to any one?'

Something in the tone of the voice touched the guide, and he spoke:

'Yes, sir, I should be glad if you would give this package to Major Shervington. It will explain enough, I think.' The grimy parcel that Lucas handed across fell upon the table, and the flimsy fastening opened. A photograph fell on the floor, and Carruthers picked it up. The sight of a grubby picture of a child's head, which the colonel laid quietly beside the written letter that formed the other contents of the little package, moved both men. 'Major Shervington will understand.'

Still Carruthers paused, hunting for the words he wanted.

'But whatever your provocation, I do not understand how a man who had the record you had among us could have done so brutal a thing as to hunt an unarmed man down—a man who was utterly at your mercy, a man who had surrendered?'

'Not unarmed, sir. He has the whole of the British army behind him. Did I not know that no risk that I might have run in killing him man to man in the open was one-tenth as deadly as the certainty I knew well enough—the certainty of being shamefully put to death by the English for doing the thing?'

There was truth in what he said. Whatever the man was, coward he was not. Carruthers could fill in the rough story as well as Shervington, and he hesitated before he said, half apologetically:

'Could you not leave it to our justice?'

'No, sir, I could not. Would you?'

Carruthers was answered indeed. 'But, man, it was the murder, not the——'

'Sir, let me tell you; it is not in extenuation of what is past. Only I should like you to know to tell the major. I saw the man. I killed him. What matter the instrument employed? I was as Ehud before the Lord. What matter who was looking on? There was no British force present for me. Whether in the streets of Throndhjem or alone on the veldt together, there was not, nor ever would be, another thing there but he and I wherever and whenever we were to meet. Do you think that the whole army would have deterred me one moment, or the solitude of the karoo would have hurried me one moment? I knew my work, my weapon, my opportunity, and I knew my punishment. Sir, I have not flinched from the death that you will put me to. I have not feared the disgrace of a felon's death. It is all written, from the beginning it has been all written, and I have accomplished the will of God. You too will accomplish His will at daybreak to-morrow. It will be a just sentence on your side; but on mine also it has been a just sentence that I pronounced and have carried out after many days. May there not be utter truth on both your side and mine?'

Carruthers was silent. 'You will be shot to-morrow at daybreak. You will not be hanged, and your eyes shall not be blindfolded. I can say nothing to you, I can only do my own duty. But thus much you shall have, that I may not seem to judge one who is in God's hands already.'

Lucas smiled and said: 'I thank you; I would have asked that and no more, had I thought that I might be understood. You will pardon me that I have so long held my tongue?'

And the guard was summoned and Lucas went out.

Early next morning there came even before daylight a stern order from headquarters that the prisoner should be brought in to Pretoria, to be made an example of with due form and solemnity.

The messenger waited in the grey streaming dawn, and took back the answer.

'I have given my word that he should be shot, not hanged, for reasons that seem to me to be sufficient. I will explain them on my arrival the day after to-morrow as my adjutant's prisoner, whom I have instructed to arrest me immediately upon the execution of the prisoner.'

And when, with a curious smile on his lips, Lucas Andersen, unafraid and less nervous than many of the firing-party, gave the signal, and fell dead without a movement, these instructions were carried out. But the reasons that Carruthers gave were understood at headquarters, and only Shervington ever knew much more about the end of Lucas Andersen, commonly regarded as renegade and murderer, but also (it was not forgotten) as the greatest guide we ever had.

# LADY

# BEATRICE

SOME time ago, as I came home, I glanced up at the windows of my flat, and noticed with some surprise that the electric light was on. I had been asked to go down to a newspaper-office as late as I could manage, and it was about a quarter-past one when I returned. Burton, my servant, had express orders to see that the light was turned out when his work was finished, and I felt somewhat annoyed. I had left the flat as soon as I had dressed, just before a quarter-past eight, and of course I put down this waste of electricity to his carelessness. I let myself in, and in the hall I found Burton himself waiting for me, as stolid as ever. I have never known Burton surprised about anything.

'There's a lady, sir, upstairs in your room. She said she would wait till you returned. Society lady, sir.'

I considered a moment, and then said:

'You had better stay up till I see you again.'

This was a quaint end to the day. It is one of the amusements of life—perhaps the only one—that one is always turning corners, and what lies behind the next may, of course, be the most interesting of them all. For once in my life, it seemed possible that I was going to find it true.

I had been rather tired, but any weariness vanished at once. I went upstairs and opened the door of my room. It is a large and somewhat dark room, chiefly furnished with books and Oriental pictures, and there was a fire burning in the hearth. By it, in a deep arm-chair, sat Lady Beatrice Combe.

I had always disliked her particularly. She was twenty-two, and a recognised beauty. Even I had to admit that, but she had once behaved badly to a friend of mine, and it had so happened that I was once obliged to give her my opinion of her conduct. She had asked for it, and I had spoken as prettily as circumstances would permit, but that was the end of it so far as either of us was concerned with the other. But lovely she was, and as she looked up at me in the firelight, I confess that she might have been Lady Hamilton herself. It was seventeen minutes past one by the clock, and as I glanced at it I noticed that she had taken off a diamond tiara and laid it on the mantelpiece. I rather pride myself upon guessing the motives of people, but I confess there never was a man more at a loss to understand the position than I. But it was no good showing it.

She looked at me and said: 'I have——'

'One moment,' I said, and turned on the other electric lights in the room. There had been only one table-lamp alight. Then I came up to the hearthrug.

'Well?'

There was a pause. She looked at me helplessly.

'It's a little difficult to explain,' she said. She got up, and stood with her hands on the mantelpiece, looking down at her foot on the fender.

I felt rather a brute as I merely answered, 'It is,' and waited.

She put her face into the crook of her elbow on the mantelpiece, and looked down into the fire.

I think if she had cried I should have been bored, but there was something convincing about a woman who did not gabble out the particular lie she wanted me to believe the moment I came into the room. Certainly she was a beautiful woman, but what on earth induced her to come and see me of all people, at that time of night, I could not even faintly guess.

'Would you mind if I smoke?'

She shook her head, and I lit a cigarette, vaguely sympathising with Mr. George Alexander as I did so. In these great social emergencies something has to be done to fill in an awkward gap. She turned round and looked at me.

'I wonder what you think I have come for?'

It was a silly remark, but she was sparring for an opening, and I accepted it.

I said with a smile: 'Well, it is a little unusual for an unmarried girl to be——'

She shrugged her shoulders and spoke: 'I am not unmarried.'

I was not quite sure of her sanity now. If ever a girl could, so to speak, be trusted to be unmarried, it was Lady Beatrice Combe. But the grey-violet eyes that had been the undoing of my friend looked at me steadily, troubled, but as sane as my own.

'Oh!' There did not seem much else to say.

'I married Lord Ellsworth this morning, privately.'

'Then what on earth——'

'He is dead!'

'Dead!'

I confess I was beginning to wonder whether it was not I myself who was mad.

I walked up and down the room once, and turned to her sharply.

'I wish you would sit down, and tell me the whole story, and how I can help you.'

'Oh, it is simple enough. I was supposed to be going to-day to stay for two months in Scotland. Lord Ellsworth married me in the Holborn Registry Office at half-past ten this morning. He went to—to see his people at Winchester, leaving me to wait for him at the Russell Hotel, where he had taken rooms the night before. He never came back. At nine o'clock to-night I got a telegram from Waterloo that he had been found dead in the railway carriage when the return train from Winchester reached Waterloo this evening at half-past six. He had written and asked that I might be told.'

Now that she mentioned it—and she did so in what seemed to me to be a very casual manner—I remembered that the posters in the street as I drove down to the office had as a sub-title, 'Sudden death of a Peer.' But even assuming that this referred to Ellsworth, I still was no nearer my original question: Why had she come to me?

In a few minutes I began to understand.

She shrugged her shoulders and said, 'There's a lot more to tell you. But I came to you to-night because I have to come to a decision by six o'clock to-morrow morning, and you are a man of the world——'

I bowed slightly. She went on with the faintest suggestion of a smile, though it was rather a pitiful one.

'—and you are the only man of the world I know who cordially dislikes me.'

To this there seemed no obvious reply, but I confess that the girl's perfect frankness and pluck revealed to me a side of her that I never suspected.

I motioned to her to sit down again, and I sat in the corner of a sofa opposite the fire. The glitter of the diamonds on the mantelpiece caught my eye. She followed my glance and said: 'You might have guessed that something had happened when you saw that.'

'Yes,' I said; 'girls as a rule do not wear diamonds. But why have you taken them off?'

Lady Beatrice shrugged her shoulders. 'I could not stand them.' Then leaning forward to me she told me half the whole truth: 'I do not know whether I am really married or not.'

By this time I was ready for almost anything. It seemed a nightmare. Here was Lady Beatrice sitting in a quiet evening gown of silk and lace, which must have cost eighty guineas at Paquin's, and the last girl I ever expected to have the honour of entertaining, telling me things that might have come out of the *Arabian Nights*.

A hansom went by outside.

'You had better tell me the whole story.'

She said: 'Lord Ellsworth married me this morning at half-past ten at a Registry Office. We went back to the Russell Hotel.'

I nodded.

'Just before luncheon—you know the sort of man he is— he said to me, "Look here, I must tell you I married a woman two years ago," and I said to him, "Is she alive still?" '

There was something about the callous, practical way in which she seemed to believe Ellsworth capable of such an act, that once and for all convinced me that there had been no great love on her side.

'He said "No," and then recollecting himself said, "At least I was told four months ago that she was dead"; and I said to him, "You must go and make certain of that." So he went down to Winchester, and he was to telegraph me that all was well. He said he could let me have the wire by five o'clock. I never got any wire. I didn't know what to do, so I dressed for dinner, and I put on those things because I thought I looked better in them. I thought he would come back!'

I interrupted her. 'Talking of dressing, where is your maid?'

She said: 'She is still at the Russell, I suppose, getting uneasy. She was not present at the wedding. I merely ordered her to stay with me at the Russell Hotel for the night.'

'But she must have thought you mad. How do you know that she has not gone straight home and told your people?'

A curious look came into Lady Beatrice's eyes as she answered: 'Fleming does what I tell her. I sent her to bed, and I am quite sure that in bed she remained.'

'Well,' I said, 'putting the maid aside, is there anybody else who knows about your marriage?'

'Not a soul; we were married under false names.'

At this I lay back on the sofa and laughed. This was the last straw.

She looked at me anxiously, and said, 'But that makes no difference to the legality of the wedding.'

'Not a bit,' I said.

There was a long pause. At the end of it she said, 'If I want to claim it.'

I said to her: 'May I ask you anything I like?'

She said, 'Anything.'

'*Anything?*'

She nodded.

'Then I don't think that I need ask you. What is to be done?'

She said: 'The only thing that is quite clear is, that under no circumstances will I return home.'

I did not know, and I never have known exactly, the reason of this determination. I think that she was on the worst of terms with her mother and was very fond of her father. Perhaps it was not unnatural.

There seemed to be no possible solution for this *impasse*. If Ellsworth had another wife still living, if, that is, Lady Beatrice was not married, it might be of course better that nothing should be said about the events of that day. On the other hand, if the wedding was valid, there might be good reason for publishing it.

I went to the telephone, and was answered with the promptness of midnight at the Exchange. I gave the number of the newspaper which I had just left, and asked to be put on to the editor. He answered, and I asked him for all the details they had of Lord Ellsworth's death. He said, 'Oh, I am very busy. If you will excuse me I will put on Draper to read to you what is going to appear to-morrow.'

'Before you go,' I said, 'is there any fact connected with this that you have thought fit not to publish?'

'No,' he said, 'nothing much.'

Then the uncertain voice of Draper took up the parable. The report of the death at Waterloo was written in the usual journalese, and, as I heard it in sentences, I repeated it to the girl. It was not a suicide. This was clear at first, and of course added enormously to the difficulty. Had it been a suicide I should have regarded it as a presumption that Ellsworth had found that he had committed bigamy. On the face of it, it seemed an ordinary case of syncope. He had been identified not only by his visiting-cards, but by two notes he had scribbled, and there was a respectful curtain drawn over any more personal matters that did credit to the *Morning Press*, but was exasperating from our point of view. The notice concluded with these words: 'There is no heir to the ancient title of Ellsworth, which accordingly becomes extinct. It is expected that his half-sister, Mrs. Pollard, will succeed to the major part of the estates in the absence of all other near relations.'

I thanked Draper and rang off, ruminating considerably. The mention of the estates was yet another complication. For if the marriage had been a legal one my beautiful young visitor could claim, and would claim, the rights of dower over a very large property, as there certainly had been no settlement of any kind. I said so, and it was Lady Beatrice herself who said at once how much. I had a general idea that the Ellsworth estates were very large. There was a good deal of land in Southampton and Portsmouth, and from the circumstances of Ellsworth's own succession—he had succeeded a distant cousin, and everything that could be kept away from him had been—it was not likely that there existed any legal encumbrances.

At a glance I saw that if the marriage at the Holborn Registry proved to be good, Lady Beatrice by her morning's escapade had at least earned for herself seven thousand a year. I told her so. 'And besides—' I said, with a shrug of the shoulders.

'And besides?' she echoed, looking into the fire.

The Westminster boomed out the three-quarters.

'The wind is in the east,' she said aimlessly.

'Why,' said I, 'did you say that you had to come to a decision before six?'

'Well,' she said, 'if the marriage is to be ignored, there's a quarter to seven train that I might take. I can explain my delay to that extent, I think, but the next train would be that which I ought to have taken yesterday, which is a nice and slow and respectable one, and does not get in till Heaven knows when.'

'But you ought to have wired,' I suggested.

She paused a moment, and then replied:

'Well, I suppose I told Fleming to do so, and I suppose she forgot.'

I think there is something in being desperately pressed for time which quickens the wits. The best work is often done when there really is not five minutes to spare. I made up my mind. I stood up on the hearthrug and said: 'Now listen to me.' She did so. By this time she was undoubtedly tired out, and the strain and anxiety were beginning to tell upon her.

'Is your case serious?'

She shrugged her shoulders.

'Then,' I said, 'we will motor down to Corlton Paulets to-night. I can lend you an overcoat.'

She stood up at once, and, after making one or two preparations, she and I went down the stairs.

I found Burton still waiting by the door, his face as unmoved as ever.

'Many thanks, Burton. You can go to bed.'

'Good night, sir.'

Leaving her in the street, I went round to the mews, and, with the most appalling amount of clattering and noise, the chauffeur and I got out the car. I took a couple of thick motor veils out of the pocket of the car, and fetched Lady Beatrice round to the entrance of the mews, where the great machine was shivering with impatience. I gave the chauffeur general directions, and we went snorting off through the empty streets of London, through the Fulham Road, and out by Putney Bridge into the cool, dark spaces of Surrey.

There is something about motoring at night that nothing in the day quite equals. To begin with, it is much safer to let out the car's speed. Birds and beasts and children and police traps are shut up for the night, and the huge white cones of my Bleriots swept forward a warning of our coming beyond even the distance that the drumming of the cylinders could reach, far as that was in the silence of the early morning. The hedges roared past us like black cataracts. There was not a minute to spare. To reach Corlton Paulets at four was our only chance if this four hours' marriage were after all to be ignored. Personally, I saw nothing in it that called for a sermon. There was no earthly reason why Lady Beatrice should forgo her legal rights if the wedding had been correct. Ellsworth had intended to confer them on her, and his death at that moment was a mere mischance. On the other hand, if the other woman were alive and the marriage were valid, there was no reason why a disastrous and wholly ineffective arrangement, of which only two living persons had the ghost of an idea, should be wantonly published as a mere piece of gossip. Anyway, the girl couldn't wait. This was the only way out of it, and even this was not more than a bare chance. My Panhard was doing all it could, but the minute-hand of the illuminated dial crept forward remorselessly.

I had lighted the lamp in the top of the car, but at a sign from Beatrice I switched it off again. Neither of us spoke. Every now and then I caught a glimpse of her by the light of a fleeting village lamp-post. She lay back in the car on my right, her face muffled in a boa, and half-hidden in the great fleecy wrap-rascal I had insisted on putting on her as we started. She was looking straight ahead at Rixon's back, and betrayed nothing of the turmoil that must have been going on within her. There was the same beautiful face that I had known and disliked for so many years, there were the same broken curves of dark hair over the ear that my eye resented; and after all, the woman was going on a mission of doubtful grace. Yet she stood the anxiety with quiet pluck, and never a moment did she betray impatience.

Every now and then a railway arch crashed overhead in a momentary darkness. Poplars swished by at orderly intervals, and now and then the steady plunging of the pistons was thrown back against us by a long stretch of low garden wall, while underfoot the cry of new gravel mingled with our rush and sweep. We halted nowhere. Steadily we thrashed our way south-west thirty-five miles an hour on the flat, never less than twenty through the towns and on the hills. Rixon and the 'Tortoise' understood that there was need of haste, and haste we made. Sometimes into the converging cones of light upon the road rabbits and stoats ran blindly, and stood mesmerised by the glare. Some we must have killed, but there was no time for sentiment. I remember yet, as if it were yesterday, the overhanging branches that swept into the headlights and out of them again over us, true green every leaf in the pure acetylene flame. Only once we slowed down. It was just where rail, road, and river become tangled up a mile or two out of Alton. A heavy-moving motor and two trailed wagons blocked the way a moment, and, as we drew clear, we passed at quarter-speed another car that had been waiting behind the road-train as impatiently as ourselves.

The light was on inside this other car, and Lady Beatrice looked full into the face of the woman within it. She had on a fur coat, and must have been in evening-clothes, but there was nothing about her that was remarkable except the diamond 'S' in her hair. Like a fool, Ellsworth—Stephen Ellsworth—had given her one exactly similar to that which he had given to Lady Beatrice. She turned to me. She didn't ask, she issued orders.

'Go back, please, at once, and follow behind that car we have just passed; follow it all the way to London.' She turned the light on. 'That,' she said, 'is the woman I was coming down here to see.'

The turn things had taken was bewildering. I believed her intuition was right, and gave the necessary orders. Rixon, good, impassive man, turned the 'Tortoise' at a crossroads and set himself back on his long journey. He was now running well within the car's powers. The little hind-light illuminating the number of the woman's car was soon recovered, and at half a mile's range we chased it back over the road we had come. We had the power of it, and could have caught it up in five miles, but Beatrice's imperious demand had silenced me. We were to wait and see what would happen, and for twenty miles and more we lay behind and watched the lights of the car ahead. It was recklessly steered, evidently by a man who could not understand that a car responds to humane treatment. It could not go on as it was without trouble of some sort, and the pace dwindled steadily. When Rixon suddenly slowed up neither he nor I were surprised. Lady Beatrice still remained impassive. I ordered Rixon to go forward, and as we came nearer, it was clear that among other disasters a tyre had been badly, and even hopelessly, punctured. The woman was out of the car, standing on the muddy road, talking and gesticulating fast. Lady Beatrice said, 'Ask her to come in here.'

The position was a pretty one, and I began to feel that fate had been good to me. I opened the door as we slowed up, and asked if I could be of any assistance. We were going to London, and might we take her with us? She—her name, she said, was Ethel Lorimer, though I have never seen any one less like an Ethel in my life—thanked me with a burst of relief. She said that she was going to London on business of the utmost urgency. Lady Beatrice's face was a mask. She said she was so glad to be of use, and that really it was no inconvenience to us. Where should we take her in London?

Ethel Lorimer was talkative. But there was no doubt that she was what is called a lady by birth. She was going to London to find her husband, who had met with an accident and she feared was dying. He had apparently written her a note on a piece of paper, just as he had written to Beatrice. I shall never forget the next hour. The two women were facing me. Neither looked at me, except that Ethel Lorimer once or twice appealed to me to know if I thought that 'Stephen' would be alive when she reached him. I could have answered her, but it was, on the face of it, a silly question, and a silly woman asked it, pretty as she was. I could only smile sympathy. It was not my business.

Lady Beatrice, as I thought, played with her as a cat plays with a mouse. There was a definite purpose in every question she asked, and as she asked them she looked ten years older. Ethel had married 'Stephen' abroad, it seemed. It was in Spain, at Burgos, she thought, and then, with a touch of colour, she said she had been wrong. They were married at Bordeaux. Beatrice let two miles go by before she put out a hand, and took Mrs. Lorimer's. Not often does a woman set her snares before a third person, but here she was obliged to; and, as I have said, I sympathised with her to some extent. There were questions asked and questions whispered, and at last Beatrice got her chance.

'Of course I understand that you must be very anxious. Has your husband—Mr. Lorimer—any relations in London?' She didn't know. The marriage had been kept secret. Mr. Lorimer had been down that afternoon to tell her that there was some irregularity in it. She didn't understand these things. She had been married in some church at Bordeaux. She was French, and a Catholic. Mr. Lorimer was not, and after a year there had been some question of the legality of the marriage. The French law was so difficult.

'Mr. Lorimer promised before he left that he would marry me again soon in England, so as to make everything right. But I didn't much mind. I am sure that if you are married in church it must be all right. But when I heard of his accident I came up at once. I hired a motor from Winchester, but it all went wrong, and if it had not been for your kindness, I shouldn't have known what to do.'

Lady Beatrice put out the light in the car. She said nothing for a long time. Then, rousing herself, she spoke, though already she had got the facts she needed to disprove the marriage.

'Mr. Lorimer married you in church at Bordeaux?'

'Yes.'

'Yet he now says that there is an irregularity?'

'I think he said so.'

'You said your marriage was entirely unknown?'

'Entirely; he wouldn't let me tell a soul. I have told no one except you; but to-night'—she was sobbing—'I must tell some one, and you have been so good to me.'

'If Mr. Lorimer is very seriously hurt, will it make much difference to your position?'

There was a long pause, and I never heard the answer, the one thing in all that night I wanted to hear. It seems that there was some doubt about the technical legitimacy of a child.[*]

'He told you that he would re-marry you in England on account of your little girl?'

'Yes.'

'Nice man!'

I nearly jumped up. But there was Lady Beatrice's eye on me, cold and forbidding. It was her affair, not mine; but I intended to tell her what I thought of her once more, before we parted.

'Oh, *such* a dear, you can't imagine. He has been very much troubled about money matters lately, he told me.'

Lady Beatrice puzzled me. In the darkness she and 'Mrs. Lorimer' sat side by side, illuminated by passing street lamps. Hardly a word was exchanged. At last London was reached, and we dived about through unsavoury side-streets till we reached Waterloo. We set Mrs. Lorimer down. She was effusive in her thanks, and as I saw her up the steps I told her who Stephen was and advised her to make herself known at once, and to claim anything there might be in the way of property. She had her marriage certificate with her.

Then I returned to the car and asked Lady Beatrice: 'Shall I take you to the Russell Hotel?' I hated the woman.

'Yes, please.'

Less often than is thought there is born to the foolish soul a redeemer. I was simply a blind ass. We went off in silence.

As she got out she put out her hand to me. 'I think,' she said, 'you have sometimes done me some injustice. Mrs. Lorimer is Stephen's wife, and if she can get Stephen's money,

---

[*]     Mrs. Lorimer eventually agreed to admit the invalidity of the Burgos 'marriage' and the illegitimacy of her child, if Mrs. Pollard would admit the Bordeaux marriage, which had no issue. It is all very complicated, and she was a quite unworthy person.

she is welcome to it. May I give you my sincere thanks—and Stephen's wedding-ring as a souvenir? I start for Scotland by the 6.45.' She pulled it off her finger, and I took it.

But I have judged people less hardly ever since. Lady Beatrice Combe, though living apart from her mother, is still unmarried. Sometimes we meet, and I am glad if she will let me take her in to supper. She has no money, and at times Mrs. Pollard passes us in her new diamonds.

# THE
# GYROSCOPE

'WERE you actually there?'

I asked the question with a certain amount of amazement and even mistrust. No one had ever yet made that claim, and the busy arguings and explainings of the scientist and the laymen as to what actually occurred to cause the famous disaster at Dover had long died down.

'Yes, I was. I was not touched. But I had had enough of new discoveries to last me a lifetime, so I came down here into the country. My friend the doctor wouldn't let me read a newspaper for three or four months, and no one was allowed to see me. Luckily for me, not three people knew that I had been there. So I had the peace I needed.'

Alston flicked at a whorl of gossamer upon the wild clematis-hedge beside him. All around was restfulness and contentment. The bees droned among the clover-flowers on the other side of the gate, and the click and clatter of a reaper sounded contentedly from the field beyond, where a central island of oats in a five-acre plot was gradually being pared down. There were the contrasting blues of the scabious and chickory along the hedge-side, and a little country lass dropped a curtsy to Alston as she passed us. We were going to kill the rats in the five-acre field as soon as they began to run.

195

# THE GYROSCOPE

Alston turned with his back to the gate, pulled his Panama brim more over his eyes, and stretched out both arms along the top rail. He hitched one boot-heel on the lowest rail, and began. I have paraphrased his story in one or two places.

Alston is a man of wide general information. I dare say he had given no particular attention to gyrostatics as an especial branch of science, but he had at any rate been interested enough in the matter to make the journey from the Midlands to Dover merely to be present at the only too famous lecture given by Retherley upon the new gyroscope in the previous March.

It will be remembered that in 1907 the question of gyrostatic action was brought to the front by Brennan in the course of a more or less popular lecture during the London season. He demonstrated the capacity of the gyroscope to maintain the equilibrium of a somewhat heavy model car upon a single railway line, and from that moment the idle experiment of a science lecture-room became the centre of a sphere of enormous commercial activity. People in the street discussed without knowing it the properties of 'objects kinetically balanced round axes of free revolution.' Eight different countries claimed the credit of the discovery for seventeen separate inventors; and then the civilised world settled down to a new aspect of the problems of transport and motion which were affected by Brennan's application of gyrostatic power.

After all, the principle was simplicity itself. We all knew that a whipping-top, properly whipped, will keep upright. For all practical purposes, the best of gyrostats could do no more. Brennan himself had long ago used the gyroscope to maintain the equilibrium of his torpedoes. He had steadied his little devils by means of a spinning spool in their ugly snouts. Later on, some of the smaller turbine craft had found themselves steering like drags in consequence of similar but wholly unintended action.

At last John Owen, of Owen, Owen and Michelham, set up his huge gyrostatic works at Dover, where half the world's steamers then called, or were going to call soon, and announced the laying down of a transatlantic liner, the *Dover*, of eighteen thousand tons, which should drive across the ocean at twenty-two knots—this was only an experimental ship, and if successful the principle was to be extended to much larger and more powerful vessels—with the stability of a railway train. For this purpose a seven-ton gyroscope had been constructed, and Owen said that that would be sufficient to keep his ship steady in any sea or swell. Public attention was aroused in the matter, not only at the prospect of abolishing sea-sickness, but because the project met at once with the severest criticism from more than one quarter.

At last Professor Morton Farraway had unexpectedly intervened in the matter by a letter to the *Times*. He contented himself for the moment by asking what would happen when a ship of eighteen thousand tons register, and probably twenty-eight thousand tons displacement, wanted to roll, and a seven-ton gyroscope revolving at enormous speed wanted it to maintain its vertical position? People thought at first that Farraway only intended to prove the disproportionate size of the proposed remedy. But he answered this with a second letter, in which he said that he had not meant to deny that a seven-ton gyroscope might be able to oppose a successful resistance to the ship's rolling. His question was quite different. He simply asked what strength of internal construction could hope to withstand the sudden conflict of two such forces.

Upon this he was denounced as a mere theorist, and the objections of *a priori* opponents to previous inventions such as railways, gas-lighting, and other successful things were freely quoted in the press. He was held up to ridicule by one

American newspaper—I remember the phrase well—as a piece of grit between the cogwheels of the illimitable wonder-working civilisation of to-day. Farraway, quite a young man, only grunted and calculated still more, while Owen went on with his gyroscope.

Besides the practical use to which Owen proposed eventually to put his gyroscope, he had given the Royal Society permission to take this opportunity of testing, on a far larger scale than had before been possible, some of the more obscure properties of the invention. The Society had commissioned Professor Retherley to make the investigation. He decided to begin with a popular lecture upon the new force, and Owen agreed at his own expense to fit up the gyroscope in the large hall of the Maritime Syndicate's buildings at Dover, and to supply the driving power. It was a good advertisement, and it was made better by Farraway's quietly written letter stating that, though his principal objection would in no way be answered by this test on shore, he believed that he would soon be able to point out another quality of the gyroscope which rendered dangerous its use on ships. He made a remark to a friend at the time which led some people afterwards to think that he intended to demonstrate the magnetic disturbances that would be set up.

The gyroscope which attracted so much attention was twenty or thirty times larger than anything that had been tried before. In height it was perhaps eight feet, and the disc was a circular mass of forged steel about five feet in diameter and eighteen inches thick. Six weeks before the demonstration it had been set up in a carefully prepared steel framework, the larger part of which was destined for use afterwards in the *Dover*. This framework was of massive proportions, and was erected in the Syndicate's hall, a large room supported on pillars, with a smooth stone floor and a couple of enormous electroliers depending from the ceiling. The ornamentation everywhere was a trifle florid. Large false windows—the hall was in the middle of the building—came down to within three feet of the floor. There was a semicircular end to the hall where a dais was built, and the gyroscope had been erected immediately in front of it and slightly to one side on a temporary staging of baulks of timber. The lecturer's raised desk was in the middle of the hall, and there was a table for reporters immediately below him. Entrance was obtained to the hall by a side door on the right of the dais. The sharp slope of the ground outside had enabled large and convenient cellars to be made beneath the lower end of the hall. Overhead were three stories of offices and board-rooms.

The 'gyre' itself—as the workmen called it—turned upon ball-bearings in a polished steel cup. The cup was filled with oil, and a trough of ice was laid round it lest the bearings should heat. The work of getting up the pace of the gyroscope was done at first by adjustable driving-bands connected with a huge petrol engine, geared for different speeds. It was impossible to run it in a vacuum.

It was on a Sunday morning that the monster was set moving. John Owen himself, with his own hands and without ceremony, pushed the daintily poised mass of glittering steel a quarter of a circle, and then with a jar the lowest gear took up the work. One could hear the distant throb from the exhaust of the petrol motor in the cellar below. The gyroscope, which Owen, with a touch of fancy rare with him, had christened 'Il Diavolo,' began its revolution as silent as death. By twelve o'clock that night she was turning well, and by the close of the week the gear had been changed ten times, and the counters were dissolving merrily in the indicator.

'I went in to see it after it had been running three weeks,' said Alston. 'The electroliers were not on, and the machineman was working by the aid of a single thirty-two candle-power lamp. A light, temporary barrier had been set round the instrument, but Owen, who was standing by his invention, invited me to climb over it. He was, he said, perfectly satisfied. The light was reflected from the polished rim of the gyrating disc as steadily as if it had been stationary. The best work had been put to its making, and Owen had some excuse for his satisfaction. The steel basin in which the axis was rotating was, if anything, over-cooled by the ice, but no great harm resulted from the thickened oil. Owen had had a stiff canvas cover made to protect the bearings from the chance of grit, and as he replaced it, he let his hand rest lovingly on the bright column of steel. "It's the greatest adaptation of the last hundred years, and I see no end to it—no end." He spoke the clearest English at ordinary times.

'The driving-bands used to transmit the power were, I remember, of web lined with some kind of close silk velvet with a nap on it, "on the free-wheel principle," Owen said, but I don't think there was much advantage in it. The revolutions were then about six hundred to the minute, and I made some admiring remark to Owen, who answered me with a tone of excitement:

' "Mon, she's nobbut walking yet!"

'Farraway came to Dover soon afterwards, but he remained at his hotel busily working at the last equations needed for his contentions. Owen couldn't work out a quadratic for his life—Michelham did all that for the firm, but Farraway was in a wholly different class from his partner. Owen trusted entirely to rule of thumb—an experienced and sagacious thumb. He said that the force to be counteracted was nothing like thirty-eight thousand tons. Farraway had never even suggested that it was. He pointed out that the weight of the ship was borne by the sea, and that eighty tons was more the figure. Farraway never contradicted this either. Owen contended that there was a certain elasticity in a gyroscope's action, and quoted Brennan's experiment in proof of it. Finally, he said that no one really knew anything about it, and that he at any rate intended to make the experiment.

'On the Friday before the demonstration morning I went again. Except that the transforming apparatus was much more cumbrous, it was difficult to see that there was any difference. The gyroscope revolved, apparently as motionless as ever. But the counters were rattling like tiny castanets; and Owen, who announced his intention of sleeping for twelve hours on Sunday night so as to be ready for the demonstration on the next day, was too much delighted to give way to his weariness. "Twenty-seven hundred steady, and we've three more transformers to use yet."

'To me there was something hypnotic in this terrific yet silent velocity. "Il Diavolo" flowed round with half-human intensity, and though I knew nothing about science, I felt through the bones of me that devils were indeed being unchained. The thought, perhaps the unfelt vibration, got between my marrow and me, and I went away. Even when I went down for a breath of air on to the Admiralty Pier, I could feel the thing at my back.

'On Monday, the day of the demonstration, everything was ready early. Workmen were everywhere in aprons carrying ferns and marguerites in pots, and hammered red baize on the platform, tucking and tacking superfluous felt in between the very framework of Il Diavolo and the dais. The accelerating machinery had been carried away by noon, and an electric motor of low power but enormous velocity was merely keeping up the speed gained. Owen turned up at half-past twelve. Farraway paid his first visit at one. The lecture was to take place at eight o'clock.

'The two champions greeted each other civilly, and Owen expressed some pleasure at seeing his critic in the flesh. Farraway, after a few moments' conversation, hastened to say that the evening's demonstration could not affect his main contention one way or another, and he complimented Owen warmly upon the brilliant way in which the practical details of the experiment had been carried out. The two men walked forwards to the still silent gyroscope.

' "What's she doing?" asked Owen of the assistant.

' "Three thousand and sixty, sir; no variation whatever for the last four hours."

' "Keep her at that."

'Farraway turned to Owen.

' "Good God! Have you ever thought of the energy stored up in that great brute?" He jotted a few notes down on his cuff. "Every speck of that circumference travels at the rate of eight hundred feet a second. And the weight is what? Seven tons?"

'Owen nodded, and then, with a grim smile, he added: "For the better peace of mind of the Mayor and Corporation of Dover and of the Royal Society, we have fitted brakes to her, ye see."

' "Brakes? Brakes??" echoed Farraway.

'Owen smiled again and showed him a huge new lever-brake, of which the leather-covered handle lay within the reach of the assistant.

' "Brakes!" repeated Farraway. "Well, all I can say is, that I hope you keep that lever properly chained up."

' "Mon," said Owen, "teach your grand-mother! Yon brake is tied up with cord, and the assistant is here just to see that no one touches it. But it imparrts confidence; and it will be useful later on."

'The two men looked over the gyroscope, and Farraway repeated his congratulations. Owen put up a match and lighted it against the flashing rim, remarking that it was the first match that had been struck along the "pre-paired surrface" for forty yards; then, dropping his bantering tone, he turned to

Farraway and asked him squarely whether he thought there was any danger in that evening's work. He had taken every precaution he could think of, but he confessed to his opponent that theoretically he knew nothing of gyrostatics, and would accept any reasonable suggestion Farraway might make. The latter thought a moment, and then assured him that he saw nothing to fear, unless, he said, one of the balls in the bearings were to break, and when Owen shook his head he agreed that that was quite a negligible risk.

' "How do you propose to stop the thing afterwards?"

'Owen shrugged his shoulders: he didn't know—he supposed it would run down enough in a month or two for the brake to be used. (Farraway smiled at this.) Even if it took months, no great harm would be done. The two men discussed the matter, and Farraway named four months as the earliest period at which it would have slowed down sufficiently for the safe use of the brake. Owen was somewhat taken aback at this. Still, once on board, Owen would of course keep the gyroscope running perpetually, so, as he said, the question had only a temporary importance. At Owen's reference to the ship Farraway nodded to remind his opponent of his unaltered conviction that no framework would stand the constant strain, and that the vessel would sooner or later tear itself loose from the gyroscope—"And then?" queried Farraway.

' "Ma worrd!" ejaculated Owen, turning the end of his straggly beard into his mouth. "But ye're wrong," he added, "ye're wrong!" '

That evening Retherley met with a great reception as he stood forward in evening-clothes at his desk under the electrolier. Beside him, in utter silence, spun Il Diavolo. The auxiliary electric motor had been detached. In front of him stretched an audience of men and women, nearly all in evening-dress also, tightly packed in gilt 'rout'-chairs from end to end of the hall. The two electroliers blazed, and the pseudo-Louis XVI. flambeaux between the two long window-recesses added to the bright appearance of the gathering. The Mayor of Dover in his chain of office presided upon the dais, and a few of the town firemen with brightly burnished helmets added a sense of officiality and security to the occasion. The Mayor was a proud but a prudent man.

'Every one had been chatting like mad,' said Alston, blinking under his Panama. 'As I wasn't dressed, I was in one of the windows and had a good view of the whole thing. The Mayor introduced Professor Retherley in a short speech. He said that they had come together to listen to his explanation of the new power that had been developed by their distinguished townsman, Mr. Owen, and that he was confident that a new era of increased prosperity was opening for the ancient port and town of Dover. They all owed a debt of gratitude to Professor Retherley for his kindness in coming that evening. Retherley stood up amid the clapping of many gloved hands. God!' (Alston was musing with his back against the gate.) 'There were a lot of women there. There were a lot of women.

'The lecture was to last an hour, and Retherley had taken half that time in tracing the history of the discovery of the gyroscope and its more elementary properties. He had a pleasant touch, and his arch reference to *mal-de-mer* was received by a genteel audience with delicate appreciation. Towards the end he was to make two little experiments with small gyroscopes, one of which would, he hoped, convince even the most sceptical—and "there still were some sceptical ones," he said—that the earth actually did revolve on its axis.

'I remember the gentle titters of superior knowledge with which this remark was received. Retherley, as he turned for a glass of water, was silent for a moment. There was a general hum of conversation, and in the middle of it there came another and quite different sound. The gyroscope was beginning to talk. I can't tell you the effect it had on me; I was nearly sick, though it was the merest purr, and for the life of me I couldn't have told you what I expected to happen.

'I believe that, under the combined weight of the audience and the timbering and the machine, one of the girders that supported the floor gave a little in the middle. There wasn't the least real danger of the floor breaking down—it would have stood six times the weight. But it sagged a little in the centre, and the framework of Owen's gyroscope, which had been pinned down for extra stability into the girder itself, dropped, or tried to drop, a fraction of an inch at one end. Of course the gyroscope did its duty and resisted the tendency exactly as it would have worked against a similar tendency at sea.

'The noise increased slightly, and at the upper end of the spindle there was a faint, grating sound. A spark flashed out. In a moment the Mayor was on his feet. He called up the firemen, and they ran up with a nozzle. John Owen at one side of the hall stood up, and his face was the colour of my Panama.

' "I consider this friction dangerous," said the Mayor. "Can you prevent it?"

' "No," said Owen, "I don't see how I can. There is no danger—no real danger."

'That qualification was the cause of the trouble. In a moment the Mayor answered him in a heavy and colourless voice: "I am responsible for the safety of this meeting, and rather than run any risk, we must, I am sorry to say, forgo the rest of the demonstration. I must ask you to stop the gyroscope."

'Every eye was fixed on Owen. There was no panic; only one or two women began to adjust their wraps. It was just an interesting situation.

' "I canna sto-p the ma-chine."

'The Mayor mistook Owen's meaning. "You shall not lose by it," he said somewhat magnificently. He beckoned to the firemen and gave them orders to apply the brakes. Owen licked his dry lips and gesticulated. Then a voice from the end of the hall, which I hardly recognised as Farraway's, said:

' "Don't touch the brake! I am Professor Farraway, and I assure you that Mr. Owen is quite right. No power on earth can stop that gyroscope."

'The Mayor paused. He was a dogged man and was aroused; moreover, Il Diavolo seemed to him quite an ordinary piece of mechanism.

' "We'll see about that!" He turned to where the firemen stood, and saw the fastening.

' "Good Lord, the brake is tied up. Cut that cord!"

'In a moment a fireman's knife had freed the lever. Farraway's high voice called out again from the end of the hall:

' "For the sake of God leave that thing alone!"

'I remember the silence there was. The Mayor's only reply was to call up the other two firemen, and the four men threw themselves upon the lever.'

Alston shook his head. 'I can't tell you how quick it all was. There was a scream of steel against steel and a stream of white sparks. Both the brake and the steel socket against which the spindle was forced fused, and the metal got into the bearings. The balls splintered, the basin broke, and with a kind of grinding roar the awful thing took charge. The spindle was disengaged top and bottom, and Il Diavolo slipped upon the steel-work of the frame and then descended upon the stone floor of the hall, still spinning as truly as ever. The reporters' table was deserted in a flash, and Il Diavolo drifted through it as a shell breaks a canvas target. One wretched man was caught and screamed. That was the signal for the panic. Those near the only door flung themselves upon it, and found that it opened inwards. I remained where I was. I suppose I was

THE GYROSCOPE.

almost hypnotised. Many of us were, I noticed. There was one woman in evening-dress who stood and looked at the thing as it slowly obeyed the imperceptible slant of the floor and spun downwards, leaving a trace of charred marble behind it. She could neither move nor cry; she put her hands over her face and the thing struck her. We all watched it. The struggle at the door suddenly ended as the gyroscope crept slowly down towards it. Some were able to run away; others dropped on their hands and knees or on their faces. A woman near me prayed shrilly to the Virgin. Some scrambled up into the sills of the false windows. Yet I don't think that even then the people understood what it was that had broken loose. They expected every moment that the force would be spent and that the gyroscope would fall.

'Quite slowly the huge top followed the slight descent towards the door, then, feeling perhaps the sustaining wall's support of the floor, veered slightly and crept on towards the wall. At last it touched it, tore through the raffle of pillar and plaster and brick, and came up against one of the reinforced sixteen-inch girders which supported the house. The purr was turned to a noise like an explosion of lyddite. The house rocked. The face of the wall fell, leaving the bent girder visible. The ceiling dropped for some yards, and one of the electroliers, still burning, descended a yard on the disengaged iron beam above.

'Have you ever played a French game called *toupies hollandaises*? Well, you spin a heavy little brass top on a table. It buzzes petulantly through rails and obstacles of brass, and you count the ninepins in each compartment of the table which the top reaches and you succeed in knocking down. If it hits an obstacle it flings itself a foot away, and creeps towards it again more angrily than ever. That gives the best idea I know of what happened. The gyroscope after the first assault flung itself twenty feet away, and roared like an angry elephant.

Then it recovered its equilibrium and again moved along the same track to deal another blow. You couldn't believe that there wasn't a deliberate and diabolical malice about the thing.

'Again it moved up, and at a touch the girder crumpled up; the whole side of the wall dropped in, killing, I suppose, about a hundred and twenty. A cloud of dust rose and concealed everything. The lights of the electroliers went out, and only the trumpeting of the gyroscope bellowed in the darkness. This time the blow had been greater, and it had been thrown farther. It was impeded by its own wreckage. Just then an inner wall fell on the other side of the hole, and a ray of light from an office came through into the pandemonium in the hall. I remember that it was a cosy little office. There was a turkey-carpet on the floor, and a very up-to-date bureau with papers lying loose upon it. The man at work there, whoever he was, had evidently fled on hearing the first disaster.

'Through this ray of light, which hung like a blanket through the dusty air, the gyroscope travelled. I could see the perfectly steady column of steel and the flying disc for twenty seconds. No escape was now possible, as the inner wall of the hall had fallen across the door, and a twelve-foot heap of stones and twisted iron girders barred the way. Moreover, the upper stories of the house began to fall through in a long cataract of bricks and mortar.

'The steel brute passed, as I say, into the ray and out again into the darkness. It was nearing the other end of the hall, splintering the chairs in its way like tissue paper, and probably killing some wretched man or woman at every yard. Very few of them screamed. We were all either paralysed with terror or hypnotised. We knew that we were doomed; perhaps for that reason we were still. It is the chance of death that causes terror, it is the chance of life that causes a panic, and we had none.'

The little girl, who had been up the lane twenty minutes

before, returned with a basket of flowers and curtsied again cheerfully to the Squire.

Alston, in the same monotonous voice, said to her:

'Well, and how is Mrs. Nicholls?'

'Nicely, thank you, sir.' Another curtsy, and she walked on. With an effort Alston resumed.

'What happened then was this. The slope of the floor, which would hardly have been detected by a spirit-level, spent itself about twenty feet from the other end of the room, and there the gyroscope came to a halt, just over the cellar in which the petrol motor was installed.

'As soon as it halted, the spindle of course acted like a drill, and the thing sank through the floor until the disc struck the stone and concrete and iron.

'Well, you know the rest. There was a crash like the explosion of a mine. The gyroscope split into three pieces, and each portion drove like a shell through the walls and out into the town. The Syndicate building fell in like a pack of cards, and every soul except myself was killed on the spot. I was not even scratched, though the fall of the hall buried me up to the waist in bricks and mortar and dead men. I was well enough, when the workmen released me next morning, to walk away. I could say nothing. I think they believed that I was one of their own number. You remember that several of them also lost their lives?

'I came home, and I have hardly talked of the thing to this day. But it does me good to set out the whole thing in my mind as a perfectly natural occurrence. I can tell you that it was months before I got rid of the idea that it was the devil himself that possessed the gyroscope that night. I have never left this place since, and probably never shall. I am better out here in the open air looking after the estate, and I have burned every book upon mechanics and machinery in the house. I think—I think we will leave the rats to the farm-hands to-day.'

# APPENDIX A

Perceval Landon's obituary from *The Hertford College Magazine*, No. 16, May 1927 is reproduced below. It includes his obituary published in *The Times* on 23 January 1927.

## OBITUARY

LANDON (88).—Died on the 23rd January 1927 in a nursing home in London, Perceval Landon; Scholar of the College, 1888–92. Of the *Daily Telegraph*; formerly a special correspondent of *The Times*. Aged 58.

'When the South African War broke out Landon became one of the special correspondents of *The Times*. It was an opportunity which he seized with enthusiasm, and by his vivid dispatches he rendered valuable service to this journal during the first part of the war. In 1900 he went to New South Wales for a time as private secretary to the Governor, but soon took up again the work for which he was best qualified. Joining the staff of the *Daily Mail*, he served as special correspondent for the Delhi Durbar, and afterwards travelled in the Far East. He returned to the service of *The Times* as special correspondent with Sir F. Younghusband's expedition to the Forbidden City of Lhasa in 1903–1904, of which he was also appointed by Lord Curzon, then Viceroy of India, to be the official historian. Landon's book "Lhasa," which appeared in 1905, much enhanced his reputation. It was illustrated with some of his own water-colour drawings, for he was an amateur artist of skill and taste. Indeed, all his writings show his intense love of colour and his appreciation of scenery.

Landon now joined the staff of the *Daily Telegraph*, on which he remained for the rest of his life. The mere list of his missions is a long one. He was a special correspondent on the present King's visit to India as Prince of Wales in 1905–1906, one result of which was his book "Under the Sun: Impressions of Indian Cities." This was neither a guide-book nor a record of the Prince's tour, but a vividly written description of the impressions made on Landon's receptive mind by the varied scenes of India. Thenceforward, till the outbreak of the Great War, he travelled in Persia, India, and Nepal, Russian Turkestan, Egypt, and the Sudan, the North-West Frontier, Mesopotamia, and Syria, and described the Delhi Durbar of 1911. During the first year of the war, which was full of difficulties for newspaper correspondents, Landon made the most of his limited opportunities in France. Afterwards he was present at the Paris Peace Conference and described the signature of the Treaty of Versailles. His next work of importance was the recording of the present Prince of Wales's tour in India and Japan in 1921–22 ; he described the Lausanne Conference in 1923; and in 1925 he went to China, but illness compelled him to return home last year. Landon was an able and experienced observer, not only of actual events, but also of those political and social changes which demand special gifts of insight for their accurate presentation. Personally, he was a delightful character, as the range and variety of his friendships proved. In addition to the books already mentioned, he wrote essays and travel-books, he translated "For the Soul of the King" from the French, and one of his novels, "The House Opposite," was dramatized and produced in London in 1909. A volume of short stories, chiefly ghostly or gruesome, entitled "Raw Edges," appeared in 1908.'

*The Times*, 23 Jan. 1927.

# APPENDIX B

## A SONG IN THE DESERT

### (P. L. Ob. Jan. 1927)

*FRIEND, thou beholdest the lightning? Who has the charge*
        *of it—*
*To decree which rock-ridge shall receive—shall be chosen for*
        *targe of it?*
*Which crown among palms shall go down, by the thunderbolts*
        *broken;*
*While the floods drown the sere wadies where no bud is token?*

First for my eyes, above all, he made show of his treasure.
First in his ear, before all, I made sure of my measure.
If it were good—what acclaim! None other so moved me.
If it were faulty—what shame? While he mocked me he
        loved me.

*Friend, thou hast seen in Ridaّar, the low moon descending,*
*One silent, swart, swift-striding camel, oceanward wending?*
*Browbound and jawbound the rider, his shadow in front of him,*
*Ceaselessly eating the distances? That was the wont of him.*

Whether the cliff-walled defiles, the ambush prepared for
        him;
Whether the wind-plaited dunes—a single sword bared for
        him—
Whether cold danger fore-weighed, or quick peril that took
        him
Alone, out of comfort or aid, no breath of it shook him.

Whether he feasted or fasted, sweated or shivered,
There was no proof of the matter—no sign was delivered.
Whatever this dust or that heat, or those fools that he
      laboured with,
He forgot and forbore no observance towards any he
      neighboured with.

*Friend, thou hast known at Rida'ar, when the Council was*
      *bidden,*
*One face among faces that leaped to the light and were hidden?*
*One voice among night-wasting voices of boasting and shouting?*
*And that face and that voice abide with thee? His beyond*
      *doubting!*

Never again in Rida'ar, my watch-fire burning,
That he might see from afar, shall I wait his returning;
Or the roar of his beast as she knelt and he leaped to unlade
      her,
Two-handedly tossing me jewels. *He* was no trader!

Gems and wrought gold, never sold—brought for me to
      behold them;
Tales of far magic unrolled—to me only he told them,
With the light, easy laugh of dismissal 'twixt story and
      story—
As a man brushes sand from his hand, or the great dismiss
      glory.

Never again in Rida'ar! My ways are made black to me!
Whether I sing or am silent, he shall not come back to me!
There is no measure for trial, nor treasure for bringing.
Allah divides the Companions. (*Yet he said—yet he said:—*
      "Cease not from singing.")

                           **Rudyard Kipling**

# APPENDIX C

The full review of the theatrical performance of *The House Opposite* from the *New Zealand Graphic*, volume XLIV, issue 4 (26 January 1910) has been reproduced below:

### 'The House Opposite.'

A somewhat melodramatic play, entitled 'The House Opposite,' by Mr. Percival [*sic*] Landon, was produced at the Queen's Theatre, London, recently. It has the elements leading up to a powerful situation. Based on the well-known story of Couvoisier [*sic*], in which a valet was seen from the house opposite killing his master, Mr. Landon's plot reveals how Richard Cardyne, in the boudoir of the Hon. Mrs. Rivers, was the horrified spectator of a similar crime. Richard Cardyne was the lover of Mrs. Rivers, the wife of the Right Hon. Harry Rivers, ex-Home Secretary, and it was from the windows of her room that he saw old Mr. Chancellor done to death by a man. But how can he make use of the knowledge, thus fortuitously acquired? Supposing that an innocent person— say, the house-keeper, Anne Carey—is wrongfully accused of the murder, how can he tell the truth, when every word he reveals will fatally compromise the character of Mrs. Rivers? This is the dilemma on which the play turns. A murder has been committed; an innocent person is charged with the offence; there is one witness who knows that the charge is false, but his mouth is sealed, because the lady from whose house he saw the commission of the crime lays imperative commands on his honour and his loyalty not to reveal the dreadful and compromising secret of their relations. The wife of an ex-Home Secretary, with a reputation to preserve, cannot possibly allow her lover, Richard Cardyne, to give away the fact of their close intimacy. Drawing-room melodrama, indeed! And very good melodrama, too, based, in this instance, on an actual historic fact, and replete with consequences of tragic import to the social butterflies whose wrongdoing involves them in the imbroglio.

**Who is to Confess?**

What is to be done? Apparently very little, although there is a good deal of backward and forward movement, and at one time it looks as if a maid's good name was to be sacrificed. Mrs. Rivers is in an agony of fear and apprehension; her lover is in the throes of remorse, and a fierce conflict of duties. Of course, one or other of them ought to confess, and thus secure the ends of justice. But who is to make the needful confession? No one knows better than Cardyne that if he holds his tongue, he is putting the assured position of a leader of society above the most primitive demands of ethical responsibility. In the long run, the woman herself confesses, confesses in an indirect fashion, by mentioning an analogous case to a listless husband, who is apparently too deeply engrossed in his newspaper to listen to the meaning of her words. She never knows whether he really understands the significance of her speech. After all, however, the confession itself is unnecessary. Mr. Rivers himself reveals the fact that the real murderer has confessed the crime, and that, therefore, the innocent will be allowed to go free. But Mrs. Rivers has had a lesson which she is not likely to forget during the rest of her life, and Richard Cardyne, too has discovered how the pursuit of light loves may lead him into a terrible impasse, in which the conventional and the real sense of the word 'honour' are tossed to and fro. Thus, viewing from the theatrical standpoint, the play contains a very strong situation, worked out in a series of scenes which end up in a very obvious moral.

# APPENDIX D

Review of *Raw Edges* in *The Spectator*, 4 July 1908.

***Raw Edges.*** By Perceval Landon. (W. Heinemann. 6s.)—
In this series of short stories Mr. Landon exhibits a talent for
depicting things grim and terrifying. It is not too much to say
that there is not one of these stories which does not leave the
reader either unhappier for having read it, or with a tendency
to look over his shoulder at the dark corners of the room. The
four illustrations by Mr. Alberto Martini do nothing to lessen
this effect, anything more horrible than the picture which
faces p. 64 having surely never been offered to the public by
way of an illustration to a volume of light fiction. The sketches
of the war are the most interesting in the collection, and give
the reader brilliant impressions of the incidents described. The
story of 'The Crusader's Mass' is both realistic and extremely
painful, and the reader will hardly be able to restrain the
feeling of disappointment and despair which will seize him at
the end. While all the rest of the tales are absolutely original, in
'Mrs. Rivers's Journal' Mr. Landon takes as his foundation the
story of the murder of Lord William Russell by Courvoisier.
The facts, of course, have long been public property, and Mr.
Landon's amplification of them is extremely ingenious and
moving, but it must be confessed that the apparition at the
end spoils what is otherwise a most convincing story. Though
the reader sups full of horrors, yet Mr. Landon possesses so
highly the gift of gripping the attention that no one will regret
the time spent upon this little volume.

# APPENDIX E

Review of *Raw Edges* in *The Athenæum*, No. 4206,
6 June 1908.

It is not unlikely that Mr. Perceval Landon may have deliberately chosen what is called the unlucky number thirteen when he decided how many short stories should go to the making of *Raw Edges: Studies and Stories of these Days* (Heinemann). Such a choice would, at least, be in keeping with the abundant whimsicality and taste for the bizarre appearing in these tales. But they are good stories, told with workman-like skill, and showing a creditable appreciation of the value of words. Some of them, like 'The Crusader's Mass' and 'Our Ignorance in Asking,' will leave a lasting impression upon the reader. They show a fine grip upon the grinding horrors of war, and a distinct power of literary presentation. The volume has four illustrations by Alberto Martini. These are rather clever and very fanciful, after a grotesque fashion. 'Raw Edges' is above the average of fiction of the day.

# APPENDIX F

Review of *Raw Edges* in *The Nation*, 6 June 1908.

## THE SHORT STORY OF CONVENTION.*

In his preface to 'Raw Edges' Mr. Landon remarks, 'If there is any good in these tales at all it is that they have been written from a point of view from which other men have looked.' But we are inclined to believe that the 'man of the world' attitude which is deliberately emphasised in the tales is the shoddy element in his artistic fabric. Artistic insight may, of course, be a gift distinguishing a clubman or a laborer, but there is, perhaps, no creed or code of life more antithetic to the artist than the 'man of the world's.' At the point where knowingness stops dead artistic insight begins, though the two may supplement one another, as in the genius of a Balzac or a Thackeray. But often the one checkmates the other, as in Mr. Landon's story 'Overtried,' where we have the most unnecessary 'window-dressing' of a touching and simple situation. The Rev. Richard Carteret, the Rector of Leigh Monachorum, has a 'secret that paralysed his life'; he has had an intrigue in India with a friend's wife, Mrs. Charteris, who has become insane on account of it, and he is suddenly asked by her unsuspecting husband, now settled in the neighbour-hood, to go and see her in a Norwich private asylum. A quiet analysis of this psychological situation, however, is not good enough for our author, and he must needs spoil its reality by smothering it with *comme-il-faut* accessories in which we do not believe. We not only have the ideal country house, where

---

* 'Raw Edges.' By Perceval Landon. Heinemann. 6s.

218

'the guests, scientists, pioneers, diplomats, refugees, come from the ends of the earth,' where 'dinner that evening was a meal as it is not understood by many,' but we have De Bernard, the 'well-known French Monseigneur,' in the smoking-room, with his face looking 'like an ivory carving,' embarking on confidences to the repentant Carteret in a style of fashionable melodrama befitting a West End theatre:—

  ' "One of your own Englishmen has used a strange phrase of haunting force. 'I speak to you a dying man to dying men,' to dying men a dying man. Like him, I speak to you a dying man. My name is on the list of those who will at the next Consistory be raised to the Cardinalate. Thereafter there lies a forked path. One way leads me on to all that many"—he paused—"all that most men deem best worth having. The other means that it will not be long before my work is over. Yet I have no choice. Others of us have failed. The 'handful of silver' works with us, too, and men who are valiant enough in black are often cowards in scarlet. But your case is harder than mine. The Church kills me: you it bids live on. My friend, I pray you, live on yet. Whatever your sorrow——"

  'Carteret caught his breath twice.

  ' "And I pray that though I speak to you a dying man, the other part of Baxter's great line may rest unfulfilled."

  'Almost wearily the great ecclesiastic drew himself out of the chair, and raised himself to his full height beside the fireplace.

  'Then, as one in helpless despair, Carteret dropped from his seat, and knelt with his face in his hands, as Monseigneur's fingers were raised over him, and the hackneyed words of benediction passing slowly from his lips took on a new meaning for both.' ...

  'Sir James, however he came to know these things, was right enough in his unspoken prophecy, for within six months Cardinal de Bernard, whom the "Times" described as the most liberal-minded of the College, and one whose elevation but three months before had been universally recognised as reflecting credit on both the Consistory and himself, died while on a visit to one of the small monasteries that shrink among the crannies of the Italian Alps. The Jesuits, with great alacrity, published the certificate of the doctors who had been called in from a neighbouring brotherhood, so the world now knows that His Eminence died of septic tonsilitis amid the inconsolable grief of all the faithful, but especially of the General of the powerful Order.'

This seems childish stuff to come from the pen of a 'man of the world,' but the point is that even if it were true to life it is out of place, and so bad art. Commonplace surroundings and simple human feelings are good enough for a great artist, but a worldly, leisured audience must have a rich *mise-en-scène*, 'the crucifix that hung from the heavy gold Venetian chain,' 'the carved amethyst on the prelate's hand,' the little anecdote of a 'certain distinguished princess,' &c., before it condescends to be moved. Accordingly, by the time Carteret gets to the lunatic asylum and sees Mrs. Charteris, we have got so impatient of the spiritual falsities designed to impress us that any spiritual truth vouchsafed us seems out of place. The interview between the priest and the woman is clever, but it came too late to save the story. In 'A Deathbed Comedy,' Mr. Landon sins in a more provoking way. The situation here, one between a dying child, Miriam, her beloved friend, Dick, who has made her promise that she will pretend to be 'nice to mother,' and the hard woman, Mrs. Gilchrist, who has overheard their conversation, and, bitterly repentant, sees through 'the lie and piece of acting designed to hoodwink her,' is a strong one, and, treated less sentimentally, would hold the audience. But the author, who has probably studied Kipling to his detriment, is not able to get beyond the smart unrealities affected by the latter author in moments of emotional crisis. It is almost laughable that the conventions of 'good form' should have so strong a hold on the untrained imagination, but, no doubt, even this travesty of art may impose on the plain man:—

> 'But as Lestrange began to descend the stairs at the end of the corridor, he heard the swish of a woman's skirts. Mrs. Gilchrist staggered towards him, feeling her way by the wall. She muttered hoarsely, "I can't! I heard it all. May God forgive you!"
>
> 'Lestrange stood like a pillar. "Go back at once." He swore frankly and without apology. "That dying child is playing the game; haven't you the pluck to do the same?" and Mrs. Gilchrist went back to her Gehenna like a whipped dog.'
>
> \*　　\*　　\*　　\*
>
> 'Three years afterwards there was a scuffle on a frontier, and Dick was released to keep his promise—if he were allowed to. He hesitated.
>
> ' "Bless me!" said St. Peter at the gate, "of course, your record is not much, but didn't you people on earth know that that was all that we asked for?"
>
> 'For there was a small hand in Dick's by this time, and so they went walking together again.'

The author has, indeed, obviously set out to 'write from a point of view from which other men have looked,' and he apparently does not grasp that deliberately to adopt glasses which are focussed for the conventional vision is fatal to artistic spontaneity. Proof of this is afforded by the highly conventional 'man of the world' situation in which woman is privileged to play a part in his tales. In 'The Recording Angel's Peerage' we have Mrs. Burleigh 'pleading for mercy' before the clubman, Edgar Carney, who is threatening to include her name in a book of London scandals. And the thrill comes when her daughter, Noreen Leighton, to save her mother's 'reputation,' throws Carney headlong down the staircase in Eaton Place, and kills him, and Mrs. Burleigh gasps, 'Noreen,

Noreen, can't you understand?' the incredible Carney being, of course, Noreen's father!

We should not trouble to discuss the patent limitations of vision in 'Raw Edges' if the stories were not very cleverly written, and if Mr. Landon did not show convincing evidence in 'The Crusader's Mass' and 'The Gyroscope' that he could do much finer work. In 'Thurnley Abbey' and 'Railhead' he shows great skill in thrilling us with the supernatural, and although the effect in the former story is got by a cheap trick, he undoubtedly has power and artistic range. Should he continue to mould his talent on third-rate models he may, of course, become popular, but if he can cut himself loose from the besetting temptation of 'man of the world' standards, he may prove a valuable recruit in the sparse ranks of the artists who can handle the short story.

# APPENDIX G

Review of *Raw Edges* in *The China Mail*, 2 June 1908.

RAW EDGES. By Perceval Landon, with designs by Alberto Martini. William Heinemann, London.

This is a collection of vigorously told short stories, which, as the name implies, deal with the raw edges of life. Most of them are thrilling, some subtle, and all decently told. That is the characteristic. The first story takes a hold, and the reader will be loth to postpone any of the following ones for other days. The book has a distinctive grip—a grip which does not relax until the end is reached. And at the end is perhaps the most weird story of the lot—a tale of a gyroscope, which runs amok at Dover. It is cleverly done—but so are the others. The ghost yarn of Thurnley Abbey is another which is calculated to raise the hair a little, whilst several stories having South Africa as a scene, and incident's [*sic*] in the recent war as a theme, give the author scope for some excellent writing. But all are not of the hair-raising order. Social life affords subjects, and the Recording Angel's Peerage, Lady Beatrice, Overtired [*sic*], and Mrs Rivers's Journal in particular constitute well-told stories of a unique order. Those who like a varied and select menu of well-written yarns cannot afford to let this book pass by.

# NOTES

# NOTES

18    *rara avis*: (Latin) rare bird.

19    *the Mutiny*: Indian Rebellion of 1857–58 against the rule of the British East India Company.

19    *Colonel Westmacott*: Sir Richard Westmacott (1841–1925), officer in the British Bombay Army who served in the Indian Mutiny.

19    *Nana Sahib*: Nana Saheb Peshwa II (1824–1859), Indian Peshwa of the Maratha Empire who led the rebellion in Kanpur during the Indian Mutiny.

19    *Monseigneur*: (French) Monsignor, title of prelate below the rank of cardinal.

19    *Protonotary Apostolic*: title for a member of the highest non-episcopal college of prelates in the Roman Curia (the administrative institutions of the Holy See).

19    *Tarasque*: monster from French mythology, described in the *Golden Legend* as a half-animal and half-fish dragon with a lion's head, a serpent's tail, bear claws, and a tortoise shell.

19    *corbel*: structural element that projects from a wall and supports a weight above it.

19    *rood-screen*: partition between the chancel and the nave in a church.

20    *gnostic*: relating to Gnosticism, various philosophical and religious movements prominent in the second century AD.

20    *Bourne*: Francis Alphonsus Bourne (1861–1935), English prelate of the Catholic Church who wanted Roman Catholicism to become the official religion of Britain.

21    *Simon Magus*: Samaritan magus and claimed founder of Gnosticism.

21    *Holy Office*: formerly the Roman Inquisition.

21    *Lesser Limbs*: unclear reference; possibly related to the *Confessions* by Augustine of Hippo: 'O God, most high, most deep, and yet nearer than all else, most hidden yet intimately present, you are not framed of greater and lesser limbs.' Manisty and the others may have expounded a gnostic interpretation of the Image of God.

21    *vox clamantis in deserto*: a voice of one crying in the wilderness (from Mark 1:3 and Isaiah 40:3 in the Vulgate (Latin Bible)).

22    *Comacine disciples*: disciples of the Comacine masters, early medieval Lombard stonemasons.

23    *métier*: (French) trade; skill; calling.

# NOTES

# NOTES

45    *Gehenna*: (Latin) place of suffering for the wicked after death.

47    *Brindisi*: city in southern Italy.

47    *duomo*: (Italian) cathedral.

47    *Apulia*: region in southern Italy.

49    *Il Secolo*: Italian newspaper, founded in March 1886.

49    *Levantine*: person from the Levant (countries of the eastern Mediterranean).

49    *White's*: gentleman's club (now in St James's, London), founded in 1693.

50    *Woods and Forests*: Department of Woods and Forests of the British Indian government.

50    *Simla*: Shimla, city in northern India.

52    *dak-walla*: postman or courier (dak: from the Hindustani डाक dāk (post); walla from the Hindi वाला vālā (person-in-charge)).

53    *Pannonia*: hotel in Budapest, built in 1867.

53    *Kerepesi Utcza*: street in Budapest.

53    *supporters*: figures supporting the shield in a coat of arms.

54    *flèche*: spire.

54    *repoussé*: technique of shaping metal by hammering the reverse.

55    *Barotseland*: homeland of the Lozi people (or Barotse), now part of Zambia.

56    *Pett Ridge*: William Pett Ridge (1859–1930), English author.

56    *Jacobs*: William Wymark Jacobs (1863–1943), English author.

56    *Jorrocks*: fictional cockney grocer featured in a number of novels by English author Robert Smith Surtees (1805–1864).

56    *Nat Paynter's vampire story*: unidentified work and author; possibly fictional.

59    *fishing-smacks*: fishing vessels with a well to keep catch alive.

65    *fo'c'sle*: forecastle; upper deck of a ship forward of the foremast.

66    *Sanna's Post*: settlement east of Bloemfontein in South Africa.

66    *Kornspruit disaster*: Battle of Sanna's Post (31 March 1900) during the Second Anglo-Boer War: Boer commandoes ambushed the British, capturing Bloemfontein's waterworks. British casualties amounted to 155 men killed or wounded; Boer casualties were three dead and five wounded. Korn Spruit is a tributary of the River Modder where the ambush took place.

# NOTES

66    *General Colvile*: Major-General Sir Henry Edward Colvile (1852–1907), British commander of the British 9th Division during the Second Anglo-Boer War.

66    *Bloemfontein*: capital of the former Orange Free State.

66    *Macdonald*: Sir Hector Archibald MacDonald ('Fighting Mac'; 1853–1903), commander of the Highland Brigade stationed at Modder River in 1900.

66    *Bosman's Kop*: Boesmanskop ('Bushman's Hill' in Afrikaans), a flat-topped hill in South Africa.

66    *Rimington's Guides*: irregular cavalry recruited from local South Africans, commanded by British officer Lieutenant General Sir Michael Frederic Rimington (1858–1928) during the Second Anglo-Boer War.

66    *Smith-Dorrien*: General Sir Horace Lockwood Smith-Dorrien (1858–1930), British major general in the Second Anglo-Boer War.

66    *Springfield*: settlement between Bloemfontein and Sanna's Post.

67    *kraal*: (Afrikaans) corral; enclosure for livestock.

67    *Modder River*: river in South Africa, tributary of the Riet.

67    *Ladybrand*: town east of Bloemfontein and Sanna's Post.

67    *Thaba 'Nchu*: town between Bloemfontein and Ladybrand.

67    *Reddersburg*: town south of Bloemfontein.

67    *Mester's Hoek*: ridge near Reddersburg.

67    *Lord Roberts*: Field Marshal Frederick Sleigh Roberts, 1st Earl Roberts (1832–1914), commander of the British forces for one year during the Second Anglo-Boer War.

67    *Zand River*: Sand River in South Africa, tributary of the Vet.

67    *Kroonstad*: town north-east of Bloemfontein.

68    *Edenburg*: town south of Bloemfontein and west of Reddersburg.

68    *Kaffir River*: Tierpoort River, tributary of the Riet River.

68    *Jagersfontein Road station*: station south of Edenburg.

68    *Riet River*: westward-flowing tributary of the Vaal River.

68    *spruit*: (Afrikaans) stream or small river.

68    *Beyer's Berg*: hill near Reddersburg.

68    *Gatacre*: Lieutenant-General Sir William Forbes Gatacre (1843–1906), head of the British 3rd division during the Second Anglo-Boer War.

# NOTES

68    *Clements*: most likely Major General Ralph Arthur Penrhyn Clements (1855–1909), commander of the 12th Brigade of the 6th Division during the Second Anglo-Boer War.

68    *pprinsloo*: Marthinus Prinsloo (1838-1903), Boer farmer, politician and general in the Second Anglo-Boer War.

69    *burghers*: fully enfranchised citizens of the Boer republics (from 'free burgher', early European settlers of the Cape of Good Hope).

69    *veldt*: (Afrikaans) open grassland.

70    *putties*: pieces of cloth used as coverings for the lower leg.

73    *'Q' battery*: Headquarters Battery of 5th Regiment Royal Artillery.

74    *Cape boy*: man of mixed ethnic ancestry, especially from the western Cape.

75    *Merlin's disguise*: perhaps the guises assumed by Merlin in the Old French epic poem *Merlin* (estimated 1195–1210) by Robert de Boron, or the disguise conjured by Merlin for Uther Pendragon.

75    *twin line out of Genoa*: possibly referring to the Genoa–Pisa railway line, which was doubled in 1910.

75    *Grimm's law*: set of sound laws describing the Proto-Indo-European stop consonants as they developed in Proto-Germanic (discovered by Rasmus Rask but extended by Jacob Grimm).

75    *l.b.w. rule*: leg before wicket rule in cricket.

75    *Lord's*: Lord's Cricket Ground, St John's Wood, London.

76    *curio number of the Friend*: as described in *War's Brighter Side: The Story of "The Friend" Newspaper*, the printers left the date line 'March 16' unaltered on an inside page of the 17 March issue, and this 'curio' issue of *The Friend* became a collector's item.

76    *Savigny*: Friedrich Carl von Savigny (1779–1861), German jurist and historian

76    *Montesquieu*: Charles Louis de Secondat, Baron de La Brède et de Montesquieu (1689–1755), French judge, historian, and political philosopher.

76    *Eldon*: most likely John Scott, 1st Earl of Eldon, PC, FRS, FSA (1751–1838), British barrister and politician.

76    *northern Abbey*: Westminster Abbey, London.

76    *St. Mark's*: St. Mark's Basilica, Venice.

76    *Shwé Dagon*: Shwedagon Pagoda, Yangon, Myanmar (Burma).

# NOTES

77    *aas-vogel*: (Afrikaans) vulture (literally 'carrion bird').

77    *In Nomine Patris et Filii et Spiritus Sancti*: (Latin) In the name of the Father, and of the Son, and of the Holy Spirit.

77    *Je ne crains pas Dieu s'il sait tout*: (French) I do not fear God if he knows everything.

78    *Adeste fideles*: (Latin) The carol 'O Come, All Ye Faithful.'

78    *Venite adoremus*: (Latin) 'O come, let us adore Him.'

81    *valse*: waltz.

81    *Of no mean city*: 'But Paul said, I am a man which am a Jew of Tarsus, a city in Cilicia, a citizen of no mean city: and, I beseech thee, suffer me to speak unto the people' (KJV, Acts 21:39).

81    *Kitsie*: Kitsie was also the name of Milbank's horse in *The Crusader's Mass*, suggesting a possible connection. However, the events of *An Outpost of the Empire* take place in or before 1896, while *The Crusader's Mass* is set during the Second Anglo-Boer War (1899–1902).

81    *Mother of Cities*: most likely London in this context.

82    *galop*: galoppade, lively French country dance.

82    *Rhodesia*: at the time *Raw Edges* was published, Rhodesia was a region north of Transvaal Colony (formerly the South African Republic), administered by the British South Africa Company.

83    *Belmont*: railway station in the former Cape Colony, close to the border with the Orange Free State.

84    *three-pair back*: garret at the back of a house, reached by three flights of stairs.

84    *filosel*: filoselle; soft silk thread.

84    *gimp*: narrow fabric used as trimming for dresses etc.

84    *chenille*: thick, soft yarn.

84    *crape*: crimped fabric, usually made of silk and often used in mourning clothes in 19th century Britain.

86    *track*: most likely 'tract,' with the 't' replaced with a glottal stop (t-glottalization), a feature of the Cockney English dialect. Sal perhaps suspects that Lady Evelyn is distributing religious tracts (the Religious Tract Society was active at this time).

89    *Argus-eyed*: vigilant, observant; Argus Panoptes was a many-eyed servant of the goddess Hera in Greek mythology.

# NOTES

90     *Sapphire throne*: 'Then I looked, and, behold, in the firmament that was above the head of the cherubims there appeared over them as it were a sapphire stone, as the appearance of the likeness of a throne' (KJV, Ezekiel 10:1).

90     *colour of quinine*: quinine solution is transparent, but fluoresces blue under UV light. Quinine was coloured pink in the late 19th century in Chennai, and so Landon may be referring to a pink sky.

90     *omnibuses*: buses.

90     *Tattersall's*: horse auction mart, founded in London in 1766.

91     *Oratory*: Brompton Oratory (the London Oratory), neo-classical late-Victorian Roman Catholic parish church.

91     *Methuen*: Field Marshal Paul Sanford Methuen, 3rd Baron Methuen (1845–1932), commander of the British 1st Division in the Second Anglo-Boer War.

92     *paste diamond*: glass hand cut and polished to resemble a diamond.

93     *Salvation Army*: Protestant charitable movement established by William and Catherine Booth in London in 1865.

94     *the grave as little as my bed*: from the hymn *All Praise to Thee, My God, This Night* by Thomas Ken (ca. 1674).

94     *the voice that breathed o'er Eden*: hymn by John Keble (1857).

94     *plash*: splash.

95     *Modder fight*: Battle of Modder River (28 November 1899) during the Second Anglo-Boer War.

95     *ganger*: foreman of a gang of labourers, especially on railways.

95     *P.M.O.*: Principal Medical Officer.

96     *Oratorians*: Catholic society of priests and religious brothers bound by charity.

97     *Mr. Creevey*: Thomas Creevey (1768–1838), English politician. His journals and correspondence were published posthumously in 1903 as the *Creevey Papers* which provided insight into the society and political gossip of the Georgian era.

100     *Carlton*: private members' club in London, originally the central office of the Conservative Party.

100     *Pall Mall*: street in the City of Westminster, London.

101     *Alhambra*: theatre and music hall, formerly located on the east side of Leicester Square in the West End of London.

# NOTES

# NOTES

# NOTES

150  *Succoth*: Sukkot, city east of the Jordan River. In the Book of Judges, the men of Sukkot refuse to provide aid to Gideon and his followers.

150  *Fourie's commando*: Josef Johannes 'Jopie' Fourie (1879–1914), a Boer scout and despatch rider during the Second Anglo-Boer War.

150  *Transvaal*: region north of the Vaal River settled by Boer farmers, and the location of the South African Republic (or Transvaal Republic) from 1852 to 1902.

150  *predikant*: (Afrikaans) minister in the Dutch Reformed Church.

151  *Winkelhoek*: settlement east of Belmont (see note on Belmont (page 83) above).

151  *Cape Colony*: British colony in what is now South Africa that existed from 1806 to 1910.

151  *Hex River*: tributary of the Breede River in the Western Cape of South Africa.

151  *commandos*: derived from the Afrikaans word *kommando*, originally referring to Boer guerillas.

152  *nachtmaalen*: (Dutch) supper, possibly the Eucharist in this context.

152  *worsted*: wool yarn, named after the English town of Worstead.

152  *unco guid*: (Scottish) pious, strict in matters of morality (literally, 'extremely good').

153  *Krugersdorp*: mining town north-west of Johannesburg, founded in 1877 and named after Paul Kruger, then president of the South African Republic.

153  *the Raid*: Jameson Raid (1895–96), in which 500 armed men under the command of Leander Starr Jameson entered the South African Republic from Rhodesia, in an attempt to incite insurrection by British expatriates (uitlanders). The raiders were met by Boer forces at Krugersdorp, and later surrendered at Doornkop.

154  *Natal and the Old Colony*: Natal was a British colony that lay east of the Orange Free State and south of the South African Republic. The Old Colony refers to Cape Colony, an older British colony that lay to the south-west of the two aforementioned Boer republics.

154  *What of Midian, of the Egyptians, of the Canaanites?*: Moses fled to Midian after killing an Egyptian, and later led the Israelites from bondage in Egypt to the border of Canaan, the Promised Land.

# NOTES

154 *President Kruger*: Stephanus Johannes Paulus Kruger (1825–1904), better known as Paul Kruger, President of the South African Republic 1883–1902.

154 *Mafeking*: Mahikeng, town in the former Cape Colony, west of Johannesburg. The town was besieged by Boer forces during the Second Anglo-Boer War.

154 *Cronje*: Pieter Arnoldus 'Piet' Cronjé (1836–1911), Boer general during the Anglo-Boer Wars. Cronjé commanded the Boer forces at the start of the Siege of Mafeking in 1899.

154 *Dopper*: member of the Reformed Churches in South Africa.

154 *voice from Gerizim*: 'And it shall come to pass, when the LORD thy God hath brought thee in unto the land whither thou goest to possess it, that thou shalt put the blessing upon mount Gerizim, and the curse upon mount Ebal' (KJV, Deuteronomy 11:29).

154 *Calvinism*: branch of Protestantism derived from the theology of John Calvin (1509–1564).

155 *Gideon's Triumph over Midian*: recounted in the Book of Judges of the Bible (Judges 6–8).

155 *kopje*: (Afrikaans, archaic) small hill in a flat region.

156 *buck-sail*: tarpaulin, especially that used to cover a buck-wagon (a wagon used for hauling loads); from Afrikaans *bok* (beam of a wagon, stand, male goat).

156 *krijsraad*: (Afrikaans) war council.

157 *Viljoen*: possibly fictional, but may refer to Benjamin Johannes 'Ben' Viljoen (1869–1917), Boer general during the Second Anglo-Boer War.

157 *Naauwpoort*: town south of Mahikeng in the former Cape Colony.

157 *De Aar*: town in the former Cape Colony, situated on the railway line between Cape Town and the Kimberley diamond mines.

157 *Plevna*: Pleven, city in Bulgaria, formerly in the Ottoman Empire. During the Russo-Turkish War of 1877–1878, Ottoman forces built extensive fortifications outside the city, and were able to hold out for nearly five months when besieged by the Russian Empire and Kingdom of Romania.

157 *rooinek*: (Afrikaans) Englishman (literally 'redneck').

# NOTES

# NOTES

163   *Great River*: the Orange River (see note on the Orange River (page 162) above).

163   *fights at Belmont and Rooilaagte*: the Battle of Belmont took place on 23 November 1899, ending with victory for the British (see note on Belmont (page 83) above). The Battle of Rooilaagte, also known as the Battle of Graspan or the Battle of Enslin, took place two days later, and resulted in another British victory.

163   *Spytfontein*: train station and hamlet south of Kimberley in the former Cape Colony.

164   *Magersfontein*: hill south of Kimberley. At the Battle of Magersfontein on 11 December 1899, the Boers forced the British to retreat; the Scandinavian Volunteer Corps who fought for the Boers were destroyed while repelling an attack by the Seaforth Highlanders.

164   *Steyn*: Martinus Theunis Steyn (1857–1916), president of the Orange Free State from 1896 to 1902.

166   *Pretoria*: formerly the capital city of the South African Republic (Transvaal Republic), now executive capital of South Africa.

166   *'G' battery*: G Parachute Battery (Mercer's Troop) Royal Horse Artillery, close support battery of 7th Parachute Regiment Royal Horse Artillery of the British Army. During the Second Anglo-Boer War, G Battery saw active service during the Battle of Magersfontein and the Battle of Paardeberg (27 February 1900).

166   *Flygare*: Captain Johannes Flygare (1863–1899), Swedish commander of the Scandinavian Volunteer Corps during the Second Anglo-Boer War. Flygare was killed during the Battle of Magersfontein. See note on Magersfontein (page 164) above.

167   *the camps*: during the Second Anglo-Boer War, Lord Kitchener implemented a 'scorched-earth' policy of destroying Boer crops, livestock, and homesteads to deny the Boer guerrillas supplies. Boer civilians, including women and children, were forcibly relocated to concentration camps; poor conditions and overcrowding caused many camp internees to die from malnutrition and infectious diseases, including measles and typhoid.

168   *provost-marshal*: head of the military police.

168   *Major Shervington*: possibly fictional.

# NOTES

170  *Guides*: most likely Rimington's Guides (see note on Rimington's Guides (page 66) above).

171  *Carruthers*: probably fictional, but perhaps inspired by Major Wallace Bruce Matthews Carruthers (1863–1910), officer of the Canadian Militia and founder of the Royal Canadian Corps of Signals, who took part in the Second Anglo-Boer War.

171  *Lydenburg district*: district in the former South African Republic.

171  *maxim*: recoil-operated machine gun invented in 1884 by the American-born British inventor Hiram Stevens Maxim.

171  *berg*: (Afrikaans) mountain.

172  *kloof*: (Afrikaans) ravine, gorge.

172  *What though the spicy breezes blow soft o'er*: From the missionary hymn *Greenland's Icy Mountains* (1819) by Reginald Heber (1783–1826), English Anglican bishop. The full stanza quoted is 'What though the spicy breezes/Blow soft o'er Ceylon's isle,/Though every prospect pleases,/And only man is vile.'

172  *Ceylon*: Sri Lanka (see the note on 'What though the spicy breezes blow soft o'er' (page 172) above).

173  *Aasvogel Kop*: hill west of Bloemfontein (see note on aas-vogel (page 77) above).

173  *subaltern*: junior officer.

174  *donga*: (Afrikaans) dry watercourse.

175  *breech*: rear opening of a gun ammunition chamber.

178  *Ehud*: judge sent by God to deliver the Israelites from the Moabites (KJV, Judges 3:12–4:1).

178  *Throndhjem*: Trondheim; Norwegian city.

178  *karoo*: semi-desert plateau in South Africa.

181  *Lady Hamilton*: Dame Emma Hamilton (born Amy Lyon; 1765–1815), dancer, model, and actress, wife of Sir William Hamilton and mistress of Vice-Admiral Horatio Nelson. She modelled for several paintings by the artist George Romney.

182  *Mr. George Alexander*: Sir George Alexander (1858–1918), English actor, producer, and theatre manager, perhaps best known for producing and starring in Oscar Wilde's *The Importance of Being Earnest* (1895).

184  *guinea*: value equal to 21 shillings (one pound and one shilling).

# NOTES

**PAGE**

184   *Paquin's*: House of Paquin, a fashion house opened by French fashion designer Jeanne Paquin (1869–1936) and her husband Isidore Paquin in Paris in 1891. A London branch opened in 1896.

184   *hansom*: hansom cab, horse-drawn carriages for hire, common in New York and London in the late 19th and early 20th century.

186   *syncope*: fainting, loss of consciousness.

186   *visiting-cards*: calling cards, left when calling on someone; common among the upper classes in the 18th and 19th century.

187   *Corlton Paulets*: unidentified location, probably a fictional residence of Lord Ellsworth in Winchester. The protagonists reach Alton on their way to Corlton Paulets from London (see note on Alton (page 189) below), suggesting they were heading towards Winchester.

188   *motor veils*: (early 20th century) face veil tied over a woman's hat to protect the face from dirt or dust while in a motor car.

188   *Bleriots*: car headlamps, developed and sold by the French aviator and engineer Louis Charles Joseph Blériot (1872–1936).

188   *cataracts*: waterfalls; waterspouts.

188   *Panhard*: motor car developed by the French manufacturer Panhard, founded in 1887.

189   *wrap-rascal*: loose overcoat.

189   *Alton*: market town in Hampshire, England, eighteen miles northeast of Winchester.

196   *gyrostatics*: study of gyroscopes, bodies in rotation.

196   *Brennan*: Louis Brennan (1852–1932), Irish-Australian mechanical engineer, inventor of the Brennan torpedo and the gyro monorail.

198   *electrolier*: chandelier holding electric lamps.

199   *gyre*: vortex; circular ocean current.

199   *Il Diavolo*: (Italian) the devil.

203   *'rout'-chairs:* chairs hired for use at large social events (from the archaic English word *rout*, meaning a group of people).

204   *Louis XVI. flambeaux*: torch made in a style developed in France during the reign of Louis XVI from 1774 to 1793.

204   *mal-de-mer*: (French) seasickness.

207   *lyddite*: picric acid, an explosive. Manufactured in Lydd, Kent in Britain, hence the name lyddite.

# NOTES

# Redcap Manor

## A.L. Randolph

Until it was demolished in 1949, Redcap Manor was considered one of the most haunted places in England. Although little remembered today, the once renowned Edwardian ghost-and fairy-hunter Arthur L. Randolph conducted a series of experiments with electromagnetic fields in the manor in the early 20th century, with his reported sightings of boggarts, barghests, banshees, and bloodsuckers causing a considerable stir in society at the time.

The long-lost notes of A.L. Randolph were recently rediscovered and are published here for the first time. Randolph's haunting recollections of faeries and phantoms, accompanied by evocative artwork by Rustan Curman, shine an electric light on Britain's hidden world. Enter Redcap Manor, if you dare…

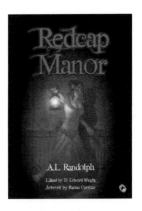

# Creepy Tales of the 1910s

## Edited by D. Edward Wright

Horror stories reflect the fears of the day, and in the ten years of the 1910s, those fears were considerable indeed. The decade in horror is a fascinating maelstrom in which the traditional Edwardian ghost story collides with both the rise of weird fiction and the nightmarish reality of total war.

This new collection includes ten stories by such luminaries of the genre as Bram Stoker, Sir Arthur Conan Doyle, William Hope Hodgson, and H.P. Lovecraft, with each tale originally published in a different year of the 1910s. Accompanied by fantastic new artwork by C. Raymond Hall, these tales of demonic curses, vampiric revenants, shape-shifting witches, airplane-hunting monsters, and otherworldly apparitions will be sure to make you grateful for the electric light switch…